BEFORE JANE EYRE

A THORNFIELD DUOLOGY

BOOK ONE

R Q BELL

INKWING BOOKS
FLIGHTS OF FANCY

INTRODUCTION

A NEGLECTED SECOND SON, Edward Rochester struggles in the shadow of his elder brother, whose jealous intrigues poison everything he touches. When Edward's long-cherished love and hopes for happiness with a childhood sweetheart are crushed by those intrigues, he is devastated.

Seeking to blot out the bitter failure, Edward takes the path laid out by his father and flees England. Certain he will never return, he embarks upon what becomes a fifteen year odyssey driven by the hope he might one day find such a love again.

But when one disappointment after another weighs him down until he is resigned to a loveless existence, Edward finds himself returning to the family home he had once forsaken, never imagining that what awaits him will change his life—forever.

PROLOGUE

ENGLISH CHANNEL—*PRESENT DAY*

It was only January when I crossed the Channel to England again.

My dog Pilot stood against the gunnel, barking at the raucous flock of gulls trailing the ship. When their cries at last died away into the mist, he lost interest and trotted back to me. Winded from his exertions, he plopped onto the deck.

I patted his head. "Aye, dog, We'll be in Dover soon and out of these cursed, rolling waters."

At least I didn't have to endure the stink of the foul engine smoke as during my crossing last summer on my journey to Thornfield, my family estate in northern England. This second visit in less than a twelve month was highly unusual. Though I never stayed long, to bring the child there and dispatch appropriate instructions to Mrs. Fairfax regarding her care had taken me but two days. And I knew in my heart that Carter would not approve the plan, so I avoided him altogether.

He was the local surgeon from Hay, the little village but three miles from Thornfield Hall. We became friends many years ago at college. Upon graduation, however, my father obliged me to go out to the West Indies, thus Carter and I had lost touch with one another. But under the tragic circumstances of my elder brother's death ten years ago, we had been thrown together again and rediscovered those early bonds of friendship.

"It is on your account, James," I murmured, "that I am coming back so soon." He was a gentle fellow, scrupulous in his morals and meticulous in his habits. I sat down on a box of cargo and pulled his letter from my cloak pocket and read it again:

Hay, September, Last Year

    Rochester—

    Imagine my shock when I discovered a little girl and her nurse living at Thornfield Hall. And Mrs. Fairfax informs me a governess is to arrive next month!

    Edward, what on earth were you thinking? Will a child be safe there?

    Certainly I am disappointed you failed to call upon me last summer and inform me of your intentions, but I must confess to another, better reason I would have welcomed your visit. Emily had recently lost our own first child—a boy. My profession well-acquaints me with death, but it was a blow for which I was ill-prepared. For all your stubborn ways, it would have done me much good to see you.

    So, write me in advance of your next visit. Perhaps like Banquo's ghost, you would rather appear without warning. What-ever your plans, I shall keep them close. But one way or the other, you will tell me how a child came to be at Thornfield Hall.

    I am yours etc,

    James J. Carter

What prompted me to pluck the little thing from the mud

and mire of Paris and bring her to Thornfield? A guilty
conscience, perhaps? No child has crossed its threshold in
years, so it is quite strange to think of a little girl—Adele
Varens by name—romping through the halls of that big,
gloomy house.

I once thought she was my daughter. But every expectation of that hope vanished in the days and weeks following
her birth. The little thing bore no trace of such grim paternity in her countenance. But surely, James, it is a noble
purpose, is it not, to rescue a motherless child?

In the wake of his letter, I knew I must tell him all. My
reply sent but a month ago ran thus:

Paris, December, Last year

Carter—

*As usual, you have managed to humble me with your kindness
and restrained reproof. That I retain the grace of your friendship
can only be the work of Providence.*

*But your claim is just—you shall have your tale. I daresay it
will be more than you bargained for. Look for me on the first
packet of the new year to Dover.*

The rough sea of the Channel was making me nauseous
after sitting so long. I put the letter away, rose to my feet and
called the dog to my side. I managed to remain upright as we
rambled about the ship. He snuffed into every corner and
cranny, every coil of rope, every box of cargo. The few hearty
passengers on deck shrank away at his approach. His size
belied his gentle temper, which kept strangers at a distance.
That suited me very well.

Spying some seabird which had wandered far out from
Dover, Pilot barked, then ran up to the bow, howling at the
bird which flitted in and out of the sails.

When I came forward he ran to me, barking again in his

frustration at the escape of his quarry. I patted his head and he gave himself over to my attentions, the gull completely forgotten. I smiled at the simplicity of his pleasures, then turned my gaze toward the White Cliffs.

I hope you are waiting for me, James. Otherwise it will be a very lonely journey back to Thornfield Hall.

BACK IN ENGLAND

Present Day

"It's good to see you again, Rochester," exclaimed James Carter.

We shook hands and embraced. "I am glad you are come to meet me."

The dog jumped into the coach before us then pushed his nose forward as we climbed in after him. I scratched his ears while Carter patted his head.

"Aye, dog. I am glad to see you as well."

Anxious to spend as little time in England as possible, I did not wait for my trunk to be unloaded from the ship, but gave instructions to send it on to Millcote. As a consequence, Carter and I were the only passengers ready to depart, so we climbed into the vehicle and got underway.

The coach settled into a rattling rhythm as we headed north along the Dover Road towards London. Early January was damned cold. We were bundled from head to foot against the weather. A morning mist hovered in the air, but the road was dry.

We bumped along in silence for awhile, until Carter

abruptly observed, "Your dog at least looks hale and well-fed, Rochester."

"I am glad to hear it." I laughed. "Can you not say the same about me?"

"To outward appearances, you are very hearty."

"Only outward appearances?"

"You seem quite distracted." He smiled. "I know you well enough to perceive your mood in spite of your attempts to conceal everything."

"That you do," I admitted. "Will you forgive my cold heart? I am truly sorry for the loss of your son. When I was in England last summer, my head was full of other things and—well, it's a damn sorry excuse is all, and I heartily regret it."

"Thank you, Edward. I have attended the deathbed of many a still-born infant and witnessed the anguish of the parents. I felt the deep sorrow of those mothers and fathers, and even grieved for their losses. But when it's your own flesh and blood—"

"It is a very different thing, indeed. But James, you owe apologies to no one. You cannot be expected to lament the death of every child as you would your own son. No man has that much mercy in his soul."

Carter nodded. He gazed at me a moment, unable to reply. Then he turned his face to the window, staring but not seeing the barren, frost-laden meadows roll by.

"I did not know him," he murmured after some minutes had passed. "He died without a name, and yet the pain was so much greater than I could have imagined." His eyes glistened with tears. "What should it be like to lose a child who has lived in the world? Whom you have seen smile and laugh and cry and call you 'Father'?"

I shook my head. "It is something no man can fathom until he must walk through that valley. But take heart. Emily is young, is she not? She will yet be able to bear children, I trust?"

He smiled at hearing his wife's name. "She speaks of it already. But," he continued more cheerily, "while I am grateful for your condolences, belatedly though you offer them, you shall not evade my questions. I never knew of your visit to Thornfield last summer until well after you had returned to Europe. I can only conclude you were avoiding me. Why?"

"After that scathing letter I received from you in the wake of my visit? I knew you would not approve my plan, so I told you nothing about it."

"Of course I would object to a child living there, Edward. And you know why. But good God! In addition to Adele and her nurse, there is now a governess as well."

"Ah, Mrs. Fairfax has been successful, then?"

He nodded. "I did mention that in my letter."

"Some hardened, upright spinster to correct every French defect, I suppose?"

"A young woman. She arrived in October."

"You have met her?"

"No. I had tea with Mrs. Fairfax sometime after the young lady had settled in. Your housekeeper seems quite pleased with her. Says she is a pleasant companion as well as a diligent tutor."

"A dual benefit, then."

"You simply couldn't be bothered to let an old friend in on yet another Rochester secret, eh? I must discover these things for myself?" He shook his head. "After all these years, Edward, still you cannot trust me?"

"I feared you would ask me to relinquish the plan, and I was in such a damned hurry to be back to the Continent. Perhaps it was imprudent of me, but I knew you would have questions and demand explanations—"

"But a child! Edward, for God's sake! Where on earth did you pick her up?"

I winced. "That, as you so plainly suggest, is what I did not do. It was rather more a case of her being left on my hands. Be patient, Carter. I have promised you the whole story."

"I am all ears," he replied, shaking his head, a deuced, all-knowing smile on his face.

I sighed.

"You must admit my supposition is justifiable," he continued. "Are you aware of the rumors?"

"Of course there are rumors," I replied bitterly. "It is the way of things. People's lives are so pathetic they have nothing better to ponder each day than hearsay and scandal. One day, a little French girl arrives at the house of an English country gentleman, and so the natural assumption is she is my bastard daughter. It merely adds to the mysteries associated with Edward Rochester and Thornfield Hall." I laughed. "I would be disappointed if such an event did not set all the tongues to wagging. But I don't give a damn for the opinion of others, Carter, only yours. I cannot abide you would unjustly condemn me."

"What else should I conclude? You have been very close over the years, and yet I have gleaned much from our rare conversations and the scattered letters I have received. You have wandered the globe—Paris, Naples, Rome, St. Petersburg—the very edge of civilization! And mistresses, Edward...how many has it been? Surely, the child belongs to one of them."

"I won't deny it—I have kept mistresses. Perhaps it would be more appropriate to say they have kept me. They provided distraction from the terrible emptiness of my life. But such society grows stale and worthless in a time shorter than you would believe. Those experiences have only added to my endless litany of regrets. But as to Adele, I plead my innocence most earnestly, and beg you would believe me. I am not her father."

He scrutinized me for a moment, then shrugged. "I suppose I do believe you. But why in God's name have you brought the child to Thornfield, man? Can it be safe for her there?"

It was the very question he posed in his letter and I must admit, it never occurred to me to consider the matter. I had convinced myself I ought to do it, for the child's sake.

Perhaps it was my own burden of guilt which motivated me. By the time I received Madame Frederick's letter, I knew that Céline had abandoned Adele without a second thought. No, she was not my daughter, but very well could have been. Would my feelings be different if she were my own flesh and blood? Her mother's declaration of undying devotion had been a mere ruse to manipulate my purse. When I unmasked her little game, oh, what a blow to pride that had been. I was as undiscerning about her as I had been about another, so many years before. Such blindness was my curse, it seemed.

"Why, Carter. Little Miss Varens is my just reward for sins well-committed. The debts charged to my account these fifteen years are heavy and deep. Much interest has accumulated. Should I not begin a repayment plan, lest at the final trump my account remains outstanding?"

He shook his head. "Putting a child in peril is not the way to gain God's forgiveness."

"God's forgiveness?" I asked angrily. "This has nothing to do with that. No doubt he has been mightily amused by all I have endured at his hand. But surely, your worries are unfounded. She has been quite docile these many years, and the child is but a small thing who now has a governess who will see to her care and education. Does it really matter what my motives are?"

But he made no reply, preferring to ponder my words yet awhile. As he sat lost in thought, I withdrew a cigar, lit it, then drew in deeply. The sweet, Havana fragrance scented the chilly air inside the coach. I felt myself sink into the cushion as the rocking motion and sedative effect of the tobacco induced a pleasant, soporific detachment.

"You haven't given up that habit, I see."

"Ever playing the physician, eh, Carter?" I held out the cigar and looked at it. "Do you suppose this shall steal some years from me? Are you going to deny me one of my few remaining pleasures?"

"I thought I might join you in your indulgence is all."

I offered him one, and he took it. I struck a match against my boot. He accepted the light.

"I am fond of a smoke now and again, Edward. I only supposed the associations with your past would be…unpleasant."

"Ah, yes," said I with bitterness. "But my preferred method of self-delusion and escape then was of the liquid variety. In truth, the cigar is the only memory of those years I choose to retain. As to the rest, may the devil take them."

"How long will you remain in England?"

"Perhaps a fortnight," I replied. "Besides my promise to tell you the tale of little Miss Adele, there is business I must attend at Thornfield. Stewart is quite capable, but occasionally, my presence is required."

"Then you've no intention to see how your little ward gets on?"

"Stewart only needs me for a few days. That should be ample time to assess the child's progress. But when business is done, I must leave. It will be far better for Mrs. Poole and her patient if I don't linger. I am nothing but an agitating presence in that house, and well you know it. Where I will go, I cannot say." I sighed. "At this moment, I find myself

rather sick of life. And certainly Thornfield holds no inducements for me to remain."

"So, once again you leave others to fulfill your duties—"

"Oh, I understand what my duties are," I interrupted,
repressing a sudden flush of resentment. "Grace was most
eager to leave Grimsby, and she is handsomely remunerated
for her troubles. Ours…is a business relationship, one she
most willingly undertook all those years ago. She has never
voiced any objections to me about the conditions of her
employment."

He shook his head. "Edward, tell me. Will you ever put an
end to your ceaseless wandering upon this earth?"

I laughed. "Do you wish the same existence for all your
friends as yourself?"

"What do you mean? That I pray you find some contentment? Yes, I do wish that for you and I don't apologize
for it."

"Am I not content, then?"

"Did you not just pronounce yourself sick of life?" he
replied, exasperated. "Does not such a declaration resonate
with discontentment?"

"But I am a man of the world, one who travels where he
pleases. Who has money to buy his way into any society,
wealth to provide any sort of pleasure his imagination can
conjure. Is this not happiness?"

"Do not mock me, Edward."

"On the contrary, James. I am rather envious. You have an
occupation which gives you purpose. You are mightily
blessed in your Emily. I hope you know that."

His countenance softened at the mention of his wife's
name. "I do indeed know it. To find a woman who would
tolerate a doctor's schedule, subsist on such a meager
income…it is no less than a miracle, to be sure. But we were
discussing your life Edward, not mine. You have been a

vagabond these ten years. Will you ever settle down and live in one place as we were meant to do?"

I shrugged. "Had you put such a question to me ten years ago, I should simply have said, 'When I find a woman I can love'."

"I wonder you undertook such a quest," he replied with sadness. "Your circumstances made that impossible."

I was silent.

In a milder tone, he asked, "In all your wanderings, you have never found such a woman?"

"No," I retorted quickly. "Not one. There is no folly so besotted that the rashness and blindness of youth will not hurry a man to its commission. And how blind I was! I had convinced myself that by severing all connection with my previous life, I could begin afresh. But little did I know I was running from Purgatory into Perdition. Having a mistress— it's a humiliation I tell you, and I had not the character to forbid it. I was a lonely Englishman, ugly to a fault, but rich enough to afford the most beautiful women in Europe. But I was a damned fool for believing them anything other than heartless creatures incapable of loving anyone, let alone one such as I. All of them sought after the same idol—not the grim blacksmith before you, but a golden one. As they gorged themselves on my gold, vitality seeped out of me until one day I no longer recognized myself and I knew it must cease. It was foolish of me to allow it to go on for so long."

"I'm sorry, Edward."

"Oh, damn it, Carter. It is the ugly truth and I have only myself to blame for it. It was like being a slave, I tell you, hostage to some perverse desire, some perceived need which time and again compelled me simply to buy companionship. Yet even when the idea became repulsive, I could not relent. The prospect of living alone, assailed by conscience and memory, was unendurable. But it was cowardly, and I am most heartily ashamed of it. Before you sits a worldly, dissipated and restless man. I have wandered the earth these ten years, but for what? There was nothing that resembled genuine affection or esteem in my relationships with any of the women I have known."

He was thoughtful. "As I told you, it was an impossible ideal, Edward. I believe you now understand that."

"Perhaps I have been nothing but a fool." I said no more, and the conversation was at an end.

VISION OF THE PAST

As THE COACH RUMBLED ONWARD, CARTER CLOSED HIS EYES
and leaned against the cushions. He had waited all morning
in Dover for the passengers to be ferried in from the packet,
and despite the bumpy ride, he soon dozed peacefully.

Pilot stood and stretched, then laid his great head across
my legs. Idly, I scratched his ears as I stared out the window,
watching the last vestiges of daylight dwindle above the horizon. The sky was clear and a bright orange glow shimmered
against the darkening blue as day faded into night.

I thought about our conversation, about my disappoint-
ments, and wondered if Carter was right. Was it an impossible quest or so unreasonable an expectation to find a
woman who suited me? In all my years of traveling the
world, occasionally I heard a voice, or beheld a form I hoped
would be her. But always, it ended in disappointment or
betrayal. Hope was starved into bitterness. Energy and
activity abandoned to recklessness.

After four long years of exile in the West Indies, I had
nearly forsaken myself. Hideous recollection! What senseless

hope drove me across the Atlantic to Europe where I believed happiness was possible? *Something* had prevented my self-destruction and reawakened a vision, infusing me with the courage to seek my dream of the ideal. From whence had come this vision?

Like a phoenix rising from the ashes of those ruinous years in Jamaica, the idea began out of a half-comprehended experience of childhood. Shadowy but strangely impressive, the memory slowly shaped itself into something more solid, and I remembered the day I had seen it in the library at Thornfield Hall.

I spent many happy hours in that room surrounded by books, where school lessons of history, poetry, mathematics and music had been conducted.

My mother's great worktable was there, arranged with her writing desk and workbox and stacks of volumes, among which would be found Donne, an atlas, her well-read Bible and especially, her beloved Sonnets. Nearby was my own little desk and chair. How often I withdrew to this retreat, and she to whom I ran—for none other would have me— gave me comfort in my sorrows over the latest ignominy rained upon me by my brother.

"Today we shall begin with Goldsmith," she would say. Or, "You shall hear of Endymion and the Moon Goddess."

And would follow a story of lands far away, exotic and strange. I wondered when she had visited such places, for she spoke of them as if she had seen them with her own eyes. The telling of those tales would transport her into that mysterious bourne, and so caught up into its wonders she became that it seemed she no longer was in the library, or aware of my presence there.

One day, my father came in unannounced. Not infrequently did he do so, generally to consult with her about some household matter. But this day, while she was thus enraptured, he paused and listened, as fascinated and caught up in the story as was I.

After some minutes, he drew near without a sound. Unusual, for generally he came and noisily conducted whatever business he had and was gone. But this morning he was oblivious to my presence. His attention was wholly engaged by his wife's voice rising and falling with the telling of her tale. I watched him, daring not to breathe, for it might break the spell.

At last she drew to the end of the story and opened her eyes. When she noticed my father there, a strange smile suffused her countenance. As he approached, again she closed her eyes and without a word, he softly kissed her upraised cheek.

The atmosphere of the library tingled.

My heart thrilled strangely as I watched. Something compelling, something mysterious had passed between them. No words were spoken, yet the effect was more powerful than an ocean of speech. That they had a profound affection for one another was apparent even to my infant brain. Her whole person changed when she saw him, her eyes aglow with some secret delight. At the sight of her smile, his gruff, brooding countenance softened, becoming almost agreeable.

And even now, as I recalled that hour, I wondered that the man I perceived my father to be had the power to stir such emotion within her. As a boy of seven or eight, I knew nothing of the ways of a man and a woman, but it only made me wonder all the more: how could he have such potent feelings for her and yet to me, his son, he showed little else but indifference?

My mother had been my greatest advocate, but even her persuasions had been insufficient to overthrow the malicious influence of my elder brother, Rowland, for whom I, it seemed, was the object of his every antipathy. And where

Rowland was concerned, Henry Rochester simply was blind. He had no will to make room for a third in his heart.

Irreconcilable and strange, it was then, and still is to me, a mystery.

PRELUDE TO A MEMORY

PRESENT DAY

The guard blew the horn to announce our arrival at the Blue Bull, a coaching inn and tavern not far from Canterbury. The noise awakened Carter, and Pilot, restless with inactivity, leapt from the coach the moment the door was opened.

It was after five o'clock, so we went inside, hoping for something to eat. A few hearty souls were gathered in the dining hall. The innkeeper himself showed us to a table near the hearth where we could converse in some privacy.

"Will you sirs 'ave supper?"

"Do we have time?" asked Carter.

"Perhaps twenty or thirty minutes," I replied. "But we are not due to our first night's destination until midnight, so indeed, we should eat something now. Bread and coffee, if you please and if you've any beef or mutton stew, bring me a portion."

"Aye, sir," replied our host.

"Make it for two," added Carter.

"There's an extra half a crown in it if you bring a soup bone for my dog!" I called after him.

The man returned in a few minutes. "There ye are, sirs, enjoy." He turned to go, but stopped. "Oh, mind ye, I nearly forgot." From the pocket of his rather untidy apron he pulled out a handsome bone, still dripping with soup stock. "Took this right out o' the pot I did." He bent to the floor. "Here ye are dog—have at it."

I tossed him the promised coin, and we set to devouring the simple meal as Pilot greedily crunched on his bone. I had just finished the last bites of my stew when the post boy came in calling, "Ten minutes til post! Coach fer the Dover Road in ten!"

"Well, Carter, time to be away. Another few hours in the rattling coach before we lay our heads upon a pillow. Have you stamina to listen while I begin my promised tale of little Adele Varens?"

Carter snatched a serviette from his greatcoat pocket, wiped his mouth and grinned. "Indeed I do, Edward.

"Pilot!"

The dog was up and at my side in a moment, the half-chewed bone still clutched in his mouth. Carter smiled as we hurried across the cobbled yard then climbed into the vehicle, only to find three additional passengers huddled together under a woolen blanket on one side of the coach.

"Good ev'nen to ya," said a plain-dressed man, flanked by a care-worn woman, presumably his wife, and a girl of about ten or eleven, presumably his daughter. "And well, a great dog, too."

Carter touched his hat in acknowledgement.

"Down, Pilot!" I muttered.

The dog dropped to his position on the coach floor to gnaw at his bone.

"Good evening, madam," I greeted the woman, tipping my hat. "I do hope my dog doesn't frighten the little girl."

Before she could reply, the child happily answered, "Oh no, sir, I 'ave a dog myself, though he is not so large as yours."

"Caroline, your manners," chided her mother.

"How far are ye sirs travelin'?" asked Caroline's father.

"To London."

"Well, I 'ope the weather 'olds clear for yer journey. 'Tis right cold, but the road is yet fair and there's no snow in sight."

"God willing," replied Carter.

As the family snuggled closer beneath their wrap, I leaned toward my friend and whispered, "I am afraid you must be patient yet awhile before you hear my tale."

"We shall be on the road a good while before we reach Millcote, Rochester. There will be time enough." He stifled a great yawn. "Besides, I believe our meager repast and warm fire was just enough to make me rather sleepy. Far be it from me to disappoint you by dozing off and missing the half of it. Besides, knowing how you manage sea travel, you ought to sleep awhile."

"These damned mail coaches may be fast," I muttered, "but with all this cursed bumping and jostling, I am decided not to endure it another night. I will hire a coach in London to take us to Millcote in a more civilized manner. I can assure our comfort and privacy if I pay for it."

"Well," he smiled, "I look forward to claiming your undivided attention for so many hours together."

If my friend had truly intended to sleep, our voluble new companion prevented him. For some miles they conversed about everything and nothing in particular, but Carter's way with people was easy. No doubt his profession had given him untold hours of practice in the art of small talk. I marveled at his friendly manner and ability to appear interested, even as he fought against the advent of slumber.

The conversation faded into the background as I stared out the window. It was dark, but the clear and cold night sky was peppered with stars. As I pondered the story I was about to tell my friend, I was sure he understood that I and my brother had been rivals. It was a natural and not uncommon occurrence between siblings, to be sure. He also knew that I blamed Rowland for Catherine Fairfax's death. But did he understand the rivalry between us bordered upon hatred? How much was I to tell him? What good might it do now to vilify the memory of a dead brother and father to someone who had been a friend to them both in their last hours upon this earth?

My brother Rowland was more than seven years my senior. As a child and youth, I was at every turn the object of his bad temper and ill will. Always the favorite of our father, he would receive the Thornfield property in its entirety, a fact which he gleefully reminded me of every day. A family estate must pass to the eldest son intact. There could be but one Master, and he would be my brother.

But in spite of my father's decided preference for Rowland, I continually tried to attract his notice. He never over-indulged me with his affection, nor spoilt me by any monetary extravagance, for his miserly tendencies were legendary. Nor by any weakness of temper on his part was I actively given my way. Rather, his attitude was general indifference. I received little guidance or correction from him save when my brother complained of some petty mischief I had wrought, or my mother called attention to behavior simply too barbarous to ignore. On these occasions, his hand was swift and harsh.

As Rowland and I grew older, our father could not abide our continual bickering. After a time, he simply ceased to reprimand us for it. Only in our mother's presence would he threaten his iron hand to enforce our obedience. And obey we did, for we feared his wrath.

I rarely complained of these punishments, however. While my youthful heart exulted whenever he exhibited interest in anything concerning me, too, did I suffer that agony peculiar to a child who wants nothing more than the attention of a parent, and willingly endures even cruelty to get it.

It had been my father's habit for as long as I could remember to make a weekly circuit of the estate, a task which took him away from the Hall for an entire day. He was a scrupulous proprietor, though perhaps not so much out of concern for the welfare of our tenants as for their pecuniary interest. And sometimes he, rather than the estate manager, would collect the rents.

Rowland began to accompany him on these rides as soon as he could sit a horse, before I was born. As I grew older, I observed these excursions, which prompted me to the saddle at a tender age. By the time I was seven or eight years old, I was an excellent rider.

Every week without fail I begged to go along. But every week I was denied. Father, rather than determine my worthiness as a horseman for himself, left it to his eldest son, and I knew Rowland would never let me go with them.

When week after week went by and still I was excluded from their company, I grew desperate. For reasons to this day I cannot name, one particular morning the rejection stung me to the heart. A desperate anger stirred within me, and I was struck with a singular idea, and so I made my decision to act!

STEALING SIROCCO

THORNFIELD HALL—1783

On the morning of my father's weekly tour of the estate, I raced down to the stables, hoping this time I could go with them.

In the yard Milo, our chief groom, held the reins of my father's horse as Rowland led another bay out of the barn. I was surprised because it was not Sirocco, the high-bred hunter of Arabian descent my father had given him for his fifteenth birthday a few weeks earlier.

"Will you not be riding Sirocco?" I asked.

Rowland pulled himself up into the saddle. "No." He frowned. "That stubborn colt was fussing about in his stall, kicking the gate and generally in a bad mood. I decided to let him cool off."

I said nothing. Rowland was not very gentle with his mounts. Sirocco, by virtue of his breeding, was already temperamental. Rowland's handling of him no doubt was the prime cause of his bad mood.

Swallowing the lump forming in my throat, I looked at

my father. "May I accompany you and Rowland today, Father?"

He shrugged then looked at my brother. "What do you think? Is little Edward ready?"

Rowland snorted. "Certainly not. I expect he would fall off at the first hedge."

"Would not!" I yelled. "I'm a good horseman, Father. Let me prove it to you."

Henry waved his hand. "Perhaps another time." Then he and Rowland spurred their mounts away.

I had not noticed Milo standing beside me. He laid a comforting hand on my shoulder. "'Ere now, Master Edward. You'll get yer chance, you wait an' see."

Tears pricked behind my eyes and the last thing I wanted was to cry in front of him. "I won't, I won't!"

I dashed away to a nearby field where stood a large oak tree. I climbed up into the lowest nook and sat there, crying and brooding over the injustice dealt me.

When the notion dawned upon me, it seemed so simple, so brilliant. Rowland didn't deserve that horse. I would show them I was a worthy horseman, and Sirocco would help me do it!

I climbed down from the tree and made my way back to the stables. I heard the grooms chattering together in the common room, but no one loitered about the stalls.

I slipped inside where Sirocco was kept. Leaving the door ajar behind me, I crept toward his stall at the far end of the stables. He was so beautiful—midnight black with a white star blaze on his forehead and silver streaks in his mane and tail. I loved him from the moment I saw him. I had visited so often he now recognized my voice.

As I drew near to his enclosure, he ears perked up at my whispered words of welcome. Without a noise, I lifted the latch of the gate and stepped inside. He nickered softly. I stroked his nose and soothed him, pondering what I was about to do.

I took his tack down from the wall and saddled him. When I slipped the bit into his mouth, he became agitated, and I knew he longed to be away to run his heart out.

I climbed to the top of the stall gate then paused. In spite of the colt's agitation, no groom came to check out the commotion, which seemed loud enough to set anyone within earshot running my way. Several minutes passed but still no one appeared. It was now or never!

Balancing on the top rail of the gate, I drew him alongside then mounted. He remained still beneath me, but I felt a quiver shudder through his flanks, as if he knew he was about to be released. A giddy sense of triumph coursed through me as I sat astride Rowland's horse, thrilled with my small victory as if I was Alexander at the wall of Thebes.

If I had taken that triumph for what it was then slipped away, no one would ever have known. As I sat there still debating the wisdom of my actions, a clattering noise from the other end of the stable startled the colt. He reared, striking his foreleg on the crossbar of the gate. His weight knocked it open, and away we bolted! I clung to his neck as we ran right past the grooms. They jumped up and dashed outside, shouting after me to stop as we thundered away down the hill.

What an exhilarating ride that day! The cold wind blew through my hair and stung my face. We galloped alongside a creek at the bottom of the hill, then raced up the incline towards the front gate. Flanked by great pillars of stone and topped with statues of rampant lions, it loomed ever larger as I made for that escape.

The cries of the grooms by now were faint. I thought I would ride on forever, and perhaps I might have, had not a sudden thought flashed through my mind: if the colt was missing when my father and Rowland returned, what curses would they rain upon me? What terrible punishment might fall on my head?

To this day, I know not how far I might have run, but something compelled me to pull up short. I turned Sirocco around and we returned to the stables. Already I had committed a most audacious deed by taking Rowland's prize colt without his leave. That would indeed anger my father. What his wrath might be as a result, I dared not imagine.

A crowd of grooms clustered about as I trotted towards the barn, encircling me when I dismounted. Milo crossed his arms and flashed me a severe look.

"Master Edward! "What have ye be'n about wif' Master Rowland's 'orse?"

He grabbed the bridle as I slid down from Sirocco's back. All the others began talking at once.

"Shush now," he cried. "Let the lad 'ave his say."

"It's all right, my brother gave me leave," I lied.

"Did 'e now?" Milo looked me up and down, a quizzical expression in his eye. "Well, then, get on wif ye back to the 'ouse. I'll see to the colt."

"Will you…tell Rowland?" I asked anxiously.

Milo cocked an eyebrow, then smiled. "I thought 'e gave you leave." He knew I was lying, but instead of reprimanding me, he made a quick gesture with his thumb. "I'll talk to the lads. Now git."

I nodded. "The music master is probably waiting for me."

I felt small and full of guilt, wanting nothing more than to be away from them all. As I reached up to pat Siroccos's nose, Milo bent and touched the colt's foreleg.

"What this? 'E's cut."

My mouth dropped open and my heart pounded. "What?"

I knelt down and saw a small gash oozing a trickle of blood.

"Rowland said he was fussing in his stall." I swallowed hard. "He...he must have kicked a fence rail."

Milo's eyes narrowed. "P'raps.

It wasn't my fault! I wanted to scream. My heart pounded as the man examined the colt's leg more closely. He had been agitated before I even entered the barn. Rowland said so.

To my untrained eye, it looked awful. I dabbed at the wound, which oozed several drops of blood.

"I...he must have hit the fence when that noise scared him. He will be all right?"

Milo looked at it again, then wiped the cut with his thumb. Only a drop or two appeared this time.

"It's not bad. Just a scratch." Milo winked at me. "Best you're not 'ere a'fore Master Rowland gets back. 'E'll be right upset. Now get along."

I patted Sirocco's neck and murmured, "Thank you," then dashed away up towards the Hall.

When I appeared in the library for my music lesson later that afternoon, my mother had no idea what mischief I had wrought.

Until my father and brother returned home.

Henry was forever changed by what happened that day, and Rowland's jealously deepened into hatred for me.

AFTERMATH OF MISCHIEF

"Aury? Aurelia! Aurelia Fairfax? Where is that boy?"

Henry Rochester burst through the front door of the Hall, his boots dripping with mud, his face flushed with heat and anger. A trail of servants followed in his wake to relieve him of his great fur-collared cloak and riding crop, but he would have none of it. He swatted them away like flies.

He was not a tall man, but broad-chested and strong as a bull. His bearing simply commanded the attention from everyone in the room when he entered. His voice thundered throughout the house, echoing up and down the gallery as though it was seeking after me like a hungry tiger. In my mind's eye I could see him marching along the hallway, throwing open one room door after another. Failure to find the object of his search—me—would only exacerbate his rising temper.

"Aurelia Fairfax! I am coming to the library presently!"

The cry echoed down the hall as the door of that very room burst open, and I fully expected that in the next moment, I should be dangling by my hair from my father's monstrous fist, his glowering countenance all rage and disapproval. To my relief, it was not my father but Rowland who entered.

He stomped across the floor to the corner near the hearth where stood the heavy oaken table at which my mother sat every morning attending to her daily correspondence while overseeing my early education. As she wrote her letters, I usually contented myself with a storybook or a slate to practice my ciphers.

Rowland was big and strong like Father, but his manner was unpolished and blundering, and his temper kindled at the slightest affront to his pride.

"Mother! Where is that worthless little snipe?" he demanded. "Let me have him. You can't hide him!"

"I suppose you have tracked mud and filth across my Turkish carpets again?" She replied without looking up from her letter.

Rowland's eyes widened, and he glanced down at his boots, squirming at this gentle reprimand.

"Have a care, Rowland. Must I speak again to Mr. Rochester about your manners? They can be so abominable."

His mouth dropped open, but the invocation of my father's name broke off his retort.

"Nor is Edward hiding," she continued. "He just finished his afternoon music lesson and is keeping me company."

Rowland heard none of this explanation, however. He planted himself firmly before her, hands on hips, and screeched his accusation.

"Sirocco, my new colt is ruined, and he did it!" He whined, pointing at me. "You! Wait until Father comes."

My brother had little patience for anything that might thwart his will. He stepped sideways to get a clearer view, then suddenly lunged at me across the table, heedlessly scattering papers and books everywhere, leaning as far as he could, trying to grab me by the shirt. I shrank as far away from his clutches as I could.

"You! Come out of there at once!" he shrieked, growing more frustrated as his groping fingers failed to grasp me. "There's no use denying it, you filthy little sneak! The grooms saw you. You took him out of the stable, didn't you? You stole him! And now he is positively ruined. Ruined! You…you little mole! Hold still! I swear, I'll—"

"You'll what?"

The deep voice of Henry Rochester, whose imposing presence all at once filled the room, visibly startled him. Like the mice surprised at the appearance of the cat, there we two were: I sat unmoving on the stool, and Rowland, ceasing his efforts to snatch me, lay on the table. Slowly, he tucked his arms beneath his chest, while his mouth gaped open in mute accusation. He glared hatred at me. Flushed from his exertions, he remained rigidly still, stretched out like a specimen pinned to a card.

My mother, quite accustomed to her husband's mercurial temper, calmly laid her quill upon the desk, rose from her chair and stepped out from behind the table.

"What the deuce do you think you're doing, Rowland?" exclaimed Henry. "Get down from there before I throw you off."

Rowland's gaze remained fixed on me as he pushed himself up and slid off the table. When his boots touched the floor and he stood upright, his stupefied expression metamorphosed into a lazy, self-satisfied smirk. I was in for it now.

With gleeful malice, he pointed at me. "Look! There he is, Father. I found him for you."

"Be silent! Pick up your mother's books and papers and put them back where they belong."

Rowland seemed unaware he had disturbed anything in

his attempts to seize me, and now saw the jumble of papers and volumes on the carpet. He stooped and gathered them up as one then dropped them in a heap onto the desk.

"Rowland, for God's sake!"

"Never mind," said my mother softly. "I'll sort them out later."

Henry looked at his wife, then shrugged. He turned again to Rowland and motioned for him to move out of his path. "Stand aside. I will deal with Edward."

"That little beggar, he's trying to hide from you, Father!" cried Rowland. "What a little horse thief he is!" He glanced around at me again, a menacing look of triumph on his face. "You do know that horse thieves hang, don't you Edward? Father, what are you going to do to him? Shall I fetch him out of there for you? Shall I—"

"Leave the room this minute," muttered Henry ominously.

But my brother would not be put off. His temper had taken hold of him, and nothing short of our father taking a horsewhip to my hide would appease his thirst for vengeance.

"But he stole my horse! You know he did!" spluttered Rowland furiously, wildly looking back and forth between myself and Henry, as if imploring the latter to act.

My father's temper, often meted out upon my person, on rare occasions vented itself against my brother. But as changeable as his disposition was, rarely was Henry Rochester goaded into action by another man's inducements, even his eldest son. He turned and leaned forward, his face no more than an inch or two from Rowland's as he gestured to the door and whispered between clenched teeth.

"Get out of my way."

"Father, you cannot allow—"

My brother never saw the blow which sent him tumbling

to the carpet. As he rolled over, clutching the side of his face which had been slapped, I could see a drop or two of blood trickle from the corner of his mouth, and his eyes, wide in surprise, rapidly filled with tears as he wiped his mouth on his coat sleeve.

Henry was unmoved. "Don't you ever talk back to me, boy. Get out. Now."

Rowland, who at fifteen tried to be as imperious as my father, had been laid out by one swift backhand. His astonishment soon became resentment, however, for as he staggered to his feet, I saw an angry scowl of hatred darken his countenance. Without a word, he stumbled out of the room, blubbering and sobbing as I had never heard before.

How I wanted to laugh out loud! For once, Rowland's attempts to disgrace me had been thwarted. More injurious, however, was the wounding of his pride. To be humiliated in front of me was unpardonable. Alas, my ecstasy would be all too brief. I knew my brother would be waiting for me. Perhaps not today, but he would have his retribution. For the moment, however, I savored this triumph. It had not been won by my hand, but still tasted sweet.

My sense of victory soon ebbed away as a more pressing concern was before me. Henry Rochester now directed his full attention to me.

"Come here, Edward."

Any hesitation to obey would not be tolerated. I stood up from the little stool and moved out from behind the table. But in my haste, I stumbled. Just when I thought I should land on my face at his feet, my mother's quick hand caught me. As I regained my footing, I glanced at her face. Her eyes beamed, and I heard her whisper, "Courage, Edward."

How her words invigorated my failing heart! Even as I trembled with the dread of what was to come, I felt my spirit expand within me, so much so that I suddenly knew whatever my father was going to do, I would not this time wilt beneath his hand.

Both Rowland and I indulged in our share of boyhood pranks, but riding his horse without leave was the most brazen, impudent deed I had ever perpetrated. For that reason alone he deemed it worthy of the severest punishment my father could inflict. What Henry Rochester's assessment of the crime had been, I was about to discover.

I stood before him, my eyes cast down. In spite of my mother's bold words and my new-found resolve, still I was trembling. I knew my father's anger was great, for his boots were still muddy. In his haste to confront me, he had forgotten to scrape them clean before entering the house. To risk my mother's displeasure, in even a trifling offense such as this, was not his habit.

Not daring to look up at his face, my gaze followed after the muddy track he had deposited on the carpet.

"Aury, you may leave us now," Henry abruptly addressed my mother. "This is between me and the boy."

"But Henry—"

"No, damn it, no! You bloody well know what effect you have on me, and this time I won't countenance it."

Aurelia Rochester knew when not to cross her husband. Without another word to him, she slipped past me and walked to the door. Henry watched her go, as did I. She stood a moment in the doorway, looking at me. Her glistening eyes seemed to smile, as if to remind me of the words she had spoken a few minutes before. Then she was gone, and I stood alone in the library. With him.

"Look at me, boy," he growled. "Stand up like a man."

It required all my courage, but I lifted my face and met his eye. And waited for the blow to strike.

But it did not come. At least, not yet.

"Well, speak up, Edward. What have you got to say for yourself this time?"

His question took me completely by surprise. I had no thought I would be called upon to defend myself. I stood there dumb, unable to utter a sound.

"Are you going to deny your guilt? Let me remind you, there were witnesses. Are you going to stand before me and contradict their testimony? That without leave, you recklessly let that colt carry you right out of the barn? You bloody little fool! That horse could damn well have broken its leg. I laid out more than a hundred pounds for that animal."

Father's agitation mounted as my silence remained unbroken. Abruptly he began to slap his boot with the riding crop, which he had hitherto been holding behind his back.

Thwack! Thwack! Thwack!

I winced as each blow struck with more force than the one before it. As he smacked the leather, the mud still clinging to his boots splattered in sticky droplets on my shirt and face. At last, his tolerance strained to its limits by my continuing silence, he paced a few steps away from me, then suddenly turned around and pointed at me with the crop.

"You damn well knew what that colt meant to Rowland. You knew it and thought to lame the poor beast, didn't you? Well, didn't you?"

Though I fought desperately to suppress them, the lump of tears gathering in my throat made it difficult to speak. I *was* guilty. I had taken the colt out of the stable, but not for the reason he ascribed. How could I explain myself to him? Week after week, I had seen them riding away, laughing and talking, a father and son together, and I longed to go with them. More times than I could count, but always I was put off by Rowland with some excuse.

You're much too young. You could never keep pace. Stick to your music, Edward, it suits you better.

Rowland would never assent to my pleas to join them, so I must *do* something to arrest Father's attention and prove I was horseman enough to accompany them. And anything concerning his eldest son was the swiftest way to achieve that end.

"No, sir!" was all I managed to say before he cut me short.

"Besides being foolhardy, it was a wicked and unkind thing to do to your brother," he thundered. "I suppose you thought he would return to find his horse crippled up, as good as dead!"

He began pacing back and forth before me, breathing faster, becoming more agitated with every step. I had, as yet, answered none of his questions, but once this notion had fixed itself in my father's mind, there would be no getting around it.

"Tell me the truth, boy!" he roared. "That's why you did it."

"No, sir!" I shouted back at him.

Henry paced wildly, all the while slapping his boot with the riding crop. His face was flushed and sweaty. "Do you hate your brother so very much, Edward?"

"No, no!" I pleaded, my eyes filling with tears in spite of my frustration. "Papa, please—"

"Rowland has told me this was so, only I did not wish to believe it. But I see it now. All too clearly. Otherwise, why would you do such a thing to his prize colt?"

"No, sir, that's not how it was!" I protested, my resentment against Rowland beginning to efface my terror of Henry's wrath. "He lied to you!"

"What?"

My brazen accusation caught him off guard. Before he could interrupt, I followed up my advantage.

"It's Rowland who lies, Father, not me! If you don't believe I'm telling the truth, go look for yourself. The colt is not lame. He has but a small cut on his foreleg." I was sobbing now. "But I wish…I wish it was Rowland who got hurt instead of Sirocco!"

"Bloody Hell!" cried Henry.

In the look of horror and shock on my father's face, I suddenly realized my mistake. Before I could retract my words, I saw out of the corner of my eye his gloved fist raise the riding crop high above him, then swing it down toward the side of my head. Instinctively, I raised my arm and caught most of the blow just below my wrist. The force of the impact knocked me over and I crumpled to the floor, blinded by my burning tears, my arm afire with an agonizing, searing pain from wrist to elbow, my hand tingling and numb. I could not move.

Unable to rise and flee, every muscle and nerve tensed in full expectation he should strike me again. I tried to roll over to bring my unhurt arm to my defense, but at length, it proved unnecessary. A second blow never fell.

After several moments, I dared to look up. My father just stood there, the riding crop hanging loosely in his hand, as though he was unaware he still held it. Something seemed to go out of him. His face had changed. The flushed, red heat of anger melted into a slate gray paleness from shock and fear. I thought for a moment he would help me up from the floor, but his expression twisted in an anguished sort of grimace. He dropped the riding crop and without a word, left the room.

THE ROAD TO EXILE

PRESENT DAY

It was after one o'clock in the morning when the coach arrived at our final destination for the night, The Red Lion.

"I'm all done in, Rochester," Carter yawned, his breath misting in the chilly night air. He tugged out his pocket watch. "What say you we meet about seven o'clock for breakfast? I believe I should much prefer sleeping to eating at the moment."

"I cannot disagree with you. Pilot!"

The dog bounded out of the coach as the ostler wrestled with our bags. The innkeeper himself, a plump, red-faced man unusually tidy and hale for such a late hour, escorted us to adjacent rooms on the second floor.

"I would be much obliged if you would rouse us at six," I said. "My friend and I will want a hearty breakfast."

"O' course, sir. Best fare you'll find on the Dover Road, I'll wager."

"I look forward to it." I turned to Carter. "Until breakfast, James. Goodnight."

He nodded. "Rochester."

The remembrance of the past and whether or not to reveal such secrets kept me from slumber for almost an hour. At last, however, I dropped into a fitful, dreamless slumber. When the knock came the next morning, I groaned, climbed out of bed, then washed and dressed. Pilot ran along the corridor ahead of me to the narrow staircase down to the common room where I let him out into the yard.

Fires from two immense hearths at each end of the room burned bright and hot. Great chandeliers of wood bearing at least two dozen candles each hung above the tables, augmenting the firelight with a soft and flickering illumination. Through the high, dusty windows, I could see morning sunlight, giving the place a more cheerful aspect than it deserved.

A boisterous cluster of militiamen gathered around a larger table at one end of the room, while guests and travelers occupied the others. A harried waiter led me to Carter, who sat waiting for me at a small table along one wall near the far end of the room. He rose and we shook hands.

"Good morning, James. You slept tolerably well I trust?"

He straightened, rubbing his back with a groan. "What little sleep I did get. How I do look forward to being at home again."

"Yes, for you have someone awaiting your return. I envy you that."

The waiter soon reappeared, arms laden with plates of apples and cheese, bread, cold ham and a battered coffee pot, steaming with the hot beverage inside. "Any thin' else I kin bring ye, sirs?"

"No, that will do." I gave him a shilling. He bit it, then went back to the kitchen as an impatient voice called out that another rack of food was ready to be delivered.

"I am sorry for dozing off last night," Carter began.

I sipped my coffee. "No need for apologies."

He swallowed a mouthful of ham and bread then washed it down with coffee. "But I am all ears now, Rochester," he grinned.

"There is something I should tell you about my brother first. When he died, I was unable to leave Jamaica, nor did I wish to tell you why. Even after my father died a year later and I came back to Thornfield, I was too proud to reveal all that happened there. I was anxious to get her settled and leave for Europe. It was rude of me and I can only beg your pardon for it. Your meager understanding these last ten years has sufficed. But there is no getting around it—I must tell you the whole of it. And when you are acquainted with every sordid detail, I can only hope you will not disown our friendship."

He peered intently at me. "I was disappointed when I learned you had brought the child and chose not to tell me about it. Angry, too." He sighed. "But I am willing to believe you had your reasons. So I am ready to hear whatever you wish to tell me. Even about Rowland."

"My unfortunate brother, yes," I began. "Perhaps you were aware—our relationship was not what it should have been, between brothers. There was nothing of friendship, and very little respect."

Carter nodded. "You never did speak kindly of him."

"There must be no questions in your mind. The depth of the enmity between us bears directly upon the point of my tale. I have never told this to another soul. Not even my mother knew all the details. I did not sleep very well last night, debating whether I should tell you." I shook my head. "But after due consideration, I knew I must. You are privy to the most intimate secret I carry. Can I in conscience deny you this knowledge which can only enlighten your under-standing?"

"You can trust me, Edward."

"Yes, I know that. But be forewarned: there is an ugliness here, and while I yet harbor ill feeling towards him, it is not my intention to disparage the dead."

"That is between yourself and God, Rochester."

"God, no doubt, had very little to do with this."

And as we breakfasted, I related to him the incident of my childhood, the purloined ride and its terrible consequence.

"I know not what explanation Henry offered my mother, but she never questioned me. I hated my father more than ever. He would always take part with Rowland, and I must accept it."

"After this incident," I continued, "Henry ignored Rowland's accusations against me. His attitude went from indifference to positive neglect." And then I smiled. "But it was not long before Miss Catherine Fairfax came into my world and changed everything."

Carter nodded. "I remember her very well. Were not her father and yours close friends?"

"Only such acquaintance as most men cultivate. Sir Basil often accompanied Henry and Rowland on their hunting expeditions, so it seemed they found each other's society agreeable. Catherine's mother was very young and pretty, but she died soon after her confinement. After her death, the baronet often came to Thornfield and he brought Catherine with him. My mother was fond of the child, and took charge of her when the others went off for their sport to Ferndean Lodge."

I continued. "Sir Basil doted on his little girl. He was near fifty when she was born, and he never remarried. Of course there were young, foolish women aplenty to appease his baser instincts, all of whom endured a place in his bed hoping to be remembered in his will. But he became a prisoner to those appetites, consuming one mistress after another until no more would have him."

By now we had finished our breakfast, and it was time to depart. I summoned the waiter and asked him to bring his master. That gentleman soon appeared.

"How may I be of assistance to ye, sirs?"

"I wish to hire a private coach. My friend and I are traveling north, to Millcote, in ____ shire. You are perhaps familiar with that county?"

"That I am, sir."

"Have you a conveyance and a driver with whom you can part for a few days? I shall pay you well of course, for I am of no mind to ramble over the roads in the damned mail coach. Much too rapid and bumpy for my taste."

"Jack's the coachman for ye, good sirs. If ye don't mind me sayin' so, his opinion about them mail coaches is much the same as yours. Too bloody fast for his likin'. He survived an overturnin', ye know, but a couple o' his passengers that day weren't so lucky. He was done wif it not so long after that. I'll send a lad to let him know he's hired out for a couple o' days."

"Now! Joe!" he yelled towards the kitchen, and a boy of about six or seven years came running out and skidded to a halt. "Aye, sir?"

"Show these gentlemen to the coachin' yard. Jack's got a private hire to the northern shires."

"Aye sir, right away."

Carter thanked the innkeeper, and we followed Joe outside. Jack, a man of perhaps forty and quite weatherworn from his years of exposure, waited by the coach.

"Well sirs, the lad tells me yer 'eading up north, then?"

"We are," I replied. "To Millcote. Do you know it?"

"Well enuf."

"Let me assure you, we've no mind to be bumped along the road like the mail. You may spare your horses along the way."

Jack tipped his hat, and after preparations were got ready, the horses stood harnessed and snorting mist in the morning cold. I whistled for the dog and he came bounding out of the stable. Pilot jumped inside the chaise, and Carter and I climbed up after him.

Soon after getting underway, I said, "Have you the patience then to endure my promised tale of little Adele Varens?"

Carter grinned. "Indeed I do."

"Recall my brief letter to you last December, that you would hear more than you bargained for. The tale begins many years ago, before I brought the child to Thornfield Hall, before even I was sent out to Jamaica. Do you remember our final year of school? That fateful Christmas holiday?"

He smiled. "Almost twenty years ago now. But what I remember most was your anxiety about going home to Thornfield. Even though you must."

"The annual Christmas ball. My mother's one extravagance every year."

"Why would you not wish to be there?"

"Patience, Carter. For strange as it may seem, the events of those days set the course of my entire future life."

A FATEFUL PARTY

His eyes went wide. "Indeed?"

"Catherine Fairfax had spent countless hours at Thornfield as my playfellow when we were young." I sighed. "But children do not remain children forever."

"You fell in love with her," he said.

"I did. And I thought she was in love with me. We talked endlessly of adventures, traveling the world, getting married. It was nothing but fancy of course, though at the time, it was real to me. I suppose I must have pinned my hopes on those dreams."

"But reality was something different?"

"Very," I replied. "She was the daughter of a baronet, but what did that mean to me if we were in love? My dreams of a future life with her let me escape a world where rank, fortune and connections were of prime importance. And none of which I would possess, of course. But I had never given the matter any thought until I received her letter a few days before we left school."

He rubbed his chin. "I do remember now. There was no talking to you. But Edward, what could she possibly have to say to so upset you? That you would even express the idea of foregoing your mother's party—"

"Was unthinkable," I replied. "What young man is not a fool when he believes himself in love? My fantasy had so carried me away, I never considered the idea she would marry anyone but me. The urgency of her letter imploring me to come home because she had something of *great importance* to tell me set my imagination on fire. I fancied some prating prig of a dandy had convinced her father to bestow her hand. Desperate to escape his unworthy clutches, she had locked herself away in her room and dashed off that letter begging me to come save her from such a fate."

He smiled. "A plot worthy of Mrs. Radcliffe."

"Perhaps. I supposed she hoped I would plead with her father and rescue her from his unjust decision. I wasn't ready for that. Nonetheless, it was my duty to go home. No able-bodied Rochester son would have the impudence to miss the annual Christmas ball. Besides, that would have wounded my mother's feelings and I could never abide that."

"You miss her still."

"I do. She was already ill with the cancer that took her, but she concealed it from everyone. That spring it overcame even her formidable will. Henry was so consumed by his own grief that by the time I had word of it at school…well, she died before I could get home."

My eyes unexpectedly watered with tears as I turned away to gaze out the window. I squeezed them shut. How I regretted my conduct the last time I saw her, that very Christmas holiday.

"Everyone in the neighborhood looked forward to that party," remarked Carter, a little more cheerfully. "And yet what has all this to do with little Adele?"

"It was true that I had neither rank nor fortune. The

Rochester estate would be Rowland's one day. But I had something else I thought just as persuasive."

"Oh?"

"My mother was Fairfax," I began. "My grandfather was Lord Humphrey Fairfax of Kennington Park."

Carter looked astonished. "The viscount? In Northumberland?"

"The very same."

"Well, well, Edward," he smiled. "I must say, I am very impressed. But Northumberland is rather a distance from Thornfield. How did your father succeed with a viscount's daughter?"

I smiled. "Apparently my mother was quite insistent," I said. "What little I know of the story is that my mother one day simply announced to her father that she intended to marry Henry Rochester of Thornfield Hall and there was nothing he could do about it. My grandfather was not pleased, of course. I supposed he threatened and stormed about it. But my father being a Rochester made all the difference."

"In what respect?"

"We have no title nor noble birthright, but we had a claim upon an old promise—a promise which beget a tradition dating to the Civil War, which perhaps is compelling enough."

He grinned at me. "A promise and a tradition? Edward, you quite intrigue me."

"My father's ancestor, the man who built Thornfield Hall, fought in the Civil War. He was a soldier in the armies of Sir Thomas Fairfax. When he died at Marston Moor, his sacrifice on the field that day saved the life of his commander, and Sir Thomas, as recompense for this debt of honor, bestowed the hand of his daughter upon that of Rochester's eldest son. At Christmas of the same year, their families were knit in marriage by the blood which had been spilt on the battle-field. The connection between the two houses therefore reaches more than 160 years into the past, that promise being the circumvention to such impediments as rank or birthright."

"And so your mother invoked this promise?"

"Her father was furious. But she would not be moved, and in spite of his remonstrances and posturing, he gave way."

"So *that* was the reason for the Christmas ball," exclaimed Carter.

I nodded.

"I must say, Edward. I have never heard of this tradition before."

"It is of course nothing more than that, an old tradition. And you are quite right; it is not general knowledge. As I said, it has rarely been invoked, and while there have been a multitude of Fairfax descendants, we Rochesters are more scarce." I smiled. "It is an uncommon occurrence. I suppose as it should be. But there has never been anything compulsory attached to it. My grandfather might easily have refused his permission, but he did not."

"Why are you smiling?"

"I just recalled something told to me by my father at that very Christmas ball so many years ago. Let us just say in her own way, my mother could be as stiff-necked as we Rochesters."

Carter laughed heartily. "I can see how you came by your own pig-headedness."

I smiled. "True, very true. But you see despite my fancies, why my notion that Catherine might become my wife was not so unrealistic an expectation. The more I reread her letter, the more worked up I became. Why could she not simply tell me what was going on? I was on pins and needles for days."

"Some things never change, Edward. You've never been patient for anything."

"Even then, I was a reckless fool. I thought I knew Catherine, but what I learned that night overturned my world."

"Tell me," replied Carter.

"I arrived home a few days before the party. The house was alive with activity: the comings and goings of the tradesmen, the staff cleaning and polishing the place from top to bottom. And the tantalizing aromas from the kitchen—it all was heavenly. But my head was full of one thing—Miss Catherine Fairfax. When at last the day of the party arrived and her coach rolled through the gates, I ran down the drive to meet it. What happened that night set in motion the events which obliged me to leave England."

CATHERINE FAIRFAX

THORNFIELD—DECEMBER, 1795

Miss Catherine Fairfax, breathtaking in her white Christmas gown edged with silver and ermine, held her brother Tom's hand as he assisted her out of the carriage emblazoned with the Fairfax coat of arms.

He grinned at me. "Devilish of me to accompany her, eh, Rochester?"

"Better you than the old man."

He kissed his sister's cheek. "Dearest Cate. We are now on hallowed Rochester grounds."

As we shook hands, he winked. "Beware the cat's claws, Edward." And bowing with a flourish, he was off.

She took my arm without a word as we made our way toward the house. The diamonds in her tiara sparkled in the light of the torches lining the drive, which flickered and hissed with the light falling snow. I pulled a folded paper from my coat pocket and showed it to her.

"Why did you write this?"

"Oh, my letter," she laughed. "I simply must be sure that you would—but never mind that now. May we just go?"

Her reluctance to answer exasperated me, but I knew her temper and it was no use pressing the point. I shrugged. "Very well, we'll go."

Women. Would I ever understand them?

Her countenance glowed with excitement as we drew nearer the mansion.

In that face I saw traces of the mischievous little girl who had long ago been my playfellow. All too quickly I must be sent to school. She must become a lady. Our schemes and plans so carefully laid as we explored the wide world must be set aside for the responsibilities of adulthood.

I touched the delicate, gloved hand on my arm. Its slender and supple fingers not long ago had been small and stubby. An image of us both on our knees wildly digging in the fields for mice flashed across my memory. The magnificent silken gown hid all traces of mud and scraped knees. She was now a young woman, and must set such whimsy aside.

We had spent many days together in one another's company, more often quarreling like a brother and sister. But looking at her now, in all her glorious womanhood—by no means did I feel about her as I would a sister. But this barrier of silence between us was unnatural.

"Kit!" I whispered in her ear. *You absolutely must come home for Christmas. I have something of great importance to tell you.* "Why would you write that when you knew very well I would be at Thornfield?"

"Oh, Edward!" she replied sharply. "I wanted to tell you… oh, can you not wait but a little while longer?"

"No!" I whispered harshly. "Tell me now."

"This party is your mama's annual grande affair, is it not?" said she, rather casually using the intimate reference to my mother. "It would be fitting…well, I thought our announcement should be made at such a festive and well-attended occasion, that's all."

"Our announcement?" I answered, quite astonished. "Would it not be premature?"

She looked at me curiously. "No, not at all."

"Of course," I echoed, still puzzling over the mystery.

I should put the question to her now, but she seemed irritated and I thought the better of it. Of course she knew I intended to ask for her hand, but not until the end of spring term. Her idea was brilliant, really. What better place to announce our engagement than at this festive occasion attended by all our family and friends?

As we approached the front door of the Hall, it flew open unexpectedly. "Ah, there you are at last, Miss Fairfax."

My little fantasy was suddenly shattered by that well-known but despised voice. Rowland. He stood at the door of the Hall, a glass of wine in his hand, and a deuced smirk on his face.

"You're drunk," I muttered.

"Not quite yet, I think…but well on my way to becoming so. What of it? It is a party, after all." He stepped aside, offering Miss Fairfax his hand. "Quite sporting of you to bring her round, Edward. Miss Fairfax, if you would step this way."

I tried to prevent him. "Rowland, what do you think you're doing? Kit?"

"Ah, Kit, is it?" He leered at her. "Is that his nickname for you? Well, then, Miss Kit." He flashed a stupid grin, and in a quick motion, pulled her close and kissed her.

Completely unprepared for his shameless deed, she laughed weakly and pushed him away, but I could not tell whether she was angry or amused by the liberty he had taken.

"Please, Mr. Rochester—"

Rowland only laughed. "Mr. Rochester, is it?" He drained his glass, then tossed it into the shrubbery adjacent the front door. "Yes, I suppose we must give way to these damned civilities a while longer, mustn't we? Very well, then." He bowed. She laid a gloved hand upon his proffered arm, and he grinned suggestively. "Now there's a good girl. This way if you please."

He removed her cloak and tossed it to me.

"See to that, will you, Edward?"

And off they went, arm in arm down the hall and into the drawing room where I spied a group of guests gathered round the pianoforte singing Christmas carols.

THE GAUNTLET THROWN

I FOLLOWED THEM INTO THE HOUSE AND STOPPED IN THE
hallway. Fury like a volcano rose within me as Rowland
hovered amidst a cluster of friends, lazily amusing them with
a joke or a compliment. Every time he looked at Catherine,
touched her hand, or whispered in her ear, I wanted to kill
him. But she seemed indifferent rather than pleased with his
unctuous charms.

He had swooped out the door and snatched her from my
arm as a hawk captures its prey. How often had he simply
taken what was mine? How fond he was of boasting that one
day Thornfield would belong to him, and when that day
came, I had best look to myself.

Not this time. I would never retreat from his belligerence
ever again!

I stormed into the drawing room. There he stood, already
a glass of Christmas punch in hand, Miss Fairfax haughtily at
his side. Familiar faces gathered around him: Captain Dent
and his wife Mariah, Arthur and Julia Eshton, and George
Lynn, recently returned from the Court of St. James where
he had been knighted.

"See to this yourself, you bastard!" I threw her cloak at him.

"What have we here, little brother?"

He snatched the cloak out of the air, not spilling a drop of his drink. Everyone around us ceased their conversations. Miss Fairfax looked at me pleadingly, her face shaded by an expression of injured pride and embarrassment.

"Edward, please," she whispered. "It is too late."

"I should have done this a long time ago." The indignation and rage within me would not be silenced. "I will speak with you alone, Rowland. Now."

His eyes widened in surprise, I suppose at my audacity to call him out in front of everyone. But I would brook no refusal, and he knew it. Would he comport himself as a gentleman and show the courtesy due our mother on this occasion? For an instant, I feared I had unleashed the devil in him.

"Well, well," he laughed. "The cub has claws after all. If you will excuse me," he bowed to the others. "It seems Little Brother desires an audience."

He signaled for a servant, who came immediately. Rowland downed the remainder of the drink in a swallow, then handed the glass and cloak over to the servant. With an exaggerated sweep of the hand, he bowed. "Shall we?"

I gave a curt nod to the others. As we made our way through the sea of guests, I felt strangely exhilarated, thrilled by their amazement as a murmur of gossip rippled through their ranks and all eyes were upon us as we strode out of the room. Among those who watched was our father, Henry Rochester.

A few moments later, I burst into the library, half expecting my mother to be sitting at her accustomed spot in the corner. But that large table had been removed years ago when I was sent away to school. She never again used this room to attend her daily business.

A fire burned in the hearth and the air was warm, but the room somehow felt cold and lifeless. Rowland's booted step behind me broke the silence.

"You're not going to away with it this time!"

"Get away with what?" He yawned.

"I will know your intentions respecting Miss Fairfax."

"Really, Edward. My intentions? What are you blathering on about?"

His self-righteous arrogance made me feel like I was ten years old, enduring his humiliations all over again. My fingers twitched to be around his throat. I got right in his face.

"How dare you take such liberties with Catherine—her father is a guest in this house!"

"Of course he is. We insisted upon it."

"What do you mean?"

He feigned a sigh, then in a low, ominous voice, said, "But it appears she neglected to tell you. Sir Basil will proclaim it to the world tonight. Miss Fairfax is to be *my* wife."

I staggered. "What? You are engaged?"

"We are." He smirked. "What do you think of your darling Kit now?"

I fell into a chair, suddenly light-headed from the unexpected revelation. "But you have no right...you know very well that she and I were meant to—"

"I know no such thing, Edward. You and Miss Fairfax? Don't be absurd." He tilted his head in mock sincerity. "Ah. You actually believed it, didn't you? That she wanted to marry you?"

I leapt out of the chair, my anger doubled at the sight of his conceited grin and I half-choked on the reply. "It has always been understood between us. This spring, after I finish school. She will be my bride, not yours!"

His voice rose to match my increasing anger. "She will not! Your idiotic notion is preposterous. You've been living in your own little dreamworld. She never had any such intention at all."

"She did, I tell you! We were always together. We grew fond of each other, and talked of it often. It is meant to be."

Again, he smiled with that withering look of judgment. "You talked about it, did you? Since you were children? Don't be ridiculous."

"There is nothing ridiculous about it. It is as I have said."

"Miss Fairfax is the only daughter of a baronet. She would never marry a second son who can bring neither rank nor fortune into such a marriage. I, on the other hand, can provide everything she'll want. Your wild fancies have carried you away for so long it seems you have forgotten the consequences of such impropriety."

He laughed again as I pushed past him and stumbled to the mantlepiece. Every feeling of bitterness and hatred of him I ever harbored from childhood rose up in my throat. I had nothing to say to these words. They were not new to me. For as long as I could remember, he had hurled them at me daily, repeating them incessantly until this reproach of my inferior position became a vague sing-song in my ears.

"You are insufferable!" I shouted helplessly. "For once, I would possess what you wanted, but could not have. That idea galls you, doesn't it?"

He laughed. "You believe Miss Fairfax is what I want?"

"You have said it yourself, Rowland. You are engaged to her. Why else would you do it?"

"You are far too trusting of women, Edward. Miss Fairfax is a pretty enough girl, and when she comes into her full womanhood, will be quite comely. To be sure, she will provide me pleasure enough, for a while at least. But unlike you, I understand men like Sir Basil. He is interested in connections, wealth, power. The Rochester estate will bring all of those things, and the Rochester estate will be mine." He laid special emphasis on that last word. "But yes, you are right. A most delightful benefit that accrues to me is that our marriage will prevent you from having her."

"Catherine could never love you!"

"Love has nothing to do with it. Besides, she is very much her father's child. You have been so smitten by your fantasy you cannot see that. But it matters not, for we both shall get what we want out of the bargain."

"You're nothing but a heartless bastard, pretending to do your duty to Father all the while you enjoy rubbing my nose in it!"

"Pretending to do my duty?" His voice rose again, for I had touched a nerve. "You are so pathetic Edward, do you know that? You have ever been so, always groveling after me to go somewhere you did not belong."

"The blood that flows in my veins is just as much Rochester blood as yours. And I will not relinquish the rights that bestows upon me."

"There are no rights where you are concerned. Birth order, my dear little brother, is everything. Casting aspersions on my paternity will gain you nothing." He shrugged. "Providence raised me above you. Just accept it."

"Providence? You have never acknowledged Providence in your life, yet now its invocation suits your purpose to justify what you have done?" I took a step towards him then muttered, "Then let the authorities consign me to His judgment after I have wrung your neck!"

How I loathed him and everything that would be his and could never be mine, for God help me, he was right! And I despised him all the more for it.

He stepped back, a genuine look of surprise on his face. "You would do it, wouldn't you?"

Just then the library door banged open and in strode our father, glowering at us both.

"What in blazes is going on in here? Everyone in the house can hear your shouting from here to the front door, for God's sake. If you think I will allow you to embarrass your mother in front of her guests, you are gravely mistaken. Keep a civil tongue, or I swear, I'll rip them out of your heads."

Rowland yawned. "It is the usual discussion, Father. Edward again is chafing at the lot of a second son."

I glared at him. "Tell him the truth. We were discussing Miss Fairfax."

"I suppose that is more accurate," he replied coolly.

Henry interrupted again. "What has Miss Fairfax to do with this?"

"Edward believes I have usurped his place," replied Rowland. "He claims they have doted upon one another since their childhood. The imminent announcement of her engagement to me has ruined his plans forever."

Henry's soft laughter cut me to the heart. "You're not serious, Edward? You, wed Miss Fairfax?"

"And why not Miss Fairfax?"

"She's a baronet's daughter."

"What should that mean to me, to her, if we love each other?"

"You cannot seriously be asking me that question," replied Henry with irritation.

"I tried to tell him the same thing," interrupted Rowland, who was beginning to sound like the toadying fifteen-year-old he had once been. "He refuses to see reason. He is so besotted by love," he sneered. "Or his lusts—"

"You fiend!" I lunged toward him.

"Enough!" cried Henry, stepping between us. He turned to his eldest. "Leave us at once. See to our guests."

"But Father—"

"You heard me. I will not have the two of you ruin this evening. Now get out."

Rowland glared at me. "Oh, very well. As usual, I shall miss out on all the fun. But I trust, Father, you will enlighten his understanding? About everything?"

"Go!" retorted Henry, his temper flaring again.

Rowland obeyed without another word. After his departure, we stood in silence for a time. I was hardly aware of my father's presence as I stared at the closed door of the library, the image of Rowland's impudent grin burned in my mind. The sounds of the party drifted down the hallway, but it seemed like a world far away, a world in which I would never have a part.

"What did he mean, 'enlighten my understanding'?"

"Sit down, Edward."

My heart went cold. "Is it true, then? They are engaged?"

"Yes."

"But how can this be? Why was I not told?"

An elusive phrase from Catherine's letter echoed again in my thoughts. *There is something of great importance I must tell you.* And then, what had she said to me, not an hour ago? *It is too late.* Oh, God, Catherine. Why? Why did you not tell me?

"How long?" I whispered.

"Only very lately," replied Henry. "I was not aware they were fond of each other."

"They are not!" I exclaimed. "Kit…Miss Fairfax, has never looked at Rowland in that way. He is more than twelve years her senior. She is but sixteen. What can her father be thinking to consent to such an unequal union?"

"The wedding will not take place for another two years at least, perhaps three," replied Henry quietly. "I would hardly call it unequal, however. The Rochester estate is a highly coveted prize. Why should not the baronet consent to the match?"

I was becoming agitated again. "He can hardly be acquainted with her. He is so much older. They have nothing in common. She is but a girl—"

I stopped, knowing that was not true. She was no longer the merry little child who had been my playfellow, but was a young woman, fresh, mature and so very aware of the world.

"Rowland does not love her," I muttered. "He's a selfish pig and well you know it."

"Hold your tongue," replied Henry ominously. "He is a Rochester, and your brother. Show some respect."

"Perhaps you will compel him to do likewise?"

He frowned. "While it is sometimes true that mutual affection has little to do with such arrangements, it is my understanding that Miss Fairfax made no objections to the match. There is nothing to prevent them from marrying."

"You must know well what that means, Father. Did not you wed above your station when you married my mother? A viscount's daughter?"

Whatever Henry Rochester's temperament, he could never remain angry when the idea of my mother was brought before him. But neither was he prepared to relinquish his displeasure with me, for he replied sternly, "Do not make presumptions about things of which you are intensely ignorant."

"What is that supposed to mean?"

"You thought to invoke an ancient promise to permit you a titled marriage. But whatever you believe about it, know this: appeal to that promise has rarely been successful, nor has it any covenant power."

"I care nothing about a damned title, but if it swayed my grandfather, why not Sir Basil?"

"It was entirely your mother's influence which persuaded her father. She refused to be wed to some stranger simply because her father believed his birth was blessed by Heaven."

I stared at him. "You mean to tell me…she *chose you?*"

He laughed suddenly, full and hearty. "She was her father's favorite, you know. But after he condemned her elder sister to marriage with that cold-blooded bastard, your mother never forgave him. He consented to our marriage hoping to win back her approbation."

I got up from the chair and went to the hearth. "Why are you telling me all this?"

"Because you know very well that Rowland is right. With her engagement to him, you must no longer think of Miss Fairfax at all."

"I must choose for myself some sort of profession, it seems. Perhaps the law? Would that not meet with your approval? A lawyer in the family?"

"Don't be an ass, Edward," said Henry in a low voice. "Of course you're not going to practice the law."

"Why am I at college, then, what is the point? You both have told me more times than I can count it all falls to Rowland. What am I expected to live upon, unless by the sweat of my own brow?"

Henry hesitated a moment, then replied cooly, "I have a plan in mind for you."

"Do you? I suppose I should be flattered. But why waste time at school? Am I there to learn something useful, or has it been merely to pass the time until you can manipulate circumstances to your own end?"

"Whether you care to believe it or not, Edward, I have given a great deal of consideration to your future. I would not have you left without resource. To that end, I have an arrangement in view."

"An arrangement?" I laughed bitterly. "I am to be a

bargaining chip then, unlike my mother, who refused the privilege."

In a growling voice, he replied, "Have a care, boy. I am in no mood for your sarcasm."

"Do you expect my gratitude? What sort of glorious future does this arrangement entail? Ah, you've purchased an officer's commission in the army for me, is that it?"

"I would never occur to me to do such a thing."

"Certainly you cannot be thinking of the Church."

"Of course not. What use have I for the Church?"

"Then what?"

"Some months ago, I received a letter from Jonas Mason, an old friend of mine who long ago settled in the West Indies."

"Where did you say? The West Indies?"

Henry held up his hand. "Hear me out. Yes, the West Indies. Jamaica, Spanish Town. We are old friends from many years ago, and when we parted company, he set off to make his fortune in the New World. And indeed, he has been very successful there. His land holdings are extensive, and his vineyards in Madeira thrive. Mason's only son spends half of the year overseeing the wine-making business there, and it seems desires no other responsibilities. Jonas therefore has no provision for the succession of his West Indian endeavors."

Henry continued. "But his eldest daughter, by all reports, is the jewel of the island, beautiful and desired by every man who sees her. Mason believes the only way left him to secure his legacy is to seek a suitable husband for her."

I laughed. "And I am to be this husband?"

"Why not? Jonas Mason wants good English blood running through the veins of his grandson. This then is my challenge for you, boy. For years you have clamored for the opportunity to prove yourself. Here, I lay it at your feet. All you need do is accept it. Do you have the courage to take it up? Go to Jamaica. Be that Englishman!"

The Dover Road—January, Present Day

Carter was thoughtful. "You had no intention of going, then?"

"I was furious with Henry, that he thought I would simply acquiesce to his scheme."

"And your mother…what did she think of this plan?"

I shook my head. "I am almost ashamed to tell you, but I presumed she was in agreement with my father about it. Rarely did she contravene his will. Why should this occasion be any different? I saw her later that evening, and curse me for it, but I never asked her. God, what an arrogant ass I was! Full of anger, pride, resentment. After the events of that evening, I had no intention of looking the fool while Sir Basil give his daughter in marriage to that devil, Rowland."

"And yet," replied Carter, "you did go to Jamaica. What changed your mind? Your mother's death?"

"The day of her funeral, something happened for which I was completely unprepared. We had returned to the house from the memorial service at the little church near the front gates of Thornfield Hall. Henry shut himself away for the remainder of the afternoon, and I retreated to the library, that refuge wherein I had spent so much of my childhood with her."

ESCAPE

I sat near the hearth, staring at the place where she used to sit composing letters, knitting, writing in a diary, or directing my early schooling. The aura of her presence still lingered, giving me comfort as it had when I was a boy.

"Edward?"

I looked up. It was Catherine. She was just shutting the door. Robed in black, a vapory veil still covered her face. I stood at once.

"Kit—Miss Fairfax. Thank you for coming."

A pang of jealousy pricked me as I thought of her and Rowland.

"How could I not come, Edward?" she answered with genuine sympathy. "The moment we received the dreadful news, Father insisted." She strode across the room towards me. "Of course, I would have been here on any account. I am so sorry about your mother. Do, accept my sincere condolences."

She held out her hand, still sheathed by a silken black glove.

"Thank you."

I pressed it with gratitude, but did not immediately release it. Nor did she make an effort to withdraw it from me. Then, as though it had stung me, I suddenly let go.

"You…have seen Rowland, then?" I asked, trying to suppress the sudden agitation I felt.

Catherine lifted the veil. Her dark eyes pierced me. "I believe he is with the other guests."

She drew nearer. "I was with him at the graveside, next to Father. Did you not see me, Edward? I was standing in your shadow."

"Were you? I am sorry for not acknowledging you. I suppose I must have seen you. Do forgive me. I…I have too many things on my mind to be of much use to anyone."

Coming closer still, she said, "Yes, your head is full of many plans I am sure, with your own departure forthcoming."

"My departure? Oh, yes, of course—"

I stopped short, suddenly wary of revealing to her any specifics about the arrangements my father had made for me. "What can you know of it?"

"Only that you are to journey to some warm and exotic destination halfway around the world and there, take to yourself a wife."

"How do you know this?"

"Rowland told me."

"Indeed?"

Rowland! How had he learned of Henry's little scheme? I remembered the argument we had at Christmas. But Father had sent him from the room before revealing any details of the plan for Jamaica. And then like a thunderbolt, his final words before returning to the party struck me: *You will enlighten him I trust, Father…about everything?*

That bloody bastard! I thought he was referring to his

engagement with Miss Fairfax, but no. He had known about the Jamaica venture all along. My hatred flamed afresh, but I would not let the demon show itself here. Not now. And especially, not in front of her.

I struggled to maintain my composure while attempting to sound resolute. "I am sorry to disappoint you, Miss Fairfax, but I have not decided whether I shall go."

She smiled, then drew a gloved, slender finger down the sleeve of my coat. Her hand lingered on mine. "I am not at all disappointed, Edward. Why would you think so?"

I shivered. I told myself she was only showing kindness and sisterly affection for a grieving brother. I should tell her to release me. But I said nothing. Her touch was welcome.

"You should change out of this wet coat," she murmured. "It is quite damp from the weather. You will catch a chill."

It had rained off and on all morning, and the fresh scent of the spring shower clung to every garment, her veil, her hair. I stared into the hearth, trying to ignore the increasing awkwardness of our situation.

"Yes. I should go upstairs directly. No doubt I am unfit to appear before our guests. Father will have no mind to attend to any such duty, I can assure you."

"Please...do not go, Edward."

"Why not? You have just admonished me I may become ill from standing here in these wet clothes, and now you prevent me?"

"I was speaking of your departure from England," she whispered. "Do not go. I do not wish it. Surely, from all you have said, you would rather remain at Thornfield."

"What are you saying, Catherine? Why should you wish me to stay? You are betrothed to my brother. You will be his wife in two years."

"Yes, I will," she replied, with the bearing and air of self-importance befitting a baronet's daughter. "Your brother was my choice for a husband, but tell me." She suddenly seized my hands. "Can you say the same for yourself? This journey which has been arranged for you? Is it truly what you want? To marry a woman you have never seen? Have you nothing to say about it? Edward, I don't believe you want to leave England." She lifted her chin. "Tell your father you have no wish to go."

"And why would I do that? It's all arranged."

She nodded. "But must you go so far to find a wife? Is there not one in England who will suffice?"

"Suffice? You don't understand. I have a duty to my family, to my father…my mother. It is what she wanted. I will not sully her memory by acting against her wishes."

I looked at Miss Fairfax again, suddenly mistrustful of her questions. The softness in her voice had vanished. Her tone had become sharp, and penetrating. I felt like a witness before a judge. "But why should you care whither I am bound? As Rowland's wife, you will one day be mistress of Thornfield Hall."

She smiled again. "Yes, I shall be. But Edward, have you not ever wished that circumstances had been different?"

"What do you mean?"

"Had *you* been the eldest son, all this would be yours!" She let go my hands and held her arms wide, pirouetting before me, almost giddy. "Then it would all be perfect, in every way."

"But I am not the eldest son. Rowland will inherit. And you shall marry him. Is that not enough?"

She threw back her head and laughed. Clear and ringing, it was full of mockery and triumph. She came towards me and again took my hand then held it to her face. When she spoke, her voice was hard and full of impatience.

"Oh, Edward, why can you not admit you still have feelings for me? I know that you do."

"Do not speak so!" I yanked my hand away, then lurched backwards, desperate to put some distance between us. "You are to marry another man...my brother, for God's sake!"

"Then it is true!" Her laughter rang in my ears. "You still love me, Edward. Why will you not say it?"

I shook my head. "Be silent, Catherine. It was never meant to be."

I retreated to the door, but she came closer, eager to press her point. Her eyes glowed with excitement.

"Oh, but it can be, Edward, if you do not leave England. I will be mistress of Thornfield, yes, but I am also mistress of my own heart, and I tell you truly. It has *never* belonged to your brother."

It shocked and thrilled me to hear such a declaration. My brother's bride-to-be, standing before me, confessing it was not him whom she wanted—but me.

"How can you say such things?" I whispered. "You would marry a man knowing you cared nothing for him, and never could? It is despicable."

"Whatever do love and marriage have to do with one another, Edward? You are so naïve! My marriage to your brother will please my father, and it will please me for I will get what I want."

"Thornfield Hall," I murmured.

"I have loved it since I was a little girl! And though I shall not be the wife of a baronet, who knows what may happen? My father's father was raised up to the rank. With enough money and the proper influence, why not your brother?"

"All our plans, our schemes were nothing but lies, every one of them?"

"No, Edward," her voice softened again. "Not entirely. I do care for you. Truly, I do."

"And yet you will marry my brother."

"Your brother will have what I want."

"You cannot want me very much, then."

"Oh, but I shall have you nevertheless, shan't I?"

"How can you say so? You will be another man's wife."

"I have no illusions that Rowland will be faithful to me. Why should I pretend to be faithful to him? Shall I remain at home, pining away while he's off to London having his fun? Certainly not! Do not look so shocked, Edward. Of course I shall do my duty: one or two offspring, and I am done. But I'll no longer share his bed, nor he mine. We shall take up with those who are more pleasing to us, that is all. It will be the usual marriage of convenience. His fortune, my name."

I stood with my back to the library door, poised to leave as she closed the last distance between us and took my hand again, a fire of defiance glowing in her beautiful eyes.

"Catherine, why are you doing this?"

"Why, Edward?" Softly, she pressed her lips in my hand, then placed it on her cheek. At her feverish touch, all the jealousy in my heart rose up before me like a viper, and I despised Rowland for everything he had, for everything he would take from me. I seized her and pulled her to me, then desperately covered her mouth with mine, exulting in triumph and longing to shout it to the world.

When our lips parted, she whispered, "It is you I have loved, Edward. Only you. Kiss me again."

She tried to pull me closer, but I pushed her away.

"No!"

I released her. The hatred I felt for Rowland was stronger than ever. But a woman who could play us one against the other? How could I ever have thought that I loved her?

"This can never be."

"You do love me, Edward!" Her voice rose in desperation, yet still she had the self-command for one last attempt. She lifted her chin. "You may not have spoken the words, but your actions have said it!"

"Love does not behave in such a manner. You will excuse me, for I have a duty to our guests." I walked to the door and grasped the knob.

"Don't go, Edward. I do not wish it!"

"And yet I shall. You have made your choice, Catherine Fairfax. I leave you to it."

I yanked open the door. As I strode away, her proud, yet frantic voice cried out, "Edward Rochester! One day your heart, too, will be divided between that which is right—and that which you love!

PRESENT DAY

Our coach stopped to change horses and have a brief rest, so Carter and I went inside to warm ourselves and have something to eat.

"I would never have believed Miss Fairfax capable of such an idea," he remarked after a waiter had brought us a brandy.

"No man with any pride would tolerate the infamous arrangement she suggested," I replied, "even if he was the most profligate creature ever to walk the earth. It is entirely hypocritical of course, but such is our nature. We must have complete victory, Carter. A divided conquest is no conquest at all."

"But why leave the country?"

"Catherine would have been merciless in her persistence. Rowland had snatched away the only thing in the world I ever thought would be mine. I was so blinded by my hatred of him, I have no doubt that one day, God help me, I would give in to her. Gladly."

He sighed. "I am sorry for it, Edward."

"And yet I must give him credit for preventing the worse agony of knowing her faithlessness. She had proclaimed her intention of dishonoring her vows to him. Might not she one day do the same to me? Let me assure you—it is an ordeal I would wish upon no man."

"And so it must be Jamaica, then?"

"All I knew was I must go away from her presence immediately."

"What was the voyage like?" he asked. "All those years ago…do you know? I intended to ship out on the HMS *Magnamine* as their surgeon not long after you departed England, but my father's illness prevented me."

"The Royal Navy, James? I had no idea you had a pirate's heart."

He laughed. "The chance for adventure, not to mention the steady wage, were irresistible. Had my father lived, I don't believe I would have remained behind. But Edward, leaving home as you did? Traveling so far to a strange place…?"

"My mother was dead. There was no one left who cared for me. Since the night of the party, the echo of my father's challenge rang so in my head I could not be rid of it. For years, I had begged to be given my due, to prove myself worthy of his respect. He had thrown the gauntlet of Jamaica at my feet, and it stuck in my vitals, haunted me day and night, till I knew I must act. Otherwise, it would only confirm his belief that I was weak and had no resource in myself. The only path I could see lay across the Atlantic. So, I took it."

JAMAICA

At last, our ship, the *Elizabeth*, sailed into Kingston Harbor. After seven tedious weeks at sea, I was more than ready to be ashore. I had spent half the time in the throes of seasickness, or walking the deck face into the wind to keep the nausea at bay.

But the last week of the voyage had been the worst. A violent storm rose up, tossing us about like a bottle cork, so truly, when the shore at last came into sight, I was relieved and grateful to see land once again.

The sun beat down as I waited to disembark. Men, wagons, carts and horses were everywhere around the docks, shouting and cursing one another they as unloaded the ships just arrived, or struggled to load and prepare others bound for foreign ports. I detected the exotic fragrance of banana, a rare fruit I once tasted in London. But the others were unknown to me. Besides, the overwhelming odors of tobacco, sugar and rum mingled with sweat, horses, and gunpowder easily overpowered them.

As finally I descended the gangway, from somewhere out

of the teeming activity, I heard a softly accented voice call my name.

"Edward Rochester?"

In the street fronting the wharf, a fine-looking coach had pulled to a stop. A man not much older than myself was looking at me out the window. A black climbed down from the driver's seat and opened the door. The occupant of the carriage stepped out, took off his hat and bowed.

"You are Edward Rochester of Thornfield Hall, in England?"

I bowed in return. "I am, sir."

We shook hands. His were soft. Not unusual for a gentle-man, I supposed. Not that I performed much labor myself, but I had been an avid horseman since I was a boy, and spent my days in the stables, looking after our stock. I attended the sales and auctions at the other estates in the county, and had become somewhat of an expert in the district.

"And you are, sir?"

"I am Richard Mason, son of Jonas Mason, who is the friend of your father, Henry Rochester of Thornfield Hall in England. Yes?"

I nodded. "I believe they have been acquainted for some years. But I confess Mr. Mason, I was unaware of the connection until my father informed me at Christmas I was to come here." I looked around him into the carriage. "Did Miss Mason not accompany you?"

"My sister? No, no. Just look around you, sir. This is no place for a lady. There will be time later—" He smiled oddly. "We shall discuss that at length with my father, after you are settled."

"I hope so," I replied. "As you must understand, I am anxious to meet her."

"Of course, Mr. Rochester, of course. Lucias," he called to the servant. "Put the gentleman's luggage on the coach."

We made our way inland to Alta Arboleta, Mason's house and plantation north of Spanish Town, up into the foothills from the Rio Cobre River. I tried to draw him into conversation, but he answered only with vague generalities.

During the intervals of silence between bursts of conversation, I observed him more closely, wondering if his sister at all resembled him. His features were regular, his eye large and well-cut. At first glance, he was a fine-looking man. But something about his expression struck me as vacant and tame. There was no command in that brow, no thought in that blank, brown eye.

What about Miss Mason? Was she as beautiful as I had been told? Would she like me? Would I like her? This uncertainty was maddening. In recalling that last, astonishing encounter with Catherine Fairfax, I felt a pang of regret for leaving England.

And yet I knew in my heart of hearts that it could never be. Rowland, damn him, had been right about her. She was very much her father's child, willing to marry a man she cared nothing for as the price to get what she wanted, to be Mistress of Thornfield Hall.

Though she claimed she loved me, I knew it wasn't true. I imagined the letter of triumph I would receive from her after she and Rowland had said their vows. How different their union would be from my father and mother, whom I knew had a deep affection for one another. For Rowland and Catherine, however, marriage was merely a means to an end. I did not envy either one of them. A loveless match and a cold marriage bed must be a misery best avoided.

I had blundered from one intolerable choice to the next. Might Miss Mason and I come to feel friendship for one another? That would render our situation bearable, at least. And perhaps, true affection could grow.

My stomach was doing flip-flops again, for still, I was suffering the effects of the voyage, and beginning to feel queasy from the bouncing of the coach. Mason noticed at once.

"Ah, Rochester. After so many weeks at sea, the change to land can be upsetting."

"Damned inconvenient," I muttered, pushing up the window and leaning against the side of the coach to take in the fresh air. "My first voyage. Is it that obvious?"

He smiled. "The long trip from England can be quite the ordeal."

"Yes," I agreed. "Seven weeks, and the last spent in a terrible storm. I was sure we were going to sink."

"The weather in this part of the world is capricious and often violent. I am sorry you had to experience it on your first journey."

"As am I."

Would that I never experienced it at all!

The road began to rise as we headed farther inland, toward the house.

"What of your mother?" I inquired after another protracted silence. "Does she look forward to the wedding?"

Mason shaded his eyes a moment. "Our mother has been dead for many years. But she would have rejoiced to see the day of her daughter's marriage, I know."

"I am sorry," I replied, the memory of my own mother's recent death still a sting. She had been ill at Christmas but no one knew. *Damn me!* I had been so upset about Kit and Rowland…I never perceived her own pain. *God forgive me.*

As the coach drove on, Mason again fell silent. Perhaps he was skeptical about this whole arrangement. Not that I could blame him. A complete stranger about to wed his only sister? Were they close? What had been her reaction to the scheme? Did she welcome it, or reject it? I grew more anxious the closer we got to the house. I just wanted to get these damned formal introductions out of the way. Give us time with each other, and I felt surely we could find some common ground.

After another hour, we turned up a long drive. A pair of forbidding, black iron gates, each decorated with an ornate letter "M" wrought into the center of its frame, stood open. The drive ended in a circle in front of a stately, Georgian mansion that spanned the top of the hill.

At the center of the long front was a large, round porch ringed with slender Doric columns supporting the balcony off the middle suite. At the center of the thick, green lawn in the middle of the circle stood an ornate fountain, a Greek nymph tilting a scallop shell out of which water cascaded into the pool in which it was standing.

An older man in a white hat stood on the porch. He was smoking a cigar. As we pulled to a stop, he bounded down the steps. Years of exposure to the tropical sun gave him a leathery, weather-beaten look, yet the image of the son was like a shadow in his countenance. There was no mistaking Jonas Mason.

"Ah, my father is here to welcome us," remarked Richard.

When the vehicle stopped, I let myself out before Lucias could open the door.

"Well now," said the elder Mason, looking me up and down as I stepped down from the coach. "Henry Rochester's boy, as I live."

"I am, sir," said I, shaking his outstretched hand.

"It's good to see you here at last, though you look a bit green about the gills, lad." He laughed. "I was hopin' the voyage wouldn't be too much for ye. But no mistake, yer standin' here, and that says a lot, I'll grant ye that. A fine beginnin'. Come in, have some refreshment. 'Tis a long passage from England."

"Indeed it was, sir. And when may I have the pleasure of

meeting Miss Mason? I am rather anxious, as you must understand."

"Oh, there's plenty o' time for that, lad. My girl is with family in Kingston just now. I'm sorry, but I did not know when to expect ye."

"Did not my father write to apprise you of the sailing?"

"He did," replied Mason, casting an odd glance at his son. "But I'd hardly call the schedules regular. Dickey has been to the harbor most every day for the last fortnight now, awaitin' your appearance. But never you mind that. Yer here now, and all's well."

This news that my bride-to-be was away sorely disappointed me. "Will she be long in Kingston, sir? Perhaps...I might go there?"

"No," he replied abruptly. "That wouldn't do at all."

Richard glanced my way with a curious expression. I could not tell if it was sympathy or amusement.

"Father, I am sure luncheon is ready?"

"That it is, that it is. The most sense I've heard out a ye for a week. This way if ye please, young Rochester."

Jonas stepped aside and let Richard lead the way to a spacious dining room, which displayed all the finery befitting a man of wealth. Several white-gloved and jacketed blacks bustled in and out of the kitchen, and within minutes, a sumptuous luncheon had been placed before us.

"Eat up if ye can, lad," said Mason. "I'll wager ye didn't keep much in yer gut that last week. I heard tell from the merchants there was fierce storm."

"Yes, sir."

We sat down to a magnificent meal, full of the strange, exotic fruits of the clime, most of which I had never before tasted. A spicy rice dish, a variety of fish and other seafood rounded out the menu. Most of it tasted quite good, though I needed copious glasses of water and rum to quell the fiery, spicy flavors. Conversation during the meal tended to small talk about the weather and my voyage, and Mason the elder inquired after my father, what he'd been doing and how fared my mother.

"She died in spring," I replied, suppressing an unexpected surge of grief.

"I'm sorry to hear that. Yer father was a right lucky man," remarked Mason. "She was a rare jewel, yer mother. I met her once, before ye were born. Yer brother was just a wee thing, barely standin' on his own two legs. But aye, a real, fine woman, and a looker, too. Old Henry was a damn lucky man, to be sure. But now," said Jonas, rising from his chair. "It was my pleasure to sup with ye, but I've many things to attend. We're havin' a celebration ball later this month," he winked. "And lots to do to get ready for it."

I stood. "I look forward to it, sir. Will I have the pleasure of Miss Mason's company before that?"

"Of course, lad, of course. Soon enough. But there's much to do before then, eh Dickey?" He turned to his son.

"Yes, Father. I will be along shortly."

Richard Mason then summoned Lucias, who came in a moment. "Rochester, Lucias will see to any needs you may have. We usually enjoy an evening on the veranda about ten o'clock." He bowed, then was gone.

I stood there, speechless.

"Mr. Edward, sir," interrupted Lucias quietly. "This way to your room."

It was clear nothing more would happen today. Bitter with disappointment, there was little else I could do but follow the servant to my quarters.

He led the way out of the dining parlor back to the staircase up to the open balcony overlooking the entry hall. The house was grand, much larger than Thornfield Hall, and in contrast to the squalor of the docks in Kingston and the ramshackle dwellings along the road toward this paradise upon the hill, it was a veritable palace.

Lucias showed me where to find anything I might require, then he left me.

My trunks and other luggage sat on the floor next to the bed. The window was open and a warm breeze stirred the curtains. I decided to write home and apprise Father of my safe arrival. Unlocking the smallest trunk, I found my portable desk, then sat down at a side table against one wall. I unlatched the box, found and uncorked the ink pot, then began shaping a quill. When it was prepared, I set to the task.

I had written a page when my insides clutched with a sudden spasm of pain. I gasped, it was so sharp, but it passed in a moment. Over-indulgence at luncheon, I thought. I soon finished my letter, sealed it, and prepared to summon Lucias to inquire about sending it out.

But before I could ring the bell, my stomach cramped again, this time with spasms so violent I fell off the chair. Gasping in pain, I pulled myself up to my knees, and fumbled for the servant's bell and managed to ring it. By the time Lucias arrived, I was doubled over on the floor, writhing in agony.

"Ah, Mister Edward," he remarked calmly. "Too much good food after seasickness," he scolded. "You get in bed. Rest. I will bring something to help."

I was in no condition to disagree with him. When he brought the promised remedy, I drank it down. What foul-tasting concoction it was I have no idea, but it eased the waves of pain enough that I soon fell asleep.

I have but dim recollections of the next several days. Lucias was my constant attendant. I slept much of the time, rising only to relieve myself, drink water or very weak tea. But neither Jonas Mason nor his son ever came to inquire after my health. This offended me. I was about to marry the man's only daughter, and still he treated me like a stranger rather than his future son-in-law.

When finally I rose for good from my sickbed, Alta Arboleta was a changed place.

The mansion had been transformed. There were twice the number of servants as before, and they ran everywhere, removing rugs, rubbing up the furniture and woodwork, cleaning the chandeliers, replacing all the candles, and polishing the vast quantities of silverplate until it shined. The kitchens, too, were alive with activity. I knew I was fully recovered when delightful aromas of cuisine known and unknown wafted through the house and awakened my appetite. I had not eaten much for days and everything smelled delicious.

I noticed too, several strange men about who did not seem to have any particular responsibilities in the whirlwind of preparations for the ball. None of them looked to be natives of the country. Two or three of them were about my age, others much older. They must be out-of-town guests, I decided. Jonas Mason was showing off his daughter and his wealth. I felt a giddy sort of pride knowing I would be envied by everyone as I took center stage to accept the hand of the beautiful young bride. *What would you think of me now, dear brother?*

I threaded my way through the chaos and found Richard Mason in the drawing room.

"I am glad to see you looking well, Rochester," he said, rising to greet me as I came into the room.

"Thank you. I must apologize for—"

"There is no need," he interrupted. "It is a common occurrence for many first-time visitors, especially after so difficult a voyage."

"Perhaps. But now I am recovered, I urgently renew my request to see my prospective bride at once. I do regret my protracted indisposition, but why is your sister not yet come? Does she even *want* this marriage? I have traveled a very long way to get here, but I am loath to proceed if Miss Mason is at all reluctant—"

"Never fear, Rochester," he laughed. "She is with her aunts is all. They are jealous of her company, you see. She is their only niece, and quite a favorite."

"I find such reassurances hollow, Mason. Your sister's continuing absence feels more like doubt to me." His round face remained placid. It occurred to me they might be hiding something.

"I tell you plainly, *Richard*. I will not marry a woman who wants nothing to do with me."

He only laughed again. "It is you who do not understand, Rochester. As I have said, my mother's family is very fond of my sister. Besides, once she is wed, she will not be able to visit them as often."

"Why not?"

He suddenly looked flustered. "Oh, a married woman is at the service of her husband, and must do his bidding."

"You make it sound as if she'll be a prisoner," I replied with scorn. "Perhaps we should leave Jamaica. Besides, will not her family become mine? If she wants to visit them after we are married, what of it? I would accompany her, as any respectable husband ought to do. Or would that be some violation of cultural propriety?"

"Perhaps not," he smiled. "It will be best to discuss such things when my sister returns."

"Which I trust she will do before the ball? Or will I be expected to pick her out from among the crowd? My father as good as told me everything was arranged. I don't understand why all this pomp and circumstance is necessary."

Just then Jonas Mason walked in, followed by another gentleman.

"Ah, lad, you look much better. Feelin' all right, then?"

"I am, sir."

He turned to the other. "This is my solicitor, Mr. Fergus Campbell."

"Mr. Campbell."

"Aye, a pleasure to meet you, sir," he said with a thick Scots' brogue as we shook hands. "Jonas here tells me you are to wed Antoinetta."

"I am beginning to have my doubts," I replied sarcastically. "I have yet to meet her.

Jonas glanced at his son, then slapped my shoulder. "Well, lad, did Dickey not tell ye? My girl will be home just in time for the grand ball. You two will have your fair chance to meet at last. What say you to that?"

"I say I would much rather have the chance to meet her without anyone else around, sir. Give us time to become acquainted. Or is she apprehensive of this arrangement?"

"Oh, I don't think so, laddie. But once you meet her, you will understand." He clapped my shoulder and laughed. Then without so much as a goodbye, he, his son and the lawyer abruptly departed.

A very strange family. Not one of them had expressed any appreciation that I had come thousands of miles to marry a woman I had yet to meet. They treated this as an everyday, ordinary business transaction. In light of their conduct towards me, it seemed ludicrous to continue this charade.

I thought about following them, confronting Mason and telling him I was done with this farce and would be sailing back to England at once. But the echo of my father's challenge still rang loud in my head. Like a thorn in my flesh, it stung me. It haunted and shamed me and I knew beyond certainty should I return home a failure, I would be forever banished. So, I took myself off to the billiards room instead.

A young man I had seen earlier that morning was just bending over the table to line up a shot.

"That really breaks a fella's concentration, suh," he said, rising upright, "walkin' right into my line of sight." Snatching up a tumbler of rum, he grinned, then took a healthy swallow. "And just who might you be?"

"I am sorry, sir." I bowed. "I wasn't aware this room was occupied."

"Just call me Val," he said, then drained the glass. "Ahl my friends do."

"American?" I inquired, shaking his outstretched hand.

"Valentine Hoyt, from the great State of Vah-gin-ya. You heard of it, I suppose?"

"Edward Rochester from England. One of the colonies, is it not?"

Hoyt laughed. "Used to be, suh, used to be. We had our little revolution that took care of that. Seems your Mr. Raleigh lost his way there a couple hundred years ago."

"I suppose he did."

Hoyt then snatched up his cigar, smoldering in an ash tray next to the now empty glass. "Well, Edward from England," he replied though a puff of gray smoke. "I suppose you're here for the same reason I am?"

"What do you mean by that, sir?"

"That Jonas Mason's offer was just too damn good to pass by."

"What offer is that?"

"Why, the opportunity to take over all of this," he said, gesturing around the room. "And considerin' the bonus included? You'd be a damn fool not to accept."

"Bonus?"

"Why, Miss Bertha Antoinetta Mason, a' course. Ain't you seen her portrait? Damn fine lookin' woman. Dark and seductive. Full, ripe lips just waitin' to be kissed. Lush, round breasts that a'hd like to—"

"That's enough, Mr. Hoyt," I muttered.

"You got somethin' against a beautiful woman, Rochester? Ahm just showin' my 'preciation is all."

The heat rose to my face. "I don't much care for your appreciation, sir. Good evening."

I managed to maintain my dignity as I withdrew from the room, biting off the sarcastic retort I had prepared. A rage stirred within me. Instead of walking into the waiting arms of my bride-to-be, it seems I had stumbled into an arena. What a stupid, blind fool I had been! *Nothing* was settled with Miss Mason. Everything they told me about this arrangement had been a lie.

I clenched my fists as I hurried to nowhere in particular. This had to be Rowland's doing. That smug bastard cared not the slightest whit for Catherine, but could not abide the thought of her as *my* wife, so he arranged this travesty to get rid of me. Kit was his chance at a title, and all she ever wanted was Thornfield Hall. I thought of our last meeting, her desperate kiss, so hungry, so passionate. I could have lost myself in that kiss, but to her, it was only a game. When all too soon the flame cooled, she would discard me as easily as a broken toy.

As I roamed through the house, even at this evening hour, servants were coming and going, placing fresh flowers, arranging furniture, performing all the last-minute tasks to prepare the house to receive its guests for the ball. I wandered down a long hallway which must be the main route to the back of the house and the servants' quarters, for a hum of voices approached. To escape their scrutiny, I ducked into one of the rooms along the corridor.

I stepped into a small, but intimate drawing room, lit by a strange, flickering light. A pair of candles stood on either side of an ornate mantlepiece at the far end of the chamber. In the shadow of the ruddy glow above the mantle was a bare, rectangular patch of wall from where a painting had lately been removed.

Ain't you seen her portrait? Damn fine lookin' woman.

What had brought Mr. Valentine Hoyt into this room, I didn't know, but certainly this was where he had seen the likeness of Miss Bertha Antoinetta Mason. I had spent so many days on a sickbed, I only now realized how little I actually knew about the place. Nor had my hosts gone out of their way to show me around. In fact, they were damn reluctant about giving me much information at all.

I sat down in an overstuffed chair and just stared at that blank space on the wall, trying to imagine what she looked like. *Dark and seductive.* Black haired? Olive skinned? A beauty quite unlike Catherine Fairfax, no doubt. *Lush, ripe lips...full, round breasts.* A woman, not a girl.

Here I was, five thousand miles away from everyone and everything I had ever known, about to engage in a battle with half a dozen suitors for the hand in marriage of a woman I thought had already been courted for me—Jonas Mason's oh, so eligible daughter.

In my mind's eye, I could see Rowland's impudent grin and imagined the ignominy awaiting Edward the Vanquished. I leapt out of the chair and paced back and forth, the portraitless wall staring down upon me, the dark-eyed gaze of the woman whose image once adorned that space fixed upon me, beckoning me closer, daring me to fight for what already was mine. There could be only one winner. Was Rowland even now laughing at me? Did he plan this final triumph to end in my disgrace, to shame me more thoroughly than he had at the Christmas ball?

A part of me wanted to shout, *To hell with you all!* I could walk out of here tomorrow and sail away from Jamaica to ports unknown, and never have to deal with Rowland or my father ever again.

But that would be the coward's way out. If Jonas Mason wanted good, English blood running in the veins of his grandson, that blood would be mine.

THE BALL

WHEN AT LAST THE DAY OF THE GRAND BALL ARRIVED, STILL I had not met my prospective bride. I was furious with all the delays and excuses, and had made up my mind to be done with the whole thing and tell Jonas Mason that very morning.

But a riotous commotion downstairs from my room got me very early out of bed. I hurried to the window and saw in the drive below a bevy of servants swarming a post-chaise just arrived. An older woman first got out of the vehicle and was escorted into the house by a white-jacketed servant. But when the remaining passenger leaned out the door, I knew it was her.

She wore a short-sleeved white muslin dress, low-cut across the shoulders, and a wide, red silk sash encircled her trim waist. Slender, brown arms held the wide-brimmed, floppy white hat shading her from the sun, already beating down hot and sweltering this early in the morning. While it blocked my view of her face, I could see plenteous, dark tresses spilling down her shoulders and a shapely form from underneath that brim. My heart raced. Here was my bride at last.

Jonas Mason hurried down the porch steps and himself helped her from the coach. Tilting the bonnet, he kissed her cheek, then clasping her shoulders, whispered close in her ear. After another minute, she nodded, then abruptly threw her arms about his neck.

Meantime, Richard Mason appeared. He too, rushed down the steps, and taking his sister's hand, gently kissed it. She laughed, then snatched it away.

With his daughter's arm in his, Jonas led her into the house. Richard started to follow, but his father whirled about. Gesturing at the servants still wrestling with the trunks, he barked out something at his son. Mason the Younger protested, but when Jonas took a menacing step towards him, he shrank back under the threat.

The son watched his father and sister disappear into the house. Then, as if resigned to his fate, he heaved his shoulders and like a chastised puppy, carried out the orders given him.

Poor Richard. No wonder he lingers in Madeira for months at a time. His father was an unforgiving taskmaster, it seemed. I laughed at the irony, knowing I had landed in nearly the same situation I left behind.

But then, was not a son always in an inferior position to an autocratic father? Yes, but a *son-in-law*, now that was another matter entirely. A man must leave his father and mother to establish his own family. Jonas Mason had no respect for his son because he would not stand up for himself. Well, I would not make that mistake.

I dressed as quickly as I could, anxious for the chance to meet her at last. After a glance in the mirror, I yanked my coat smooth, tugged the cuffs of my shirt sleeves, then descended.

But Miss Mason and Jonas were nowhere in sight. Instead, standing at the foot of the grand staircase was the old woman who'd first disembarked the coach. She was dressed in a simple gown of floral-patterned linen, and a lacy shawl was draped over her thin shoulders. Her skin was a deeper brown than Bertha's, and she was very old, perhaps near four score years or more. Clear and beady dark eyes twinkled from beneath brows which bore but a trace of the thinning, silver-gray hair, plaited and pulled severely back.

"Ah, Georgie." Her musically accented voice quavered as she held out a hand to me. "Where have you been? Your father has taken my Birdie away and I cannot find her."

I bowed. "Madam. I am sorry, but you have mistaken me for someone else. I am Edward Rochester. I have come from England to marry your Birdie."

She gasped, then slapped me hard across the cheek. Crossing herself, she exclaimed, "What devilish perversion is this?"

She raised her hand to strike me again, when Richard Mason entered. "Sylvie!"

The old lady whirled at his shout. She suddenly wailed, "Reeshard! Your brother speaks vile things about my Birdie!"

Richard embraced the old woman and spoke soothingly. "*Chère* Gran…Birdie died many years ago, remember? That man," he pointed at me, "is Edward, not Georgie. Edward is betrothed to Netta, not your Birdie."

"Noooo!" she moaned. "You took her away, I saw you!"

Mason's pale, forlorn look pleaded with me to intervene. "She is dead, Gran, for many years. We buried her."

"She died?" Gran wailed again. "Why do I not remember? Oh, Reeshard!*"*

"What's all this fuss about?" demanded Jonas Mason as he hurried downstairs.

Richard, still with a comforting arm around Sylvie,

replied, "Gran mistook Edward for Georgie, Father. She's forgotten the circumstances of his death…and Mother's." He glared at his father, who merely shrugged.

"Is that so?" Jonas clapped my shoulder. "Well, lad. I'm sorry you had to see this. This is Miss Sylvie DeCastera, my late wife's ma. 'Tis a pity, but her mind is gone. That's why my girl goes to see her and the others. Reminds Gran of her own daughter. I hope you'll pardon her foolishness."

I bowed. "No offense taken, sir."

"Good. Now Dickey," he said to Richard. "Take your gran upstairs and see that she's settled. I don't want her makin' a spectacle of herself tonight."

"Yes, sir," replied Mason. "Come along, Sylvie."

Jonas and I watched them go.

"Sir," I began. "Will I have the pleasure of Miss Mason's company this afternoon, before the ball?"

"Hmm, probably not. I believe she's upstairs with her abigail just now. You understand, the trip here was tedious, and I told her she must rest before the party. I'm sorry, lad, but she must be at her best tonight."

"Sir—" I began. But he cut me off.

"You just be there. Everything will be all right, you'll see."

THE LIVELY ATMOSPHERE OF THE BALLROOM PIQUED MY SPIRIT as I sat at a table in a shaded corner. Mason had spared no expense to put on the finest spectacle money could buy. His sizable fortune gave him power and importance enough to command the presence of other wealthy members of this insular society, including the colonial governor himself.

Every one of the gentlemen I had seen the day of my encounter with Valentine Hoyt were here, including that upstart American himself. Everyone's desire—Miss

Antoinetta Mason—a mysterious and alluring beauty, sat perched in the middle of an elevated platform centered at the front of the ballroom. My father had not exaggerated when he called her 'the jewel of the island.' My glimpse of her this morning promised more, and I was not disappointed. She was tall, with thick, raven tresses. Darkly exotic and lavishly attired, her voluptuous form drew every man into her orbit. They hovered like drones about the queen, attentive to every whim.

Rozzini appeared the most cunning of the lot. He exuded an aura of Machiavellian charm that would strike down an opponent before ever he realized there was a cobra in the room. As I watched, he oozed towards the *objet de désir.*

I shook my head, wondering at the desperate vow I had made while staring at a blank wall, conjuring an imaginary vision of the unknown bride. Let the others bow and scrape. I would not prostrate myself so. A man ought to stand on his own two feet. He must face a woman and win her love by his honor, his wit and his word, not some servile profession of adoration by which he disguises his lust. I would not flap into the fray like some crow fighting over scraps of another predator's kill.

But as the Italian drew near her chair, a ghostly presence seemed to rise up behind him. It wavered, undulating and growing into a familiar form, the shape of the Great Henry, my father. I blinked, then rubbed my eyes, certain I was seeing things. His brooding scowl only darkened, his impatience a palpable force in the room. Squirming under that glare, I glanced round, astonished that no others had felt that freezing influence.

From the moment he had spoken it last Christmas, the challenge my father had thrown at my feet reverberated over and over in my mind, its humiliating taunt a continual chastisement for my failures. And now, I imagined him scolding me for my hesitation and doubt.

Well, boy, here you are. What are you waiting for? Do you believe these fops will simply step aside for you? You must fight, you must show yourself the stronger man. Do you not yet understand? She is not the prize—you are!

My eye wandered back to the dais. The Italian had drawn up close and was whispering to her. She smiled at his words, her dark eyes sparkling with a kind of wild abandon. A thrill of envy shivered through me, when a surprising voice spoke low in my ear.

"Are you going to just stand here and watch that prig make love to *your* bride?" whispered Richard Mason.

My fingers clenched. "*My* bride?" I whispered harshly. "You've been nothing but a gatekeeper since my arrival in Jamaica, yet now you push me forward. What sort of game are you playing, Richard?"

He gripped my shoulder. "Yes, it is a game, but have you no pride, Rochester? Will you not play?" His voice trembled with suppressed emotion. "Heed me when I tell you, every man here has already lost to you, if only you will act!"

"Why should I believe you? At every turn, from your sister's convenient absence to your father's excuses, even this morning. Why would he go to all this trouble and expense for a mere show?"

"My sister can be quite charming, her allurements tempting," Mason continued. "Many a man bewitched by her has been disappointed when his suit was rejected. Jonas spoils her terribly, and he knows how to play to her vanity. But make no mistake, Rochester. My father's plans for this marriage will prevail. Though he has lived in the West Indies these many years, his ties to the old country remain strong. For a long time, he has coveted what your father has, his ancient connections, his old, English estate."

I laughed. "That estate will never be mine. I am but a second son."

"A son whose mother is the daughter of a viscount is more than sufficient for Jonas."

"Good English blood," I muttered.

"The time is now, Rochester. Behold. Rozzini's seductions are in vain."

The Italian, on one knee at her feet, held her hand in his, supplicating for favor. But she only laughed at his efforts.

"She toys with them all," whispered Mason, an odd smile on his face. "Watch her, Rochester. She has learned well. Tell me you do not burn to explore what is behind those coy, teasing looks. She is there, but your maddening indifference only encourages these fools."

On the heels of Rozzini's failure, Valentine Hoyt made his move. I remembered his vulgar words, and something suddenly kindled inside of me. The thought of even one of this prancing pack of dandies holding her in his arms made me see red.

"Rochester—?"

I strode away from Richard to the front of the ballroom where his sister smirked and giggled at the worshippers surrounding her. The closer I came, the farther into the background faded the sounds of the music and conversations as I fixed my gaze on her form, all the while moving with purpose and determination. When at last she turned, her eyes burned into mine, her smile spreading into a feral look full of desire.

Slowly, she rose from her chair, her dark eyes intent upon me as I approached. When all the men swarming about her realized something was happening, as one they followed her gaze to where it was riveted, and watched as I drew nearer. They redoubled their pleas but to no avail.

With elegant deliberation, she pushed them aside, then

sauntered around the front of the tables on the platform, and waited near the center from where a set of stairs descended to the ballroom floor. I paused at the foot of that stair. Her gaze swept over the crowd, as if demanding their attention. The noise fell to a hush. Conversations ceased as all eyes turned upon us. She threw back her head and laughed, then descended the steps and took my outstretched hand. The orchestra began to play a new dance, the waltz. I led her to the floor, and we began.

The guests watched for several minutes as we spun about the room. Neither of us spoke until several other couples at last joined us on the floor.

"You are Ed-ward," she said simply. "Ed-ward Rochester?"

"I am."

"Where have you been?" she scolded. "Papa told me you came all the way from England to marry me."

"I have wondered the same about you, Miss Mason. You were away visiting your aunts when I arrived."

"Oh," she laughed. "I forgot. Papa made me go." She suddenly pouted. "But I did not want to."

"Then why did you?"

"Papa made me," she repeated. "And I must never refuse Papa."

"He said your aunts were delighted to see you, that you remind them of your mother."

"Do I? Why would they not visit Mama for themselves?"

I smiled. "They wish to see a living reminder, not her grave."

"Her grave? She is dead?"

"For many years. So says your brother."

"Oh, poor Dickey," she lamented, as we whirled about the floor. "Papa made him do it."

I had no idea what she was talking about, but as I did not wish to stir any unpleasant memories, I asked about her visit.

"Tell me. Did you spend those days with your aunts in seclusion then, since you did not wish to be there?"

"Oh, no!" she laughed. "There were so many parties, and dances, and men who adored me."

"Ah, then what I was told is quite true. You *are* the Belle of this Island."

As the orchestra concluded with a flourish, the couples stopped and clapped their hearty approval. I took her hand and led her from the floor.

And now," I pressed her fingers to my lips, "you shall be my belle, and mine alone."

"Of course I will," she retorted with sudden sarcasm.

"Come. Let us return to your place of honor at the top of the room."

She suddenly took my hands and put them around her waist. Pulling my head towards hers, she kissed me hard, open-mouthed and hungry. Laughing again, she broke away from my grasp, while tugging me towards the door at the back of the room.

Recovering from my astonishment, I asked, "Where are we going?"

"If I am to marry you, Ed-ward, we must be lovers."

I pulled her back. "We will be, we will be," I smiled. "But *after* the wedding."

"Why must we wait?"

"Because it is custom," I said stupidly. "Besides. What would your father say?"

She scowled. "The same thing he always says. He gets angry. As he did with Mama. But now you are here." Pulling me close again, she looked up at me with a pouty, seductive smile as she trailed a red-colored fingernail up my coat sleeve. "But you will never be angry with me, will you, Ed-ward?"

SPANISH TOWN

Aᴌᴍᴏsᴛ ʙᴇꜰᴏʀᴇ I ᴋɴᴇᴡ ᴡʜᴀᴛ ʜᴀᴘᴘᴇɴᴇᴅ, ᴛʜᴇ ᴡᴇᴅᴅɪɴɢ ᴡᴀs over. It was a very grand affair, attended by everyone of importance in Jonas Mason's circle of influence. The aunties from Kingston all were there, and duly lavished their congratulations upon my new bride, who adored being the center of their attentions.

Miss Sylvie DeCastera, on the other hand, spent most of the wedding day and the reception afterwards hanging on the arm of her grandson, but she barely spoke three words to me the entire day. Richard was very apologetic for her "bad behavior" as he termed it, but I was grateful she did not repeat that ludicrous scene on the morning of the ball.

My bride and I traveled only as far as Kingston for the honeymoon. Mason feared his daughter would not tolerate sea travel well, and I did not look forward to another voyage of misery, so I agreed.

I know not what other groom ever experienced such a fortnight, but it was filled with party after party, and every night she came lustily to my bed. At first, it seemed like a dream. A woman who wanted me all the time, whose appetite could never be satiated? What man would not revel in that? I thought of Catherine Fairfax and her outlandish proposal, and felt pity that she and Rowland, through their own selfish ambitions, would consign themselves to a cold and loveless marriage bed.

But I soon discovered how narrow was my new wife's range of interests. As her behavior grew ever more erratic and unpredictable, I became more disinclined to accommodate her. On such occasions, she pouted or got angry, sometimes violently so, especially after she had consumed too much wine or rum, which was rather too often. When she threatened to take her desires elsewhere, what could I do but give in?

Mason had outfitted an entire wing of *Alta Arboleta* for our benefit. I protested vigorously, saying I wanted a separate house, someplace we could have our own staff of servants, establish a family, and have some privacy. But Mason scoffed at this idea, and absolutely would not relent.

"It's for yer own good, lad. And hers. But you'll see. A father knows best."

When Mason wasn't pestering me about whether or not his daughter was with child, he was keen on me learning the business of the plantation as soon as possible. Most of the duties I found to be tedious, some repulsive. By far the worst was having to deal with the traffic of slaves. It was a loathsome duty that degraded me and was cruel and inhumane to the poor men and women who suffered under it. I was grateful that *Alta Arboleta* was a mountain plantation. Our primary crop was coffee, therefore we had fewer slaves than the sugar plantations of the lowlands.

Once, and only once, Jonas forced me to accompany him to an "auction," as they termed the ghastly marketing of these poor creatures. We were in town and when the appointed hour for the sale came, the doors of the yard were thrown open. Mason and the other owners like a herd of wild animals stampeded in, seizing such of the blacks as they could lay hold of. A man with numerous handkerchiefs tied together encircled a dozen bodies at once, claimed them all as his property, and demanded to know the final price to bear them away.

Mason soon decided, however, it would be best to let me deal with the financial side of his enterprise, which had its own drawbacks. For one thing, it required me often to be in company with the most unscrupulous, disagreeable sorts of men who would cheat their own mothers out of whatever profits they could, all the while trying to defraud us on their side of the bargain. For another, many of them were old acquaintance of Jonas who did not appreciate having to deal with his green, new son-in-law.

While I could find ways to endure the rank unpleasantness of the business I must transact on Mason's behalf, it was becoming increasingly difficult to cope with my wife's ever more disturbing behaviors as the days and weeks went by. Rarely could we converse in peace, for always the subject of conversation was either uninteresting or beneath her notice. If the latter, she abused my intellect, calling me tiresome and commonplace. If the former, she got angry and accused me of neglecting her. I assured her it was my earnest wish she be happy. But she only laughed in my face, then called me a liar and declared she knew where to find someone else who would give her everything she wanted.

The first time she disappeared from the house, I became frantic, calling Lucias, Zabel, and the other servants to mount a search. But none of them moved. I got angry, and asked if they were not concerned their mistress was missing. I confronted her ladies' maid, a young Jamaican girl named Libbee.

"Surely, you know where she is. Why did she not take you along? It is not safe for her to travel alone."

She burst into tears. "Oh, Missah, I know. But she make me promise not to tell."

"She go into Spanish Town," said Lucias softly.

"What? How did she manage that? It's miles down the hill and she does not ride. That is a very long walk."

Lucias hung his head. "The old coachman, Simeon. He took her."

"Why was I not informed?"

"Miss Netta is mistress of the house. Who is Simeon to question where she go?"

"You are right, of course," I answered wearily. "Go down to the stables. Tell them to prepare a horse, then bring it up to the house. I will go after her."

I was on my way upstairs to change, when Jonas Mason confronted me. "Rochester? What's yer hurry?"

"My wife, it seems, has taken it into her head to go into Spanish Town unaccompanied. I am going to fetch her back."

"Ach, I told you my girl had a will of her own," he boasted. "If you were man enough—bah! Tis yer own fault—"

Then suddenly, he burst into a fit of coughing. He yanked a handkerchief from his coat pocket and covered his mouth, but the spasm went on for several minutes. When at last it subsided, he wiped his mouth. Before he could shove the cloth back into his pocket, I snatched it away. There was bloody spittle all over it.

"Mason. You are not well."

"Don't ye think I know that? I thought you could manage her, I thought you could get me an heir. But what bloody good are ye? She's run off, and it's likely I'll die before ever I see my grandson."

"You are a bastard," I said. "Your daughter is not fit to be my wife. If you think I would inflict her upon a child, you are sorely mistaken. Besides, you already have a son. Why not summon him back from Madeira?"

"Dickey hates me, lad. He would never do it. And I would never ask such a soft, weak-willed coward. That's why I needed you. That girl will rut with any man that would have her, just like her mother, the whore. I thought a fine, young man of good English stock could get me an heir. But I can see, you're as pathetic as all the rest." He grabbed the bloody cloth then stormed out of the house.

Any man that would have her?

A feeling of sick hopelessness washed over me. I suddenly knew where to begin my search.

THE RIVER WHARF NEAR SPANISH TOWN WAS A RAMSHACKLE collection of seedy bars, squalid inns and dilapidated warehouses, as well as the slave market I had been to but once. A feeling of forlorn desperation took hold of me as I rode into town, scanning the streets and side alleys for the white and black cabriolet bearing the *Alta Arboleta* crest. And at last I spied it, parked near the end of a long, narrow alley not far from the water. Its hood was drawn, and Simeon sat perched in the seat, probably ordered by his mistress to remain there rather than leave the coach unattended. I doubted she was concerned about him witnessing something which might compromise her virtue. *I wonder. Did ever she possess that quality?*

He startled, then bolted upright when he glimpsed me riding towards him. As I drew closer, I could see the fear in his face.

"Missah." He bent his head in shame when I rode up next to the vehicle.

"Simeon. Look at me." He did. "Do not be afraid. I know

you have come here at the command of your mistress and you must obey her. Can you tell me…how long has she been inside?"

"We come down the mountain at sunrise. She make me stay with the carriage, so here Simeon sits."

I dismounted. "Take my horse and return to the house. I will fetch your mistress. And Simeon?"

"Missah?"

"You will never bring her here again, do you understand?"

"But she get angry—"

"I know. Nevertheless, you must do as I say. I will deal with Miss Netta."

"Yes, sir."

He climbed down from the driver's seat, then walked over to where I stood with the horse. I gave him a boost up into the saddle, for he was a small man.

"Off you go." I slapped the horse's rump, and away they trotted.

If I thought too much about what I had to do next, I knew I would not be able to go through with it. So I simply strode into the bar. Through the murky haze of smoke and dust, I could see about a dozen patrons seated in groups of two or three at the grimy tables. The cacophony of chatter ceased almost at once. All turned their suspicious eyes upon me. What it was that betrayed my identity to them, I cannot say. But they all looked at the bartender, who looked at me. I thought I caught an expression of pity as he jerked his thumb upward. "First room on 'a left."

I nodded, then slowly climbed the stairs. The stink of cheap perfume, stale beer, rum and sweat mingled with other noxious odors nearly overcame me. I paused a moment at the door of the chamber, took a few deep breaths to steady myself, then turned the knob. It wasn't even locked.

In the dingy light, I could see an undressed woman—my

wife—stretched out on the bed, writhing and groaning, urging her companion to hurry. A shirtless man next to the bed frantically fumbled at the buttons on the front of his pants.

"I'll be there in a moment, swee' heart," he said, leering at her.

"I think not."

Abruptly, he turned. "Who in 'ell—?"

One well-placed fist to his chin dropped him like a sack of grain. He crumpled to the floor.

She sat up and screamed as I stepped over the man's prostrate form.

"You!" she shrieked at me.

"Get dressed," I replied calmly, snatching up her underthings off the bed. "I am taking you home."

As if suddenly embarrassed by the sight of me, she pulled a shabby blanket over her nakedness.

"Libbeeeeee!" she screamed. "Where is Simeon? Go away!" She crawled to edge of the bed and looked over. "My friend loves me. I'll kill you! Bastard!"

I tried to pull her to her feet. "Come, Netta. It is time to go home."

"No! No!" she screeched. "I hate you!"

She squirmed and clawed at the clothes as I tried to pull a linen shift over her head. While cursing and screaming, she flailed wildly, beating on my chest and head, trying to scratch at my eyes, but at last amidst the fiercest howling, I managed to pull it on. Gripping her wrists firmly, I held her still. "We are going home, Bertha. Stop fighting me. I'm not going to hurt you. You are ill. Let me help you."

"You swine! I'll kill you!"

I would never be able to get her home while she raved thus. On the small table in the corner of the room, I spied a half empty bottle of rum. Already she reeked of it, but I knew she would drink another glass or two if I offered, and it would calm her enough that I could carry her downstairs.

"Would you like another glass of rum?" I asked. "You have tasted it already today." I flashed an acrid smile. "Let us celebrate me finding you."

She ceased thrashing about and gave me a wild-eyed grin. "Oh, is it a party? I adore parties," she cackled. "Pour it for me."

I filled a tumbler and eagerly she snatched it from me then drained it in a swallow. Quickly, I poured another. As she gulped it down, I heard "her friend" on the floor beginning to stir, and I knew we must be gone before he became fully conscious.

Her capacity for drink was copious, but as they had already consumed half the bottle, the two glasses she downed had the effect I hoped for. She grew less combative, and her eyes began to droop. I felt her relax and easily lifted her as she went limp and passed out.

I brought her downstairs then outside, gently placed her upon the seat of the small carriage. She slumped against the hood. Swiftly, I removed my coat and covered her with it, then climbed up next to her. I took up the reins and urged the horse away up the alley towards the main road leading home to *Alta Arboleta*.

And so I drove us back to the house upon the hill and away from Spanish Town.

A WORLD FAR AWAY

PRESENT DAY

After a brief stop to change horses, Carter and I climbed back into the coach. I sighed, breathing out a cloud of vapor into the chilly air as we got under way again.

"Can you now understand, James, why I never told any of this to you before?"

"Good God, Edward. No man would want to relive such memories."

"I was never given a chance to know the woman who was betrothed to me, yet there were hints, and odd things that should have given me pause."

"Sylvie DeCastera, perhaps?"

"What a strange and awful encounter! Why did it not make me question everything? With the continuing excuses about my bride's absence, why did I never follow up my suspicions? That very first conversation with her on the dance floor was rife with secrets and conspiracies, yet I blindly ignored every feeling that something was not right. That night at the ball, if I would have stopped to think, I might have realized what was going on."

"And yet you did not," whispered Carter.

"To my eternal regret," I sighed. "After such a long journey, I admit, I was as curious about her as the rest of them. At all appearances, she was everything I had been told she would be: a dark, hypnotic beauty to drive men mad. I was wholly entranced by her seductions. When Richard Mason whispered that all I need do was act, a mighty struggle raged inside me. On one hand, I felt like a lamb being led to slaughter. On the other, I could think only of my father's disappointment, of my brother's smug satisfaction when I returned to England a failure. He would ridicule me, and I would forever lose the chance to earn my father's respect. While I watched the others crowd around her, this opportunity, tossed to me like a bone to a starving dog was slipping through my teeth. It was now or never."

Carter sat silent for a long time as the coach rattled onward. I continued.

"Recall James, how I spoke to you of treachery. It wasn't until well after Jonas Mason died that I discovered how deep it ran. And it came at the end of that terrible year heralded by Catherine's death in the carriage accident."

"I remember." He shaded his eyes as if to forget. "Less than a year before her wedding to your brother."

"That selfish braggart!" Carter flinched at my sudden vehemence. "Always the show-off, heedless of the danger to anyone else. It was as good as murder—"

"Edward!" Carter interrupted. "Do not be so unjust. Of course it wasn't murder."

"Perhaps not in the eyes of the law," I replied bitterly. "But he should have known better."

"And do not forget," he continued. "I was there. Everyone suffered that day. Your father, Catherine's father. But especially Rowland. His injuries were very grave. I feared he would never use his hand or arm again."

"You would defend him?" My anger rose again. "His arrogance and recklessness killed her!"

"Let it go, Edward. She chose to ride with him that day." Then unexpectedly, he smiled, a sad smile though it was. "Have you never done anything foolish trying to impress a woman?"

"I—"

No words came out of my mouth. Since leaving Jamaica, my life had been one useless attempt upon another to do that very thing. I leaned against the cushion and let the rattling coach shake my bones awhile. When the anger was gone, I apologized.

"I'm sorry, James. My father had commanded me to forget all about Catherine Fairfax. Then he banished me to that world so far away and promptly forgot me. I must admit I thought more than once what it would have been like had I remained in England, had I become Catherine's lover."

He sighed. "Nothing good, and you know it. After you left college, I thought you might write and tell me where you had gone. But I never heard from you."

"I was angry and ashamed, desperate to conceal everything about my situation. Mere weeks after the marriage, I wrote to my father, begging him to keep it a secret. I described everything in disgusting detail so he would have no choice. The consequences of this marriage were far worse than he could have imagined. If word got out, it would be a blight on the family name he could never eradicate. Most willingly did he comply with my request."

"Catherine, poor girl," said Carter. "She lingered many hours after the accident." He closed his eyes to blot out the grim memory. "God, I am sorry, but there was nothing I could for her. Rowland was yet unconscious, his leg broken, his hand and arm mangled and useless. Your father was beside himself."

"No doubt," I replied with contempt. "Did Henry tell you nothing about me? Did you even ask?"

"Of course I did. He told me you had left England to seek your fortune, but nothing more. He spoke not a word about your marriage or where you had gone. I asked so I might write to you, but he never answered me. It wasn't until your brother's death I learned you were in the West Indies. But what is this treachery you speak of? What fresh duplicity did Jonas Mason's death uncover?"

I smiled grimly. "It's almost laughable now, but Henry himself revealed the intimate details of the arrangement. It was most peculiar, and by a means I'm sure he never thought possible. Jonas Mason had been dead perhaps a year, when one afternoon, Lucias, the old butler, informed me a visitor was come to *Alta Arboleta* looking for me."

TREACHERY DISCOVERED

"Mr. Edward, there is a gentleman to see you. Will you receive him?"

"Who can it be, Lucias?"

"Mr. Campbell, sir."

"Campbell?" I repeated distractedly. "Ah, yes. Jonas' solicitor."

What could he possibly want? Some devilish construction in Mason's will to thrust more indignities upon me?

"Well, send him in. I should be glad for the company—we have so few visitors these days."

The old servant bowed, and a minute later, Campbell appeared.

I rose from behind my desk and approached the man whom I now remembered. I met him briefly when first I came to *Alta Arboleta.* It was he who had conducted the reading of Mason's will not long after Jonas died, but that was months ago. He held forth his hand.

"Mr. Rochester, sir." His grip was firm and his Scots brogue as thick as ever.

"To what do I owe this unexpected pleasure, Campbell? May I offer you some refreshment?"

"No, thank you. My business requires a few minutes only."

"Won't you at least sit down, then?"

He nodded, set his valise on the floor, then sat in the chair facing my desk.

"Well, Campbell? I thought all matters respecting Mason's will had been settled."

"Aye, that is true enough. But I found something he never told me about. As I took an oath to execute my duties faithfully and with the utmost integrity, I must see to this final task."

"Of course. But what more can that duty have to do with me? Or his daughter?"

"A few weeks ago, a gentleman came to my office claiming he had found some property belonging to Mr. Jonas Mason."

"Oh?"

"Yes, he had been one of Mr. Mason's business partners, if you understand my meaning, sir. What he showed me was a locked strongbox, one I had never seen before. Apparently Mason had brought it to their business establishment for safe-keeping. When this gentleman was clearing out the premises to put the building up for sale, he came across the box. Thinking perhaps it might be worth something, he brought it to me."

"And was it?"

Campbell reached into his valise and pulled out a wrapped and bound packet. "The box contained only these seven letters, sir. And all of them bear your family name —Rochester."

"Indeed?"

"There are three letters written to Mason by a Henry Rochester of Thornfield Hall, in England."

"My father," I said.

"Aye. And three of the letters are fair copies of the replies sent by Mr. Mason. As my client left me no explicit instructions concerning the disposition of this correspondence, the ownership properly reverts to their author."

"The last news I had of my father, Mr. Campbell, he was dying. I expect the next letter I receive from England will inform me he is dead."

"Then the law recognizes you, sir, as the rightful owner. When the author dies, his closest living relative becomes the possessor. And as you are husband to Mr. Mason's daughter, I must give you the fair copies of his letters for safe-keeping." He cleared his throat. "I am sorry to say it, but—well, it's not very likely they will ever be of any use to her, is it now?"

I sighed. "No, Campbell. You are quite right about that. But you said there were seven letters. Three from my father, and Mr. Mason's three replies. From whom is the odd letter?"

He untied the string and removed the wrapping from around the packet. Handing me the topmost missive, he asked, "Will you swear this is your father's hand?"

I took the document he proffered and unfolded it. There at the bottom was Henry's unmistakably bold scribble. "Yes, certainly, this is his signature. Not a doubt of it."

After thumbing through the letters, he took up another. "Here is the odd epistle, sir. It is addressed to Mr. Mason. But it was not written by your father. It is signed by a Mr. *Rowland* Rochester."

"Rowland? He was my elder brother, but he is dead."

"Well, sir…may I offer my sincerest condolences?"

I nodded then accepted the letter he held forth. My eye

dropped immediately to the valediction. "Yes, this is Rowland's hand."

I returned it to him. Arranging them back into the bundle, he retied the string. "I thought you might like to have these, sir."

"Is there a receipt, or something I must sign?"

He smiled. "Indeed there is."

He pull a thrice-folded paper from his coat pocket then laid it on the desk, smoothing the creases so it would lay flat. "Sign here, at the bottom."

I took up my quill, dipped it then signed the paper.

Campbell sanded the signature, then blew off the excess. "I am much obliged to you, Mr. Rochester," he continued. After placing it in his folio, he took up the bundle and handed it to me. "Your letters."

"Are you certain you will take no refreshment?"

"Thank you again, but no. This is the first among several errands I have this afternoon."

He stood to take his leave. I came around the desk to shake hands. "Good-bye, Campbell."

"Mr. Rochester." He gave a little bow, then departed.

I watched him go, then dropped into the chair in which he had been sitting. For several minutes, I just stared at the stack of correspondence resting there, wondering. Three letters, all written by Henry Rochester to Jonas Mason. I recalled my father mentioning just two letters: the first, wherein his old friend claimed to be looking for a suitable match for his daughter, and the second, wherein Mason had accepted my father's offer of his youngest son, and agreed upon the arrangements.

What was in the third letter? And how was Rowland involved in the negotiations? I always suspected he played some part. Perhaps here was proof.

Suddenly burning with curiosity, I quickly untied the packet, fumbled through them and found the oldest letter, which was dated five years ago, a year before ever I came to this cursed place.

Thornfield Hall, January, 1796

Mason,

Though it has been several years since last we've seen one another, the news of your prosperous endeavors in the West Indies reaches me here at Thornfield Hall. I congratulate you.

I understand there is a daughter for whom you are urgently seeking a husband, one who can bring good blood and a fine English name. Consider my youngest, Edward, who must have some means to secure his future. He has taken it into his head to pursue an occupation, but it is misguided ambition and will come to nothing. If your fortune is as large as you claim, send me proof. I am certain we can come to an understanding—

Misguided ambition? Will come to nothing? Good God, would the intrigues never end? Here was evidence of further deception. My own father had initiated the contact with Mason. Just who the hell did he think he was?

Resentment roiled inside me as I scattered the other letters across the desktop, wildly seeking the next. When I found it, my eyes devoured these words:

Thornfield Hall August, 1796

Mason,

—your wife's affliction is unfortunate, but with respect to her daughter, likely it is nothing more than excitable, animal spirits. I see no undue cause for alarm, therefore let Edward remain ignorant. We have every hope for reasonable success. No undue delays must thwart our purpose—

My hands shook with rage as I read the last one:

Thornfield Hall January, 1797
   Mason,
   £30,000 is an offer I can accept. If you are as you proclaim to be, anxious for our English name and blood, let me advise you of this: Edward is sensible of recent failures and therefore will be eager to succeed. Some incentive to ensure his whole-hearted participation would not be imprudent—

A red haze filled my vision. With ever mounting fury I snatched up the letter from Rowland. The picture it painted, a conspiracy so absolute and devilishly wrought, sent me reeling:

Thornfield Hall October, 1796
   Sir,
   Your son, Richard, has informed me there may be regrettable circumstances respecting the bride, though my father assures me it is but a trifle. Your son believes the match will benefit her, therefore I urge you to let them marry at once. My brother is inexperienced and raw, but lusty enough to get her with child if you act with alacrity. Whatever inconsequential difficulties of temper or character may exist will be of little consequence once your heir is conceived and your legacy secured—

PRESENT DAY

Carter stared at me, pale with shock, unable to speak.

"I read the letters a dozen times over, James. What they revealed was contemptible. There is no doubt. My own father initiated the plot, and what's worse, they all understood the fate awaiting me in Jamaica."

"My God, Edward. They knew!"

"They did," I replied bitterly. "No words can express the outrage, the utter humiliation I felt in that moment. How Rowland must have laughed at the idea, for no matter how it played out, he would be the victor, and I, the vanquished. If I refuse to go, they brand me a coward. If I go but fail, I must return home in shame. But, I exerted my powers and won the day. Yet my triumph was hollow. It was a rigged game after all. And the prize? A fetter of servitude to madness!"

"But surely," said Carter, "someone on the island must have known something?"

"Miss Sylvie knew. Yet how could I give credence to the rantings of an old woman who had mistaken me for her dead grandson? Besides, Jonas Mason was respected, perhaps even feared by others in that society. I doubt not he paid well to buy their silence."

"An old story, to be sure."

"These were vile discoveries, but before I found out, the doctors had diagnosed my wife's affliction: insanity. Her behavior was such that she must be confined, for her own safety as well as others. By now, most of our servants had fled, fearful of her violent temper. I was forced in every way to become her warden. As the months dragged into years, I sank deeper into despair, my only comfort a bottle."

"Rochester," he whispered, "however did you endure it?"

"Not very well, James. When the terrible truth in Campbell's letters came thundering down upon me, I had nothing left to withstand the torrent, and it swept me away to a place I had been more times than I could count: Spanish Town, its streets littered with the sordid watering holes to which her lunatic fascinations and monstrous appetites had time and again enticed her.

But this time, I did not go to extricate her from the clutches of some drunken sailor, but rather to seek oblivion in whiskey and rum. I began to frequent one establishment in particular for the company of a young woman I had met there..."

OBLIVION

Spanish Town—*September 1801*

The murmur of a dozen conversations ceased as I entered the pub. Never before had I come to this wretched establishment as a patron, and yet the denizens all knew me. They had heard the stories or witnessed that English-man who returned again and again to the shantytowns, searching for his wife, the madwoman from up the hill, to bring her home again.

Their curious stares followed me as I took a bottle and glass then retreated into a dark and dingy corner of the tavern. But the novelty soon wore off and everyone went about his business. It seemed even such a den of thieves as this honored the unspoken code respecting a man's right to drink alone, even a man everyone knew to be rich.

I had finished a glass when I noticed a gaudily painted young woman watching me with dark, eager eyes and a smile she hoped would elicit an invitation. I beckoned her to my table.

She approached. "May I…?" she asked shyly.

I nodded.

As she sat down, I waved at the bartender to send another glass. After a girl brought a tumbler, I half filled it with whiskey. My companion stared wide-eyed as I pushed the glass towards her. She touched her throat, as if to ask, 'For me?'

Yes, I nodded once. With some hesitation, she lifted it, then held it to her lips but did not drink. I encouraged her again. When finally she filled her mouth, it was obvious she had never tasted whiskey before. She tried to swallow, but instead, spluttered it all over the table. She coughed and choked then looked up at me, horrified at her blunder.

"*Dios mío!* Oh, I am sorry, forgive me!" she sobbed, rising from her chair, shaking her head, her eyes filling with tears. She glanced at the bartender with a look of fear. I reached over the table and snatched her wrist, and smiled. "There's no harm," I said gently. "Sit down. Sit down."

Surprised by my reaction, she sat.

"Not much of a drinker, are you?"

She shook her head.

I pulled a handkerchief from my pocket and held it out. She took it and dabbed her cheeks.

"Dry your eyes, my girl. You had better develop a taste for liquor if you're going to work here. I doubt many other customers would be as forgiving."

"I am grateful," she sniffled. "Since you did not send me away, you must still want me, yes?"

Poor girl. She had no idea how soon her youth and pretty face would be ravaged by the privations of her trade. Yet there she sat, wide-eyed and innocent, fully expecting me to take her upstairs.

"What is your name?"

"Maria."

"A pretty name, Miss Maria. And how did you come to work in a place like this?"

"My brothers and sisters…they have no one but me to take care of them."

"Is that so? You love them very much?"

She looked away, as if I had shamed her. "Yes, sir. But—"

"It is enough that I know that, Miss Maria. I am sure they love you."

Her eyes again filled with tears.

"It appears, young lady, you need someone who will teach you how to drink whiskey and rum." I poured a small amount into her glass.

Her nose wrinkled as she sniffed the beverage. She tipped the tumbler slowly, until the dark, golden liquid just touched her lips. She swallowed a taste, then looked at me.

"Very good," I nodded. "Take another."

She did so, this time with a little less hesitation.

"It is an acquired taste," I said. "But now." I placed a coin on the table. "Tell me all about these brothers and sisters."

"Now?" She looked around, then leaned towards me over the table. "You wish only…for talk?"

"Yes." I pushed the money all the way across the table. "Only talk."

She shrugged, picked up the coin, wrapped it in the handkerchief, then stuffed it down the front of her dress, its bodice cut to enticingly display the tops of her small, rounded bosom.

Maria told me that after her mother died, her father said she was old enough to work and she must do whatever was needed to bring money into the family. The fields were too brutal, she said. Besides, her father always told her she was very pretty, that any man would love her. It seemed like a much better choice than the plantations, so she came to Spanish Town to "make men happy."

She had not seen any of her brothers or sisters for many days, but it was clear they meant the world to her. She interrupted herself several times to ask if I wanted to lay with her yet, but I only laughed. Again and again, I assured Maria the money was hers to keep. She had earned it with her stories. When finally she understood I was in earnest, she relaxed, and together we talked and laughed and drank into the night.

PRESENT DAY

"For weeks, Carter, whenever I met her, all we did was talk. It was enough. When finally she realized I wanted nothing else from her, she ceased asking why I would not bed her. Of course, everyone in Spanish Town knew about my mad wife, and I am sure they thought me a fool for refusing to take advantage of the cheap and easy access to Maria's favors."

Carter said nothing.

"How could I explain it to them?" I pleaded. "All I longed for was intimate conversation, not a confrontation fraught with screaming and violence. My arrangement with Maria allowed me a scrap of dignity, somehow. Certainly, I could have her anytime I wanted. But I was bound by a promise. Yes, my wife was insane, but nevertheless, she was still my wife. Unlike her and every other party to the contract, I vowed I would not dishonor that promise. And," I continued, "I might have kept that oath, but for your letter with news that my father was dead."

"I was sorry to have to write it, Edward."

"All that day and into the night, I sat alone and got very drunk. I was so angry! I felt cheated somehow, knowing I could never curse him to his face for what he had done to me. Come sunrise, I stumbled my way to the stables and managed to saddle a horse and once again, found myself on the road to Spanish Town…"

SPANISH TOWN RIVER WHARF—*DECEMBER 1801*

I staggered into the tavern where we always met. She was at my side almost as soon as I blundered through the door. Unsteady on my feet, Maria helped me into a chair at our usual table.

"Sir, you are not well today."

"I am perfectly...fine," I muttered. "Just get me a glass of rum to quell this damned headache! Bartender!" I shouted. "A bottle. Now!"

He brought it himself. "Well, Mr. Rochester. We ain't used to seeing' ya here so early in the mornin'."

"What of that?" I choked out. "Is my money not good enough?"

"No disrespect meant, sir."

"Where is Maria?"

Still standing beside me, she touched my arm.

I clasped her hand. "Good. Good." I slurred out the words. "Sit down. Drink with me."

She obeyed.

The bartender set down two glasses, then half filled each. He recorked the bottle, left it on the table, then returned to his customers.

"You are upset this morning," she said. "Something—what has happened?"

"Oh, yes, my dear, indeed has something happened." I swallowed a mouthful of rum, then peered at her through hazy vision. "And I'll wager you know all about such things, don't you? That every father whoever lived...is a bastard!"

"No, no!" She shook her head. "My papa *loved* me."

"Did he? Is that why he forced you to work here, in this god-forsaken place? To drink with disgusting men who play with you like a toy to be tossed aside when they are finished with you?"

She looked away. "I give them…love."

"Love? You think two bodies writhing in a bed is love, do you? You silly chit. You have no idea."

"Why are you so angry? Did I do something to displease you?"

"Of course not. Just look at you. What a pretty little thing you are."

"Then what is it?"

"My father is dead."

"Oh, I am sorry—"

"That swine doesn't deserve your sympathy!" I slammed my glass onto the table, shattering it into pieces. "He banished me from the world. He hated me, I tell you. All my life. But why—?" I sobbed once. "How could he hate me when he loved my mother? Oh God, how could I have done that to her?"

Maria touched my arm. "You are bleeding."

"What?" I held up my hand and stared at it, trying to focus. Blood oozed from a cut on my palm.

"It's nothing."

Before I could wipe away the trickling gore, Maria took my hand. She tugged out a handkerchief, the one I had given her, from where it was hidden in her bodice. Slowly, carefully, she wrapped the linen to bind the wound, then knotted it tight.

She gazed up at me. Her round, dark eyes shimmered with unfallen tears that reflected a hollow emptiness, a kind of desperate longing. Caressing my bound hand, she then held it to her cheek.

I should leave. Now. It was only by blind luck I hadn't fallen off my horse on the way down the hill. If that luck held, I might make it all the way back. If I walked out before it was too late.

Her cheek was warm, her eyes eager, almost hopeful. I fumbled in a pocket, took out a coin and tossed it onto the table.

She picked it up. "So much money? For stories?"

It was a gold coin. I shrugged, then stood up. Looking down at her, I whispered, "Yes. Stories. All day and all night."

She picked up the coin and hid it away in her bosom, then took my hand again. Together we left the bar and I followed her up the same stairs I had so long ago climbed in search of my lunatic wife the first time she had run away to Spanish Town.

Maria led me to a room at the end of the same, dingy hallway, then opened the door. It had an east-facing window, and the morning sun shone through dirty, ragged curtains, brightening the room enough to illuminate the bed, neatly made up, its grayish-white spread covering two or three pillows and a thin blanket.

Maria disappeared behind the privacy screen in one corner of the room. Some moments later, she stepped out, wearing only her corset. The sun reflecting off the coppery, smooth skin of her face, her arms, her ripe little breasts, made me ache with all the loneliness and humiliation I had suffered in the mockery of my marriage.

I wanted her. Desperately.

Turning her back, she asked, "Help me?"

I obliged. As one by one I undid the laces, a voice still screamed inside my head. *Can a man hold fire and not be burned?*

I didn't care. Henry, that sorry excuse for a father, deserved this. How quickly he complied with my request to keep the marriage a secret! But he did nothing to extricate me from this snare. He must protect his precious reputation, but his son he could leave to rot in obscurity.

But there was nothing left to protect anymore. Rowland was dead. And now Henry. Was. Dead.

The corset fell away. Maria turned around and looked up at me with dark, hungry eyes. She took my hand and together, we fell into oblivion.

Present Day

"Edward, don't do this to yourself," urged Carter as our coach arrived at our final destination for the night, a small, wayside inn near Harbury. "Does it really matter anymore?"

"Perhaps not," I replied. "I had broken every other promise I made to myself. Now, this last shred of my self-respect lay in pieces all around me."

He sighed, then opened the door. After Pilot jumped out, Carter touched my shoulder.

"Come, Edward. A cup of tea and good night's rest will do us both good."

I laughed. "They say curiosity killed the cat, but James Carter? Never."

"If it were not so late," he scolded, "I would sit you down at a table inside and demand the next chapter at once. But I can barely keep my eyes open. By breakfast tomorrow, however, I will be all ears."

"Is that a challenge, James?"

"I daresay I will be downstairs before you are."

"We shall see about that. Until tomorrow, then."

RICHARD MASON

MORNING CAME AND I GROANED. BAD DREAMS HAD WOKEN ME several times during the night. I felt wrung out. But my friend was waiting for me, so I dressed then hurried downstairs. After letting the dog out into the yard, I entered the common room of the inn about half past six. Carter sat alone at a table near the hearth basking in the warmth of its steady blaze. On the table sat two steaming mugs of coffee.

"Edward." He rose and shook my hand.

"James."

"How did you sleep?"

"Not well."

"Bad dreams again?" he asked.

I nodded but did not elaborate. I sipped my coffee. "Breakfast?"

"On the way," he replied.

A sleepy-eyed lad soon set before us a platter with ham, cornbread and eggs. As we filled our plates, I picked up the story.

"The morning after I had been with Maria, I fled back to Alta Arboleta, full of shame and self-loathing. My humiliation now was so complete, I thought nothing else could bring me lower. But an unexpected visitor waiting for me proved how wrong I was."

Alta Arboleta—December 1801

A cock crowing roused me at sunrise. A ray of light fell on Maria still slumbering beside me. My gaze lingered a moment on her face, fixing that image in my mind as a reminder of the hope of youth and all its lost dreams. Without a sound, I dressed, left a handful of gold coins on the nightstand then stumbled downstairs. Hurrying out to the stables, I found my horse then crawled up onto his back and we trotted away.

A sudden squall drenched the riverfront and me as I rode out of Spanish Town. It washed away the stink of whiskey and lust clinging to me like a fever. Hammer blows of misery and regret pounded at my temples as I slunk away back to the house upon the hill.

By the time I passed through the gates, my clothes were dry. The stables were deserted so I tended the horse myself.

Weaving my way towards the house, I caught sight of a fine-looking carriage in the drive. Its details were unclear through my headache-blurred vision but I knew I had never seen it before. After months without a caller, who might dare cross the threshold of my chaotic and desolate world?

Stumbling around to the back door, I saw Lucias on the porch waiting for me. But he never waited for me—unless there was trouble. Oh God, what has she done now?

"Lucias?" I eyed him suspiciously. "You are here to scold me, I suppose?"

"No sir, Mister Edward," he sighed. "Mister Richard has come."

"Ah." Relief washed over me. "And what could have pried him away from his precious vineyards?"

My steward shrugged. "He is in the library."

"Well, then, we must have coffee. And," I winked, "bring a little something more robust to enhance its flavor, hmm?"

He nodded with a knowing glance as he surveyed my rumpled, unshaven appearance. The silent rebuke stung me. Lucias took great pride in his duties as steward. He still ran the place as if he had an army of servants at his command. In his years with the Mason family, he had seen and experienced awful things. But no one else could sympathize with my plight as did he.

While he fetched the coffee, I hurried upstairs to change. My reflection in the glass startled me. The man looking out seemed much older than my six and twenty years. Was it only four years ago I came here, desperate to make my mark upon the world? I would give anything to have those years back.

But such musings were best left to another hour. I had a guest. It would be ill-mannered to keep him waiting. I made myself presentable, then went downstairs to the library. My brother-in-law stood near the hearth.

"Well, well. Good morning, Richard. What brings you to my riotous little corner of the world?"

He stiffened as I drew near.

"Buck up, Dick. You look as if you've seen a ghost." I thumped my chest. "Let me assure you, I am alive and breathing."

After a few minutes of agitated silence, he replied, "Rochester, I am just returned from Madeira."

"Jonas is dead so you decided to come back. Why?"

"There was little love between my father and I. Campbell wrote about a few matters regarding the estate, but that is not why I have come."

Lucias appeared at this moment with the coffee service. Mason fell silent as the old man poured out two cups then departed.

"There is nothing you can say that ought be kept from him." I beckoned Mason to the table. "He is aware of everything that goes on in this house, so do not pretend otherwise." I hoisted the bottle of whiskey which the old servant had brought. "Care to add something a bit stronger than sugar?"

Mason shook his head, taking one of the cups. I added a few drops of whiskey to the other, then sat down again. I waited for him to continue the conversation, but he merely sat there.

"Your father," I prompted. "I know you and he did not always see eye-to-eye."

He nodded.

"Don't let it be of concern. It is the way of all sons with fathers, I fear. They have no way of overcoming their differences short of violence. So instead, they settle for uneasy silence, or as in your case and mine, separation by great distances."

"It is not something I am keen for others to know."

"The reason Jonas wanted a grandson, I suppose?"

Again, he nodded. "There was nothing for me here."

Richard Mason was the last of my wife's blood relatives. Miss Sylvie died shortly after the wedding, and the two aunties fell victim to an outbreak of malaria which had devastated Kingston. Etiquette dictated I should consider him family, but I never could. He remained a virtual stranger before the wedding, yet afterwards, attached himself to me like a devoted dog. I found it all quite insufferable. I thought it was out of concern for his sister, but the letters Campbell had given me revealed his motives to be far less noble.

"Why have you come back, then?"

He rose from his chair. "My concern must now be for the living. I am come to investigate certain reports I have heard. I wish to believe them false, but I could not in conscience ignore them."

"What reports?"

"Rochester," he pursued quietly. "There are rumors of a most disturbing nature."

"Reports? Rumors? Which is it?"

He sighed. "I am worried about my sister."

"After all this time?" I rose, swallowed the rest of my coffee then set the cup on the service table. Moving closer to Mason, I said cheerily, "Ah. I suppose her wanton, adulterous conduct has brought you back here, then?"

Almost shaking, he whispered, "It is not my sister's conduct which has brought me back—but yours."

"*My* conduct?"

"I have heard—that is to say, my sources inform me that you have been—"

"That I what?" I glared at him. He flinched, then turned away. "Dammit, Mason! Face me and say what you mean."

Still shaking, he turned. "You mistreat her, Rochester!" He blurted. "You have been beating her, and—"

"What the devil are you talking about?"

He stood a little taller. "I have received letters—

"From whom?"

He did not reply.

"I have a right to know who accuses me of such despicable things."

Still, he was silent.

"Tell me, Richard. Do you believe these accusations to be true?"

He looked away again. "I…I don't know."

"Now there's a fine thing. You come all this way to condemn me on the word of a stranger?"

"For my sister's sake, I must."

"Believe that if it makes you feel better, but I'll wager you've come for another reason. You want to assuage your conscience, to make sure you got your £30,000 worth out of this sordid, little arrangement. Well, didn't you?"

His mouth dropped open, and he went white, quite white.

"Oh, I know all about the devilish bargain between Jonas and Henry. I have seen their letters."

He sat down again, his face ashen. "How…is that possible?"

"Your father hid them in a strongbox at his business. After he died, one of his associates found the box and brought it to Fergus Campbell, thinking perhaps it might be worth something. But it was only the correspondence between your father and mine."

"Oh!" He shuddered, then mumbled to himself.

"Well, Richard?" I paced before him. "Are you going to deny what I read in them?"

"Rochester," he whispered, without looking up. "It is what we…what I thought best."

"And how could you possibly know what was best? The opulent parties were mere exhibitions for everyone's benefit, weren't they? Especially mine. And all the while, you lurked in the shadows like a spy, watching and waiting. How many times did you rehearse that devilish little speech of yours?"

I strode to the table, filled a cup with only whiskey this time, then drained it in one, burning draught. Still seething at Mason's accusations, I drank down at least two more shots straight from the bottle. Since I had eaten no breakfast, I was on my way to getting drunk again, but I did not really care.

"Now Dick, you *will* tell me." I wiped my mouth then came and stood before his chair. He sat hunched over, his head in hands, rocking back and forth. "Who is this weasel who wrote such things to you?"

When Mason realized I was standing over him, he looked up at me with the bleakest expression. His lip quivered as if he wanted to say something. In that moment, I almost felt sorry for him.

"Perhaps my correspondent has exaggerated," he finally whispered.

"Yes," I replied, irritated. "Perhaps he has."

I could feel the iron restraint I had forced upon myself these four years slipping away. My resolve to repress the deep antipathy I felt towards all who had conspired in the plot was beginning to fail me. The whiskey worked its rancorous charm, loosening my tongue, imperiling the tenuous hold by which I yet held my temper.

"But you cannot deny, Rochester," he managed to say, "that she is no longer mistress of this house." Snatching a kerchief from his pocket, he sat up, wiped his damp forehead then rose from the chair and faced me. "I am informed that her servants have been dismissed, that she is now held in close quarters, like a captive in her own home."

"Oh no, you are not at all mistaken," I assured him. "But only a fool would believe she is the captive. It is quite the reverse, Mason. Everyone in this house is a prisoner: we are all at the mercy of her demons. She is mad, you know. Quite insane."

He staggered.

I grasped his arm. "Surely, this cannot surprise you? You wrote to my brother about it."

He pulled away, and his eyes narrowed in suspicion. "What did you say?"

"You heard me. One of the letters in Campbell's box was from my brother, addressed to your father, discussing what *you* had written about your own sister. You were certain she would one day fall into the same madness as your mother."

"Rochester, please." He collapsed into my chair. "It cannot be. It is too soon for this."

"What do you mean?"

He sighed. "We believed…I hoped marriage might do her some good."

"You hoped? There is nothing to be done for her, I tell you. I have tried. God knows, I have tried!"

His round, smooth face was blank. "You have no idea, do you, Mason? I assure you, the violence perpetrated in this house has not been by me." I drew up the sleeves of my shirt and held up my forearms. "Take a good, long look then tell me who is the guilty one."

Raw, angry welts and cuts crisscrossed the flesh of my forearms, some deep enough to have required a surgeon's ministrations.

"Not a fortnight ago, when I went to her room, she seemed quiet and content. I asked if she wished to go outside to the garden. She seemed pleased with the idea. Then without warning, she attacked me with a hair comb she somehow had sharpened to a knife point. I managed to stop her before she could inflict more serious injury."

Mason shook his head. "I am sorry."

"Somehow I don't think you are," I replied, pulling my sleeves down to cover the silent witness of her affliction. "But surely—you now understand the necessity for her confinement?"

"You admit it, then?" he cried, leaping from the chair. "You are nothing more than her jailer!"

"I am!" I shouted. "And whose fault is that? My brother, your father and mine—and you, Richard. I came here to be a husband, not a prison warden. Yes, she is locked up, but for her own safety and that of others."

"My little *pajarito* was such a sweet child," he murmured.

"But she is no longer a child. She can be dangerous. Truly

dangerous. But don't take my word for it." I grabbed his arm and pulled him towards the door. "Why not judge for yourself? Come, Richard. I will leave you alone to get truly acquainted with her again."

His eyes widened in fear and he tried to pull away. "No, I beg you. We did not know how soon it would—come to this."

"You keep saying that!" I cried, letting go of him. "Every one of you knew her fate. That's why you lied about your own mother and pretended she was dead. Everyone except Miss Sylvie. But all along, you knew. You knew she was interred in that hellhole of an asylum in Kingston and said nothing!"

The bitterness and anger building these four long years suddenly choked me with its acrid taste. And I wanted him to suffer, just as I had suffered.

"Did you visit her, Richard? Do you know what it was like?"

He began to cry. "I could never bring myself to it." He buried his face in his hands and wept softly.

Seizing his wrists, I forced him to look at me.

"Well, I did go there, after your wretched mother was dead. At last she had found some peace, for God knows, she had none in that Bedlam. They could find no one else willing to claim her mortal remains for a decent burial. Your father was quite ill, but had he been hale, he would have refused, having washed his hands of her welfare years before. And where were you, Richard?"

"I should have come. I am a coward."

"It was horrible," I murmured.

I shuddered at a sudden memory of following the warden to the asylum morgue. As we passed through the dark and dank corridors, my skin crawled at the phantom touch of icy, skeletal hands groping and clutching at me, trying to drag me into the bottomless pit with them.

"The warden told me it was your mother's body laying there on the slab. But I had never seen her before, so I had to take his word for it. Filthy and emaciated, it was covered with sores—"

"No more, I beg you," he cried.

"Oh, but there is so much more, Richard, and you will hear it. Do you know they sometimes lock up men and women together? No matter the age? Whether healthy or ill? And of course, few of them are restrained. It seems their antics constitute the entertainment for those who are supposed to care for them."

He threw his hands over his ears. "Please, no more, Rochester." He whimpered like a whipped dog. "Have mercy!"

"Mercy?" I cried, grabbing him by the lapels of his coat.

"No more, no more," he sobbed, clawing at my fingers.

"You will hear the truth!"

I slapped him across the cheek.

His eyes went wide, more with fear than pain. He ceased struggling and let himself be supported by my grip.

"Listen to me, Mason," I whispered, still clutching his coat. "Night after night, I would be summoned into town—whatever quarter, whatever sin-hole she had crawled into. Wherever there was drink and men willing to buy, she would find her way there, seeking appeasement for her monstrous appetites. And when she chose not to wander into wild company and partake of their bacchanals, she spent her maniac fury against those of her own household!"

I breathed fast, and when I realized I still gripped him by the coat, I let go. He fell back, stumbling into his chair, still smarting from the blow across his cheek and trembling with shock. But I had more to say, and again, began to pace before him.

"Except for Lucias, Zabeth and a handful of others, the

servants have fled for their lives. Her orders were senseless or unreasonable. She could be exceptionally cruel while raging about imaginary defiance. Brandishing a butcher knife, she once chased down a laundry maid for that offense. But instead of stabbing the frightened thing, your sister, *my wife*, bit off her ear, claiming it was a just punishment for a servant's disobedience. When I questioned the poor child, the orders she had been given were nothing but gibberish."

He slumped over, his shoulders heaving with his sobbing cries. Good God, I thought. He really had no idea how far she had sunk.

"Richard—"

He threw up his arms, as if to ward off another blow, and still weeping softly, shrank into the shadow.

Further explanation was useless, I knew. He no longer wanted to listen. Exhausted and wrung out, I too, dropped into a chair, too weary to say more.

"Mason?" I inquired after a protracted silence. "I only want you to understand." A dim regret that I had given way to my temper passed through my mind. "In spite of her conduct and the obvious danger she was to herself and others, I would not condemn her to the horrible fate suffered by your mother."

He made no reply.

"Of course I loathe her behavior. Its fetid shadow has darkened my own existence, and robbed me of a future inheritance. I am mocked behind my back. Their heartless pity sickens me. I am the cuckhold of the lunatic, who in her sickness abused herself ruthlessly. They shun me and those of my household as if it were plague-ridden or worse. But do you not understand? Your sister is nothing to them. They think of her only as another inmate to provide fresh amusements to the keepers of Pandemonium. Whether you care to believe it or not, I do bear a conscience. Though her natural flesh and blood has abandoned her, she is my wife, and a duty by which I am bound. I could never consign her to that place."

He sat in the chair, still holding his face. He had ceased weeping but was too overcome or ashamed to meet my eye.

"All the doctors agree," I continued. "And believe me, there have been many of them. She is mad, and unpredictably violent. That is why she must be confined. I, of course, bear the full force of her rage and hatred, for I am the executor of the business. I hold the key to her cell as it were, and she hates me for it. Given the means and opportunity, I know she would kill me."

He said nothing. I got up and went to the other end of the room and looked out to my garden, obscured by an afternoon rain shower. The graying mist washed out its colors of sweet rose, brilliant yellows, green and orange. How like my own existence: dull, colorless, lifeless! My head ached from too much whiskey, too much argument. I was ashamed of having lost control, if even only for a moment. But in that moment, I had given vent to feelings I had long kept close, feelings I had never before confessed to anyone. I walked back to where he still sat in silence.

"Richard?" He lifted his head. "I tell you plainly, I should have divorced her the moment I discovered her adulterous ways, your £30,000 be damned. But I waited too long. The doctors pronounced her mad, and it was too late."

Still, he remained silent.

"I know how my father profited from the arrangement—may his sorry soul rot in Hell. But what was your part? What did you stand to gain from ruining my life?"

He turned away. "I am a coward, just as my father before me was a coward. My sister and our younger brother were destined to suffer the same fate as our mother. Georgie died of fever before the madness truly took hold of him. But

Netta was strong. She had no idea—" He paused and shook his head. "I tried to protect her."

He buried his face in his hands. His shoulders shook as he sobbed again. When at last he raised his head, his eyes were dark with hatred.

"One day my father found our mother gone away into town again, and his anger was terrible to behold. So he decided to be rid of her. But would he do the deed himself? No—" He paused. "I, his son, must take her to that place. I watched as they dragged her inside, screaming and shouting obscenities. And then," he paused again then shuddered. "She cursed me to my face. I swore that day I would never go there again. When Jonas showed me your father's letter, it was as if Providence had intervened and given me a way to prevent that fate for my sister."

"You give credit to God for all this, do you?"

"You cannot possibly know what it was like, Rochester. I watched my mother sink into madness, and then Jonas forced me to deliver her to that unspeakable asylum. On that day she cursed me, it was as though she had died to me. I shuddered to think my father would do the same to my sister."

"So you all saw fit to deceive me?"

"You were as eager as any of the others."

I could not say I was entirely without guilt. But none of the other suitors had ever been genuine contenders. Their presence was necessary to assure my participation, a vicious rivalry to spur a young man past the warnings of conscience.

He stood. "I am sorry, Rochester. I hoped to find something better than what we had given her, which was nothing. Perhaps she might have a husband who could...care for her."

"Go on and keep telling yourself that little lie. You were simply grooming a new warden, and that's the truth."

He looked away.

"You still don't understand, do you? You were the only one of your family who ever gave the slightest damn about her. And yet knowing the dirty little secret, you could foist that upon another man. A man who thought he was taking a bride to love and honor him. A woman he might one day cherish? A man imagines a family, sons and daughters..."

The agitation was beginning to stir again, and I knew prolonged discussion could only end badly.

"You came here full of malignant rumors and false accusations, Richard, but now you know the truth. Just take it and go."

I rang the bell. Lucias soon appeared with Mason's hat and coat. He paused at the library door and without turning around, said, "I am truly sorry." Then they both left the room.

I stood before the hearth, staring at the fire, mulling over the events of the past and how I had come to such an end. A soft voice soon interrupted my musings.

"Mister Richard has gone."

"Yes, he will go back to Madeira and I shall dine alone again tonight."

"Mister Edward, you eat something now."

I surveyed the tray and cup he brought, and remembered I had not eaten since breakfast the day before. I took a sip of the steaming coffee, which was sharp and strong. "Thank you."

His old face wrinkled with a sad smile, showing his still fine, white teeth. I lifted my cup in salute. Then he was gone.

EPIPHANY

I sat in the library until very late, pondering my encounter with Richard Mason. But losing my temper like that? It only gave credence to his accusation that I was a drunken, boorish rogue who mistreated the pitiable creature who was my wife. He was remarkably narrow when it came to his sister, but I now understood why.

When at last I retired upstairs, my night shirt and robe lay on the bed, placed there by a meticulous, tender hand. While I brooded in darkness, Lucias went about his work, leaving a pitcher of cool water and a bowl of fresh oranges beside the bed, the latter already shriveled in the heat. Nothing escaped its vampiric power.

All was silent at this hour. But how many times her ghoulish ravings had awakened the household these last months, I knew not. The events of recent days had strained me to the breaking point. I had no wish to face her demons tonight.

As I lay wrapped in silence, I suddenly thought of my mother. She had died during my last year at college, and with her death, the voice of prudence, the advocate for my good was gone. When Catherine deserted me then proclaimed her adulterous intentions, what choice did I have but to flee? Henry laid his ambush and in blind arrogance I stumbled into it.

These memories of deceit and betrayal kindled hot resentment while impotent fury welled forth in vexation and tears. Poor, duped, fool! I craved independence to *prove* something to him. When the chance for liberty presented itself, I, with all the swaggering carelessness of youth, grasped it. And is not independence now mine? Am I not the Master of this house? No doubt. But at what cost? I was ashamed of how I had passed my time last night, only to come slinking back like a thief to his lair. Richard Mason's unexpected visit only made it worse.

Unable to sleep, I got out of bed, donned my robe, then went to the balcony overlooking the garden. Long past midnight, it was still hot. I felt a swaying heaviness gathering in the darkness overhead. A storm was coming.

I took a cigar from my robe pocket, lit it then exhaled a cloud of smoke. Leaning on the balcony rail, I stared through the fragrant gray haze. In the other direction away down the hill was the wharf, its scattered lights still flickering along the riverbank. I thought of Maria—her wide-eyed look at the gold coin, marveling I would tender such a sum for so commonplace a service.

Did she really believe it was love between us? I saw in her eyes a hopelessness mirroring my own profound unhappiness. But at that moment, I no longer cared about noble self-promises. For a time, two desperate and lonely people found consolation in a rush of empty pleasure.

But in the aftermath, I felt degraded and full of guilt. No one would condemn me for seeking out such solace. No doubt it had been expected of me long ago. But it was not what I expected of myself. My resolve had vanished like fog in sunshine. I squandered away my honor, and now my cherished vow lay broken and in ruin, like the rest of my wretched life.

I had sought in vain for what I would never find there. A momentary lust was all she could offer. After the hour of time that is not time, there was no deep communion, no abiding respect, no tender passion of soul and spirit between us. Where was she whose sympathies met my own? Where was that woman whose heart beat as one with mine, whose very blood flowed in my veins?

How was it accomplished, this strange melding of natures? How did men and women sojourn together, beings as unlike the cold blasts of winter winds are from the gentle rains of summer? The one is composed of flint and steel, prone to inflexibility, while the other is of softest silk with a disposition inclined to harmony. Yet in the secret place known to God alone, the true confluence of souls somehow permits the nature of each to influence the other, so that together they are better than each alone. It was a mystery, but how well I knew of what I spoke, for I had seen it! It had substance and depth, yet was as measureless as the seven seas, as constant as the seasons of the sun and moon. *An ever fixed mark that looks on tempests and is never shaken.* Such a treasure, if ever it was to be found, would not be there in that place.

It has all come to end in this insignificance, this worthless existence which means nothing! The low hum of insect voices sounded an eerie sort of harmony to the dissonant Greek chorus of my own thoughts, which condemned me in a heartbeat. *All is vanity and there is nothing new under the sun.*

There can be no doubt. I *will* die here.

Is there anyone in the world who cares?

I thought of Carter, who had faithfully attended upon my brother and father in their last hours upon this earth. By

God, you are a good man, James! What a pity we shall never meet again. I regret all your efforts have been in vain, but you have my gratitude, nonetheless.

Weary of introspection, I snuffed my cigar and went back inside. The house remained quiet, and I lay down, hopeful for an uninterrupted night's sleep. Its peaceful unconsciousness would remove me from present troubles for a time, and I welcomed such a gift.

"GREAT GOD!"

A shrieking, eerie cry rent the night in twain, vibrating every nerve, wrenching me from sleep.

Momentarily disoriented, I sat up to listen. And I knew what it was. Her demons had wakened her, and she must for a time give way to their torment. Impossible to remain abed now. But scarcely audible above the noise, I could hear a faint knocking. Someone tapped at my inner chamber door.

"Mister Edward, you awake?" whispered a low voice. It was Lucias.

"Yes, come in, Lucias. I am awake now."

The faithful servant opened the door and peered round. He held aloft a single taper, its yellow glow illuminating his wrinkled, black face. This ritual was not new to either of us, yet one never got used to it. Before I had my robe on, however, he was taking things in hand.

"This time, I go. You been up much lately, habn't been sleepin'. She sound bad tonight. You stay. I call Zabeth. We take care of her."

I smiled weakly. Though it was my duty to go, I was ill-prepared to argue with him. Even when I had not been where he expected I should be, he understood. But Lucias was an old man. She might try him beyond his strength.

"Lucias—"

He held a bony finger to his lips. "You go back to sleep now. Lucias knows what to do." Without another word, he softly closed the door.

Grateful to be spared, I slumped on the bed and pressed my ears in vain effort to shut out the wolfish howls echoing throughout the house. As blackness fills the night, there is no avoiding it, no relief from its wailing torment. Even now, those sounds worked their foul spell, buzzing my frayed nerves, setting my flesh aquiver with a thousand hateful recollections.

The night air, steamy and hot with the coming storm, made it hard to breathe. I staggered onto the balcony, desperate for relief. But there was none to be found. Mosquitoes whined round me in a cloud. With every labored breath, the sodden air irritated my eyes, filled my mouth and nostrils. I was drowning.

"Oh, God! Deliver me from this wretched existence!"

Sinking to my knees, I pressed my face between the posts of the balcony railing. The dingy alehouses away along the river wharf now were dark, their silence a contrast to the wailing fury around me. Tears filled my eyes, and I shook with despair as I wept afresh, my anger dissolving into grief. I would never escape this misery.

I lifted my gaze toward the horizon and could see its thin, gray line separating the turbulent waters of the Atlantic from the night. Sinking into those dark depths was the moon, its bloody orb like a hot cannonball melting the very fabric of darkness. Hopelessness encircled me like the hangman's noose. The knot would be drawn tighter and tighter until at last, all my life was wrung from this earthly garment.

Desperation enlarged as a mocking voice whispered its condemnation, promising that liberation was near and the means were at hand, if only I had the courage to act! I struggled to repress the accusations, but in the fullness of time, my resistance had completely broken down.

My doom was nigh.

"No more," I muttered, rising to my feet.

A sudden wish to end my misery swept me back inside. From beneath my bed, I dragged forth a wooden box and knelt before it. Within this elegant little trunk the means of liberty awaited. I took a chain from my nightstand drawer upon which was threaded a little brass key. I opened the box. Coiled in the dark, velvet lining like sleeping cobras lay a brace of loaded dueling pistols. They had been a wedding gift from Rowland. That bastard! He hadn't the courage to deliver them himself.

The deadly beauties lay in their casket. I touch the barrel of one, and strange! Despite the heat, the metal feels cold. I imagine myself taking up the pistol, then calmly placing its chill steel against my temple. Will it be very loud? I wonder? Will I feel the ball tearing through hair, flesh, bone, brain? Will I see my own blood spattered on my hands ere the light goes out of my eyes? Will there be pain, or grief, or regret as my life drains onto the floor?

Her screaming continues as I frame these thoughts.

"This life is Hell," I murmur, tears again filling my eyes. "It is Hell!"

No future awaiting me could be worse than this present hour. Can I not climb out of this pit of Sheol to find peace with God? This misery would never be over until she or I was dead. And the power to end it lay cold and naked before me.

It would be easy, echoes the mocking voice. *Do it, Edward. Do it!!*

My resolve, fixed on the knife-point of the desperate agony of my plight, frames itself for an instant before me. I pick up one of the pistols, cock the hammer, then place the barrel against my temple.

Do it, do it! urges the relentless voice.

I will!

My eyes squeeze shut. My finger rests on the trigger.

Count to three, then do it!

One...

Two...

Three!

I held the gun steady. The barrel yet pressed against my temple. But I didn't pull the trigger.

I could not do it!

At the moment of decision when destinies are fixed or altered, I came to myself. The zenith of despair had passed. My hand started shaking as I uncocked the hammer, then lay the pistol back in its cushion. I closed the lid, locked the box then pushed it back under the bed. Unlike her, I am not insane. Perhaps for an instant, hopelessness felt crushing, but only for an instant. I must remain here then, until one of us was no more.

I threw myself on the bed, angry I could not summon the courage to do the deed, when all at once I became aware of silence. The howls had ceased. The house was quiet. Blessed, unearthly quiet. Thank God for you, Lucias!

A wind had risen, and the air felt weightless. Steady and cool, its force collected in the power of the storm, hastening it to fruition. The hurricane blasts blew open my balcony doors, and they banged against the wall. The wind rushed through my apartment, and in a great shout the storm heaved itself onto my world. Ere half an hour had elapsed, it was over.

In its wake blew a cool breeze. A silence, not of dread or expectation, but of peace, came over me. The mosquitoes had fled, driven off by the storm's fury. The air smelled fresh, pure—clean! Rising from my bed, I went out onto the balcony, where the unsullied drafts flitted across my feverish brow.

The pungent scent of orange blossoms, pineapples, pomegranates, even orchids, mingled with the storm-cleansed atmosphere. Awakened by the rain showers, the richness of my tropical garden burst forth. Its heady rush of sweet, spicy odors like an aromatic physic cleared my mind, and the enticement of that perfume beckoned me.

I rushed down the balcony steps and ran into the garden where I was surrounded by lush, appetizing fragrances. The trees dripped and their fruit shone bright, replete with ripeness. As a schoolboy delights in the taste of a purloined apple, I snatched a glowing orange from a branch, twisted it in two, then bit into its succulent center. Its sweetness was a shock. I tasted it again, then flung both portions deep into the orchard. The tart oil of the rind stung my lips, but I cared not! I wiped it on my sleeve, and laughed at the simple plea-sure of such delights again.

Standing among the trees in my drenched nightshirt, I savored the tang and flavor of the fruit. Somewhere out there, the waters of the Atlantic rumbled into shore. I ran along the gravel-strewn path to a flowery arch at the bottom of the garden. Passing beneath it, I walked to the cliff's edge where in the coming light of dawn, the mighty ocean waves leapt landward, celebrating their life and power.

A cool breeze off the water rushed into my lungs. My soul stirred within me. Long withered and scorched, it swelled anew with warm, living blood. With Hope! The tempest, borne upon a wind from Europe, reawakened my yearning for home. I longed for regeneration, a renewed spirit purged of the memories of this infernal place.

"*Go!*" murmured a voice.

But unlike that mocking demon of Despair, this voice

whispered in a soft sigh and daring expectation. With the coming of dawn, my spirit quickened, and my insides fluttered wildly. A tingling sensation flooded over me from the inside out, some vestal force stealing into this mortal flesh which had lain torpid all the years of the mockery that had been my marriage. It seemed the polluted mantle of this life was being shed, and a clean one emerging in its place. I envisioned a new path leading back to the Old World where my prospects were becoming clear.

My brother and father were dead. I was now the Master of Thornfield Hall. My responsibilities were there in England, not here. I would write to Carter and let him know I was coming home.

He had been exceptionally kind to my father, who had been unable to accept his eldest son's terrible fate. But what about the fate of his youngest son? Did I not come here out of respect for that father and my duty to him? What has the discharge of that duty gained me? Is there a woman who cherishes me? Is there a child which lives and grows beneath my hand and care? No. My bed was empty, my house unfilled and its nursery barren, void of life, all but abandoned by hope. And that most elusive prize of all—the esteem of my father? Was it now mine without question? Would ever I hear him utter those words, 'Well done, my son, well done'?

I would not. For he was dead.

I felt tears rising again as my frustrations kindled afresh. There was no future here, I knew. As I watched the waves roll into shore, a plan began forming in my mind. Am I not a free Englishman who now possesses such wealth that borders are meaningless? It was for family I made the fateful decision that day to honor him, and it has brought me nothing but misery and ruin. Perhaps it is true, I thought, that a friend sticks closer than a brother. But when there is no friend, and when the brother who should act as a friend does not, there is nothing left to follow but the compass of one's own conscience.

Growing ever more restless with each new possibility, I walked back to the house, moisture still dripping from the sweet clusters of fruit, plentiful and ripe all about me. An idea was shaping itself in my mind, a course of action that would re-establish me into the world of the living, a world wherein the opportunity for happiness would once again be within reach.

I hurried up the balcony stairs, then glanced back towards the sea and knew: that was the path to happiness. Never-more, I vowed, would any man's whim guide my steps. Come what may, I would be the arbiter of my own destiny.

A PERILOUS VOYAGE

We left Harbury after breakfast. The tale of my near self-destruction had carried us as far as the Old Crown Inn near Nottingham. We had just finished supper and dawdled over a cigar and sherry before retiring to bed.

"And so, James, that very next day, I began making plans to leave Jamaica."

Carter sipped his drink. "I knew nothing about your situation. Henry never told me where you had gone or why you left. But I had the distinct feeling you were never coming back to England."

"That was my dear brother's intention, I'm sure."

"Perhaps," he replied. "But after Rowland's accident, your father became less guarded in his conversation and let slip hints and names sufficient for me to deduce you were somewhere in the West Indies. But when I received your letter with news you were returning to England, it quite surprised me."

"I hardly believed it myself. But a privilege I thought never would be mine had been thrust upon me. I was the

Master of Thornfield Hall, and as the last Rochester, my duty required me to take up the position as head of the family. I could not do that from Jamaica."

"And Richard Mason? I assume you wrote to him about what happened?"

"He went back to Madeira some days after that unfortunate, final interview. After all the arrangements had been secured, I wrote and advised him to contact Fergus Campbell. But Richard never replied to my letter. I have no idea if he accepted the offer."

"Offer?" Carter was surprised. "You left it all to Mason, then?"

"Everything Jonas did was with one end in mind: to get an heir to supplant his son. But it never happened. After his scheme came to nothing and he was dead, I gladly gave over what belonged to his rightful heir. I kept only what remained of the £30,000—the blood money Jonas paid as dowry. It seemed to me that both she and I had earned it."

He sighed. "A strange and tragic tale. But I am grateful to know all these things, Edward. It has clarified certain… conjectures I had with respect to your past.

I laughed. "About what?"

"When you returned to school after your mother's funeral, you were a different man. You shunned every opportunity for fellowship. As I was caught up in my naval preparations, I just assumed you were mourning her death. But now I understand. You had far more on your mind than ever I imagined."

I smiled. "Had you actually shipped out to ports unknown with the Royal Navy, I know not how things might have turned out. But if my character has at all improved after hearing this woeful narrative, I am glad for it."

Pilot, who had been at my feet under the table, stood and

stretched then gave a great, bellowing yawn. "A moment, James."

I got up to let the dog out into the coaching yard. When I returned to our table, Carter looked around, then leaned forward.

"Surely, the challenges of sailing back to England with one in her condition would be formidable. And with your terrible propensity for seasickness…Edward, however did you manage it?"

"I must confess to a small deception which enabled me to get her on board without inquiry into her ailment."

"Oh?"

"You recall the story of Abraham, what he told Pharaoh about his wife, Sarah?"

"So you lied, did you?"

I felt rather like a mischievous lad. "Yes, to the captain. I even used Abraham's very falsehood: that she was my sister. I will never know if he believed me, for of course, we looked nothing like brother and sister. But who knows? Perhaps he thought I was adopted."

Carter smiled then shook his head.

"My additional embellishments were outrageously exaggerated," I continued, "which of course only elicited more sympathy. I told the captain she had recently suffered a terrible tragedy, that severe melancholy and shock were the result and sometimes appeared as the ravings of insanity."

"My dear Rochester! Have you no shame?"

"I suppose not," I smiled. "But it worked. The first two weeks of the voyage went by without incident. But my hopes for an uneventful passage were dashed when our ship escaped a near-fatal disaster."

"What happened?"

I snuffed the stub of my cigar. "The only thing that would ease my seasickness was fresh air, so I spent as much time as

I could walking the deck, which kept me away from our cabins during those intervals. I had restricted her to the compartment next to mine. But the weather during those first weeks as well as her temper were so mild she actually allowed me to bring her on deck a few times."

"What changed?"

"About a fortnight after we departed Kingston, our ship encountered a storm. All passengers were ordered below decks. It was late afternoon by the time the weather cleared. She eagerly accepted the small glass of wine I offered to help her sleep, while I went topside to clear my head."

ATLANTIC CROSSING TO ENGLAND—*FEBRUARY, 1802*

The sky was a bright blue as the late afternoon sun sparkled off the water. The ship bustled with activity as sailors clamored over the deck and up the riggings, unfurling sails and putting everything to right after the storm. I threaded my way through the chaos, meandering to the stern. By the time we got underway again, it was dusk.

The darkening sky on the eastern horizon flickered with a thousand points of starlight as night fell. Behind us, sunset glowed like a reddish, golden fire burning on the water. It was quite peaceful. I had just lit a cigar when the captain approached.

"Mr. Rochester." He nodded in greeting.

We shook hands. "Captain Smollett."

"You appear to have weathered the storm very well, sir."

I exhaled a cloud of smoke, then laughed. "You would not think so if you had seen me two hours ago. I spend time on deck because it's the only thing that keeps the damned nausea at bay. That little squall nearly did me in."

"In these waters, the weather can change at any moment."

"I am well aware of that," I replied, shuddering at the memory of my first disastrous journey across this very ocean, most of which I had spent in a fog of nausea and vertigo.

"And your sister? How did she fare?"

"She was not so seasick, but sorely afraid. I gave her a little wine after the tempest to help her sleep."

"I see," he replied.

"Is there something I can do for you this evening, Captain?"

He cleared his throat and seemed hesitant to speak. "I would have come to you earlier, but the weather made that impossible."

"Of course," I agreed.

"My first mate informed me that prior to the storm, one or two of my crew were overheard talking to your sister."

I snuffed the cigar then flicked it into the sea. "No one was nearby when I reported to our cabins," I said. "I admit I was terribly seasick, but we had no visitors that I recall."

Captain Smollett appeared rather embarrassed. "The conversation that was overheard no doubt will offend you, sir. But several of the crew were gossiping about it like old women. I fear there may be those who will take the suggestion seriously."

"And what suggestion is that?"

"There is no way to say this delicately, Mr. Rochester. Apparently your sister has—" He coughed into his fist. "Ahem, well, this crewman believes she has offered herself to him."

"She did what?"

"You heard me correctly, sir."

"I appreciate your frankness, but let me assure you, Captain, there is no cause for worry." I showed him a key.

159

"She has not the power to grant him access." I held it up for his scrutiny.

With obvious relief, he took it, and nodded. "I am very glad to hear this, Mr. Rochester." He returned the key after inspecting it. "I regret the circumstances, but I felt it was my duty to alert you. Whoever had the temerity to make such an offensive remark will be severely reprimanded. Be assured, sir, our bargain remains intact. My crew know nothing of her condition."

"Thank you for informing me. I will see to her at once."

He lifted his cap, then I hurried to the companionway and descended below deck. Of course this revelation was most disturbing. It required all my resolve to remain outwardly composed. But I knew her ways, and if these crewmen proved more persistent or resourceful than Captain Smollett supposed them to be—besides, some reckless youth who had spent weeks at sea would be ill-prepared to resist such alluring promises.

The glow from the setting sun was near gone, its last light a mere shimmer of red on the horizon. The corridor approaching our quarters was dim. I could scarcely distinguish the cabin doors from the bulkhead. I rattled my door. Still closed and locked, just as I had left it. I breathed a sigh of relief. Taking up the glass of the sconce on the opposite wall, I intended to light its candle, but it was missing. My pulse quickened as I moved towards her room, where I discovered the captain's warning had come too late. Someone had gone in, or come out. The door was ajar.

I entered the berth. As my eyes adjusted in the fading light, I distinguished the shapes of the bed, the dresser and chair against the dimness. A moaning sound coming from somewhere on the floor, followed by the clatter of an empty bottle rolling across the planking, alerted me. My foot kicked against a prostrate figure. Kneeling over, I could see it was one of the crew. He was shirtless. The drop-flap of his pants was unbuttoned and he and reeked of rum. I heaved him to his feet.

"Get up, sailor. What are you doing here? How did you get into this cabin?"

His clutched his trousers, belched, then blinked slowly, trying to focus. "She bid me come in. An' besides, I 'ad the key, sir."

"You're drunk."

"That I am, sir."

"You say you had a key? But that's impossible."

He grinned lazily. "Oh no i' tain't. Mr. Kenge has th' master key to all these 'ere passenger berths, 'mergencies an' all." He held it up, grinning again. "I took the liberty of borrowin' it from 'im, Captain."

"I am not your captain," I retorted sharply, snatching the key away. "But we shall find him directly."

I dragged the man up on deck and found Captain Smollett with his first mate, Mr. Price, who at once confirmed this was the sailor he heard earlier in the day bragging about his expected rendezvous. I told them where I had found the youth. Of course his condition was obvious. The captain was furious.

"Jones, you bloody ass!" He clutched the latter by his hair.

Jones again grinned. "I 'ad a key, sir. An' besides. The lady invited me."

"Mr. Price!" Smollett hailed the first mate. "Take this fool below and lock him up. He shall feel the lash when he can stand up straight. Harker!" he beckoned a nearby sailor. "You and Mr. Price escort this man to the brig at once."

"Aye aye, sir," shouted Harker. He and Price supported the inebriated seaman between them and half carried, half dragged him to his fate. The captain then turned to me.

"Mr. Rochester, I must apologize—"

"There is no time for that now, sir. She is missing. Jones was falling-down drunk, but I cannot believe he consumed an entire bottle of rum alone. She must be wandering somewhere on board."

"I will order a search party immediately."

I held up my hand. "Do you smell that? Something is burning!"

The deck lanterns which had been lit within the last hour cast enough light to reveal a thin white plume of smoke rising up from the cargo hold. "She must be there. I will go at once!"

Without waiting for his leave, I dashed to the companionway and descended below deck into the hold. There were several compartments, some for ship's stores while others were for the cargo and passengers' luggage. I followed the stench of smoke and found her in a corner of one of the forward compartments, standing among several crates of fabrics being brought back to Liverpool.

The missing candle from the sconce lay atop one crate near where she stood. It burned into the wood, albeit slowly. It just smoldered now, but soon the embers would flame hot and catch anything combustible around it.

A smaller crate from atop one of the stacks lay broken open on the floor, its sides ruptured apart exposing a variety of fabrics within. Bolts of silks, cottons and fine linens lay strewn about her in a jumble. She had unraveled yards of fabric and even now was wrapping white muslin around herself like a shroud.

She startled at my appearance then cackled her greeting. "Ha ha ha ha!"

Her dark eyes wild and wide, she grinned then laughed like a hyena. Her disheveled linen shift was torn near the shoulder. As she pirouetted about, the bolt of fabric wound around her waist then suddenly was yanked off the floor. It struck the candle which tumbled into the tangle of fabrics. They burst into flame.

"Bertha!"

The fear in my voice made her halt. She watched as the flames of the blazing pile of cloth grew higher, licking dangerously near the bulkhead ceiling. At first it dazzled her as she stared at the undulating glow. But somehow she sensed the danger and began beating at the blaze with the canvas sailcloth which had lined the broken crate.

Dashing across the hold, I kicked the burning pile and scattered the bolts, which immediately diminished the flames. By now, several crew had arrived to take up the fight. Soon, the blaze was extinguished, the only loss being the contents of the crate which had smashed onto the floor.

The excitement and danger of the fire so soon after her rendezvous with the sailor, as well as too much drink, quelled her thirst for mischief. She willingly came back with me to her cabin and passively submitted to my every attention. I bathed her hands and face, then helped her into a clean nightgown. She drank a glass of water, then lay down like a child in her bed, curling into a ball beneath the blanket. When at last she slept, I blew out the candle, locked the door, then found my way back on deck.

MRS. POOLE

When I came down to breakfast the next morning, Carter was already waiting. Pilot, who had gotten himself tangled up with a badger the night before, crept in alongside me then plopped apologetically under the table.

"James." We shook hands. I poured a cup of coffee while Carter plied me with questions about the after-effects of the fire at sea.

"I cannot really blame her," I replied. "I had assumed the diluted wine she drank would be sufficient to make her sleep, but it was not. The sailor's offer of rum was a far more enticing offer because she had not tasted it in a long time. They drank the entire bottle in less than two hours, and its effect was potent. The excitement of her little adventure rendered her tranquil for a few days. But my penchant for seasickness made the last weeks of the voyage very unpleasant. I had to maintain a close vigilance and could snatch but an hour or two topside while she slept. By the time we arrived in England, I was quite ill."

He shook his head. "Thank Providence your ship did not sink."

"Providence?" I muttered. "It was rather owing to the quick actions of the crew that so many lives were spared."

"You know what I mean—"

"Is it not enough that Richard Mason throws Providence in my face for these wasted years of my life? I don't need you to do it too, James."

"Do not ascribe the same motives to me as you assign to Richard Mason."

I sighed. "I am sorry, old friend. But it is hard to recount these events without dredging up all the bitterness and anger associated with them."

"I understand. But I hope our friendship can survive a few harshly spoken words."

"It can." I smiled. "But only because of your generosity and kindness." I shook my head. "Whatever did I do to deserve it?"

"We've known each other a long time, Edward." He sipped his coffee then smiled. "Force of habit, I suppose. But now," he continued. "After you came back, what then?"

"As soon I felt fit, I began searching for a caregiver. I went weeks without success and finally took your advice respecting the Grimsby Retreat."

"As usual, you were too proud to listen to anyone else's counsel, even respecting matters for which you had no experience." He shook his head. "But I never imagined your choice would be the superintendent's mother."

THE GRIMSBY RETREAT—JUNE, 1802

"You are certain this is a good idea?" I asked Carter,

pacing back and forth in the waiting room at the Grimsby
Retreat.

A new kind of hospital for the care of the feeble-minded
and mentally unstable, it was conducted on a more humane
system than other institutions of its kind. Among the
reforms they had embraced was the elimination of straight
coats for immobilizing patients. They eschewed such
barbarity as the stocks or other ghastly forms of restraint.
Patients were not permitted to roam the halls, nor were men
and women ever housed together.

"Yes, as I have affirmed many times," he replied calmly. "If
you had just listened to me, you would not have wasted so
much time."

I had spent weeks interviewing a dozen candidates at
least, none of whom were remotely qualified for the work.
They were either too young or too old. When the only question any of them asked me was how much was the salary, I
knew I was out of my depth. Exasperated, I had turned to
Carter, who reiterated his recommendation of Grimsby.

Its superintendent, a Mr. Josiah Poole, all too frequently
had seen his own mother labor as a nurse under the horrific
conditions found in so many sanitariums purported to
provide care for those who could not care for themselves.
Being a philanthropic-hearted young man, he assembled a
group of like-minded friends and investors who proceeded
with the establishment of Grimsby. In his reply to my letter, he
wrote that he had taken the liberty of mentioning my need to
his mother. It was she whom Carter and I were about to meet.

"Gentlemen."

Carter rose, and I stopped pacing. We faced an amply
bewhiskered young man, not much older than myself, next
to whom stood a coarse-looking, large framed woman, on
whose countenance the cares of her profession had been

deeply graven. One could tell at first glance they were mother and son.

Josiah Poole heartily shook Carter's hand. "You must be Mr. Carter, the surgeon from Hay?"

He nodded. "This is my good friend, Mr. Edward Rochester of Thornfield Hall. I believe he also wrote to you."

"He did," replied Mr. Poole. "And I am pleased to make your acquaintance, sir." I shook his proffered hand. "May I present my mother, Mrs. Grace Poole?"

She curtsied. "Mr. Rochester."

"Mrs. Poole."

"Mr. Rochester," continued Josiah Poole. "I want to assure you I showed your correspondence to my mother with only the best of intentions. You see, she's had considerable experience with the very type of patient your letter described."

"I suppose it will save me the trouble of a lengthy explanation," I replied.

He bowed.

Carter interrupted the ensuing awkward silence. "I must commend your efforts, Mr. Poole. The progressive work you are doing here does not receive the accolades it deserves."

"We do our best, sir. It is but a small effort when one considers the unmet needs of society."

"True," agreed Carter. "But one must start somewhere. If you would oblige me, I am curious to know more of your methods."

"An excellent notion, sir. Mother?" Mr. Poole turned to Grace. "If you have no objections, I will conduct the doctor on a brief tour."

She nodded her assent.

"I would like that very much," replied my friend. "Edward, you don't mind?"

"Not at all. It will give Mrs. Poole and I some time to become acquainted."

After the two men left the room, I beckoned Mrs. Poole to sit.

"As my son informed you," she began, "I am aware of your need, sir. That you have someone requiring…care?"

"I do," I replied. "And I intend the nurse should live at my house." She began to protest, but I forestalled her objections. "Mrs. Poole, let me be frank. My experience of institutions to care for the insane was brief but extremely unpleasant. Such places create the unsavory reputation which you are trying to overcome through the enlightened methods utilized here at Grimsby."

She nodded. "While we have accomplished a great deal of good here, there is much yet to be done. However…" She trailed off.

"Most people are not as open-minded as yourself and this establishment's Committee members, I perceive?"

"In my experience, sir, people do not wish to acknowledge the existence of individuals who are so afflicted as those who reside here. They would much rather have them locked away and forgotten."

I passed my hand over my eyes as images of that asylum in Kingston flashed through my mind. *Locked away and forgotten*. Precisely what Jonas Mason had done. And I was now contemplating the same thing.

Grace Poole continued.

"Many of our patients are healthy, yet their minds are as broken as their bodies are whole. It is difficult to care for them. Many of them have no comprehension that their behaviors are at odds with proper society. Because they are so misunderstood, they are often the victims of violence and cruelty."

When I had answered that summons to collect my mother-in-law's mortal remains, the appalling conditions in which she had existed all those years sickened me, and made me even angrier about the circumstances which had brought me to Jamaica. And yet, God forgive me, when the temptation confronted me, I understood how Jonas Mason could make such a choice.

"Let me get to the point, Mrs. Poole. I would provide everything needed. In addition, there is a generous salary."

I waited for the question, but instead, she asked, "Do you think it the wisest choice, sir? There are resources here at Grimsby."

"The patient about whom I speak is like one whom you have so aptly described. There is nothing physically wrong with her, but every doctor who has attended her has pronounced the same diagnosis—insanity. She has on occasion been violent, but such behavior generally has been directed against me. By removing myself from her presence, I believe such outbursts will cease."

"If true, that would be a wise precaution, sir."

"I am glad you agree."

"Would you live nearby?"

She was all business, I gave her that. Perhaps even a bit arrogant. But she was someone who understood what such duty would entail.

"I am undecided," I replied. "My father had business interests in Paris which I am inclined to revitalize. I thought perhaps I might begin there."

She nodded, but said nothing.

"Would you find such an arrangement to be unusual, Mrs. Poole?"

"Perhaps not, sir. Yet, when there is such a place as this Retreat at your disposal, I must question the wisdom."

"I do have good reasons for wanting this to be a private situation. The circumstances are unusual."

"How is that, sir?"

What did it matter if I told her? I would be gone in a few minutes and she would never see me again.

"The patient I speak of is my wife."

"Indeed?"

"I was very young," I added hastily. "Ours was an arranged marriage. More than four years ago, at the behest of my father, I traveled to Jamaica—"

In brief, I related the whole, sad story, including the unforgettable visit to the asylum in Kingston. Grace listened with interest as I recounted the incidents, the outlandish behaviors, the temper tantrums and acts of real violence which had been perpetrated against myself and a few others.

In the handful of questions she asked, I felt a kind of sympathy. Yet as I spoke, her mouth hardened into a thin line of reticence. Her dark eyes fixed upon me, but that unblinking stare conveyed a shrewd understanding. When at last I had done, she rose from her chair. "I am sorry, Mr. Rochester."

"Thank you, Mrs. Poole." I stood to take my leave. "You have been very patient. I apologize for having burdened you with my troubles." I gave a curt bow. "Good day."

I turned to go.

"Sir?"

"You have another question?"

"All I meant to say, sir, is that I am sorry for all you have endured. I well know what it is to deal with such a one. But never in my own family."

I held forth my hand, and she took it. "May I call you Grace?"

"Of course, sir." She gave a quick curtsey.

"Your kind attention has lifted my spirits. I hope you and your son will continue with the good work you are doing here."

"I'll no longer be here if am I to enter your employ, sir."

"But I thought you were not interested in my business?"

She smiled. I perceived a sharp mind behind that plain-looking countenance, and a will which harbored a self-interest sufficient enough to keep my secret.

"Is there something else you wish to ask of me, Grace?"

"I heard a rumor or two when old Mr. Rochester died, sir. That things were left in a bit of confusion?"

"Let us just say there were a few legal entanglements that could not be sorted out until I returned from the West Indies. But if, as I suspect, you are inquiring about the solvency of the estate, you needn't worry on that score. Your salary as I said will be quite generous."

"I never doubted that, sir. But I do have a request."

"And that is?"

"We have found that method and routine is very important to the treatment of the patients here at Grimsby. I would carry on that policy in a private situation. It is imperative I be allowed to make the day-to-day decisions concerning her care."

"Done."

"Do you wish me to sign any sort of agreement, sir? A pledge of confidentiality, perhaps?"

"You and I will get on very well, Mrs. Poole."

She curtsied. "Be assured, sir. Mrs. Rochester will be well cared for. On that you have my word."

WE DEPARTED AFTER BREAKFAST AND HAD BEEN TRAVELING ALL day. Our coach arrived late to the King's Head Inn, where we cajoled a midnight supper of bread, cheese and beer out of the proprietor.

I sipped my ale. "Grace has, on whole, proved a decent companion for her, James, you must admit."

"I do wish you had informed me of your wife's propensity for violent behavior," he replied. "In my opinion, the arrangement you settled upon is less than ideal."

"Are you suggesting I should have left her to rot in that god awful asylum in Jamaica?"

He shot me a withering look. "Of course not."

"Am I no better than Jonas Mason?"

"You would not have brought her to England if that was true."

"God, what an end, Carter," I murmured. "My entire family, dead. I came back as Master of Thornfield Hall, but knew I must leave again as soon as possible. When Stewart and the lawyers had sufficiently unraveled things, I left to make a new life for myself in a place where no one had ever heard the name of Edward Rochester."

A FRESH START

Present Day

When the next morning our coach rattled away from the inn, I sat lost in thought, thinking over everything I had revealed to my friend. This scrutiny of my past had rekindled long-dormant feelings of resentment against my dead father and brother. The ten, long years of wandering and self-indulgence had blunted those feelings, but always they were there. The memories would sometimes rise up and haunt me for days. This deliberate invitation to them was almost dangerous.

"Do you suppose it will snow ere we arrive in Millcote?" asked Carter as he peered through the coach window. The sunrise glow tinted the eastern sky bright orange as we set out on the road. The landscape had become more rugged and wild and the air colder as we drew closer to the northern shires and our final destination.

"I hope not," I replied, scratching Pilot's ears. "We have been fortunate thus far."

"Well, that would never do, would it?" He laughed. "To be delayed by the weather? You may be forced to endure my company yet another night and reveal even more of your mysterious past."

"I am afraid today's chapters will only confirm your suspicions of my profligate ways all these years—the sorry saga of a man who began the pursuit of a dream full of hope, but like every other fool who preceded him, ends up on the same, ruinous path."

"And tangled up in all this is the mysterious little girl at Thornfield Hall, whom you insist is not your daughter. Why, I keep asking myself, would you bring another man's child to live in your house?"

"When you hear about my experiences in Europe, you will understand how it all came about. It took the lawyers about six months to untangle the estate matters. Once Grace had settled in and I was no longer needed by anyone, I ventured across the Channel to the Continent. By a happy coincidence, on my first voyage I met Monsieur Philippe L'Argent, and we became friends."

ENGLISH CHANNEL—*September, 1802*

A man perhaps fifteen years older than I stood next to me near the bow of our packet ship as it made its smoky, noisy way across the Channel. It was cold and windy and as usual, I was fighting against the rising nausea. The older man seemed unaffected by the boat rocking over the rough sea.

"You look very green about the gills, young man," he observed.

By his accent, I supposed him to be French.

"Perhaps a sip of wine would help?"

I nodded. From inside his overcoat the man produced a smallish *bota*, the Spanish style wineskin used by Basque sheepherders. He demonstrated its use, pulling the cork, lifting it high and tipping it towards his mouth. He gave the *bota* a gentle squeeze, then gulped the thin, flowing stream of dark, red wine.

"Simple, eh? Now you try."

He handed me the wineskin and I emulated his actions. With the first squeeze, the wine hit me in the nose because I was holding the bag too high and too far from my mouth. He laughed.

"Hah, hah, hah." He snatched a handkerchief from his pocket and gave it to me. "Try again!"

I wiped my face then repeated the steps, this time with success. A cool squirt of flavorful wine shot into my mouth.

I handed over the *bota*. "Thank you. I'm sure the wine will help settle my stomach."

"This appears to be your first sea voyage, young man?"

I shook my head. "No, I've sailed to the West Indies and back, but had the same, damned seasickness on both voyages."

After dabbing a stray dribble of wine on my chin, I held out the handkerchief, but he refused to take it back.

"Keep it, monsieur. At the moment, you need it more than I." He sighed, then shaded his eyes while looking toward the French coast. "Crossing *La Manche* is always a challenge, *n'est ce pas?*"

"This is my first trip to France."

"*Vraiment?* An Englishman who has never been to France before? *Mon Dieu!* That is terrible!"

I smiled. "I never had the time to go to Europe. But now I am determined to explore to my heart's content."

"Ah, that is well," he replied with satisfaction. "Allow me to introduce myself. I am Philippe L'Argent, from Paris. Is that your destination?"

I gave a curt bow, then extended my hand. "Rochester. Edward Rochester. Yes, I plan to go there first."

Instead of shaking my hand, he suddenly pulled me to him then kissed me once on each cheek. After seeing my shocked expression, he patted my shoulder. "Ah, forgive me, Monsieur Edward. May I call you Edward?"

I nodded.

"We Frenchmen are very emotional. The *baiser sur les deux joues* is a traditional greeting, even between men. I know you English. You are so *stoïque*, so reserved, but we Frenchmen cannot help ourselves. *Peu importe!* Do not be embarrassed. If you are going to spend time in Europe, you should prepare yourself for similar customs elsewhere, eh?"

I nodded. "Thank you for the advice, Monsieur L'Argent."

"Please, please!" he scolded. "If I am to be your guide, you must call me Philippe."

"My guide?"

"Of course, *mon ami.* Since this is your first visit, it must be a memorable one. Paris is the pearl of Europe, *La Ville-Lumiere!* I will take you there and show you all the famous sights, if you will allow me." He winked and laughed. "And perhaps some which are not as well known, eh?"

Again, I smiled. "Thank you, Philippe. I am much obliged to you. If what I see pleases me, I may reside there permanently."

"Of course, I am biased, monsieur, but you could not make a better choice."

"WITHIN A WEEK OF MY ARRIVAL, JAMES, I GOT SETTLED INTO an apartment in a fine quarter of the city. Philippe and I spent the next few weeks together. We dined out most every evening, attending party after party where he introduced me to his many acquaintance. At one of these soirées, I had my first glimpse of Céline Varens."

"Adele's mother," said Carter.

"We were only just introduced that evening for she was ever surrounded by flatterers and admirers. One newly arrived Englishman was nothing more than a curiosity. But after three months of the Paris party scene," I continued, "the other sights and cities of Europe beckoned. I went first to Vienna. After some weeks there, I visited Venice, Florence, Rome and Naples. With plenty of money and a good name, I was accepted into fashionable society everywhere. For two years, I roamed about, indulging in the nightlife wherever I went. But soon, I grew restless in my disappointment—was there not one woman who would sympathize with my plight, one woman who longed for a constant companion, someone with whom to share her life?"

Carter sighed. "You really believed such a woman existed? One who would simply live with you after discovering you could not marry?"

"My story was in earnest, James, my desires natural and simple. If I pledged myself to her, and stayed true, would that not content any woman?"

"Not any worthy woman. You are fool if you think so."

"There are more women than you would believe who were very willing to engage in such an arrangement. But they were shallow creatures seeking a man rich enough to keep them in a lifestyle they enjoyed, one to which most of them were accustomed. Their petty talk of jewels, wardrobes, fine living arrangements and their endless propensity for entertainment was appalling."

"What else did you expect?" replied Carter thoughtfully. "Is it not always the same everywhere? Those with plenty seem bent on destructive self-indulgence."

"In those days, I was caught up in the very middle of it. My naiveté made me blind to everything. The women I encountered in those circles were more than ready to exchange their favors for access to my bank account, but nothing more. That bitter discovery hardened my heart. I descended into recklessness and self-indulgence. If distraction and amusement was all they wanted, that is what I gave them. That is what I took from them. In short, all the idle pleasures that being rich could afford me. As I reflect on my behavior, I can hardly believe with what callousness I proceeded."

He shook his head. "The same old tale, eh?"

"Decidedly unoriginal of me, but true. I wanted to forget, to blot out the awful memories of the years in Jamaica. The sweet concoction of dissipation was the remedy for such gall, and I indulged myself heartily."

I continued. "My one true enjoyment in those early years was music. My childhood had been filled with it, for my mother was a proficient. She recognized my own ability at an early age and engaged a master to instruct me. When I wandered my way back to Paris, I was drawn into that world."

"Where you again encountered Mademoiselle Varens?" asked Carter.

"Precisely," I replied. "One night out on the town, my friends and I were particularly bored. I was the only musical fellow among us and as a joke, suggested the light opera. To my surprise, they heartily agreed, hoping they would see on stage *beaucoup des belles femmes*. And so we went. And I saw her again that night. Céline Varens, *Le Petit Oiseau Chanteur*, the darling of Paris nightlife. She dazzled me afresh. Her beauty and poise entranced me, and I was riveted by her performance. My heart swelled with desire as I watched. During the final act, she glimpsed my way. My blood raced. I knew I must meet her again."

CÉLINE

"Rochester, *allez, maintenant*! Do not waste the night like this! Bah! Wait for your little song bird if you must! Perhaps you will have luck in love tonight!"

"*Adieu, mes amis*! I am counting on it!"

Backstage, I threaded the crowd of cast members, stage-hands, wardrobe women and others hurrying everywhere, at last finding my way to her dressing room.

The door was closed to visitors, of course, though theatre folk, as well as a few gentlemen who apparently were not connected with the opera, had leave to enter. These people came and went for over two hours. But when each man who had gone in came out again, he was quite obviously disappointed by his reception.

By the time the chaos subsided, I and a handful of admirers lingered in the corridor. But one by one, they drifted away. When at last she emerged, I had been waiting more than three hours.

Looking fresh and vibrant, languid in her shimmering black gown, her slender neck encircled by half a dozen silver chains, a red velvet cloak draped over her arm, she smiled up at me, for I stood head and shoulders above her.

"*Vous avez beaucoup de patience, monsieur.*"

"I would wait as long as necessary, Mademoiselle Varens, for a chance to speak alone with you."

She held forth her ungloved, delicate hand, which I pressed to my lips. She scrutinized me with large, dark eyes, which all at once beamed with recognition.

"Ah, you are Monsieur Rochester, *n'est-ce pas?*" she inquired almost shyly.

"Why, yes," I replied with a bow. "We have met before, but only briefly."

"I remember. *Vous êtes un ami de Philippe?*"

"We are friends, yes."

Her countenance lit up with her smile, and her eyes shone like black diamonds, bright and alluring in the flickering candlelight of the theatre corridor. Truly, I knew not what to make of such a look. Coy, inviting, exasperating all at once. I was enraptured.

"Well, Monsieur Rochester. Though we were introduced so long ago, I am acquainted with you by reputation."

"And may I inquire," I began, "to what reputation you might be referring?"

What delight was this? From our brief meeting nearly two years before, she remembered me?

She smiled again. "Ah, our friend has told me of your travels throughout Europe. That you thoroughly take plea-sure in—" she paused, then demurely said, "the entertain-ments of every city you visit? That you spare no expense for your own enjoyment."

It seems I had acquired quite a name for myself as the wild, extravagant Englishman who lived for parties and spent money like it was water.

"He is anxious about me, is that it?"

"*Au contraire*, monsieur." Her eyes gleamed with a kind of restless fascination. "I find it—how do you say—enticing, that you would so boldly seek after your own pleasures. *Mais, il est triste*. Philippe has told me that *toujours*, you are alone. Would you not appreciate *un amoureux* to accompany you on such pursuits? Would it not be more...*mémorable?*"

Again, I lifted her hand and pressed it to my lips. Warmed by the heat of her presence, in slow motion I fell into the bottomless depths of her eyes. "Will you have dinner with me tonight, Mademoiselle? Perhaps we might discuss it?"

Her dark gaze met mine. I held my breath, waiting for her refusal, when all at once, a smile spread over her face and her eyes, like ebony gems, glittered up at me.

"I am surprised at you, monsieur."

"Why is that?"

"I did not think you would take so long to ask me your heart's desire."

I exhaled a sigh. "Grant my request and you will make me the happiest of men."

"Can you doubt, monsieur, what I want?"

She held up the black glove for her unsheathed hand. As I reached to take it, she let it go and I snatched it out of the air. Lifting her arm, I trailed my fingertips along the soft under-skin from shoulder to wrist. She watched me, her eyes half closed, her lips parting ever so slightly as I slid the glove onto her hand. She pushed into it as I pulled it to her elbow. I leaned over, cupped her cheek, then brushed her lips with mine.

She stepped back and laughed, then handed me her cloak. As I wrapped her shoulders in the plush, sable-trimmed garment, she leaned into my arm, and sighed. We stood for moment unmoving, when suddenly she reached up and pulled my head down and kissed me hard on the mouth. She gazed up with an innocent though knowing glance, as if to assess the result of her brashness. I pulled her close, and lost myself in a long and lingering kiss.

Finding our way to one of the finest restaurants in Paris, we ate and drank, talked and laughed until the early hours of the morning. When I escorted her back to her tiny apartment near the theatre district, she invited me up for a brandy. I did not return to my hotel that night.

We went out again the following evening, and the next night, and the one after that. For uncounted days, I attended each performance until I knew every note of music, every gesture, every movement on stage. Afterwards, we would go to a fashionable cabaret somewhere in the city, inevitably returning by the wee hours to her flat.

She was a favorite in that society and soon, we became the talk of the town.

"Rochester!" exclaimed a casual friend. "How does a man who resembles a shaggy, black bear capture the heart of so delicate and fawn-like a creature as The Varens? Truly, you are a man to be envied!"

"But was I, Carter? Men hovered about, basking in her shadow, clamoring for her notice. But as her attentions seemed wholly devoted to me, I fancied myself the envy of them all. It seemed that everyone in that social circle cared only for money and the vainglorious attentions of everyone around them. Oh, how she flattered me. And like a fool, I once again was taken in by the honey-coated tongue of a vixen."

"But in my heart, I knew Céline was not the kind of woman I wanted. She could never imagine an existence apart from the bright lights and glittering excitement of the theatre. As the darling of that set, she excited everyone's

admiration. To secure her regard against all rivals, I show-
ered her with clothes, jewels, furs, all of which she adored, of
course."

"Your mistress," said Carter.

"I never used that word," I replied. "But she loved being
escorted among the admiring crowds, adorned in the expensive garments and glittering gems I had bestowed upon her.
At the height of my infatuation, I leased her a spacious and
elegant apartment. How well I remember the night when
first I took her to see it."

"OH, *MON AMOUR*, EDWARD! *TU ES TRÈS GENEREUX!* THESE
rooms are charming…everything I see… *c'est magnifique!*"

She threw herself into my arms, proclaiming eternal love
and gratitude. I listened with a perverse kind of pleasure as
her small, slippered feet pattered throughout each room.
One after another, she glanced in at the furnishings, silken
draperies and the Turkish carpets, expressing her utter
delight.

"Ah, *mon Dieu*! What parties I shall have! Oh, Edward,
dozens of our friends will come to eat, drink and be merry."

"HOW MAGNANIMOUS I FELT THAT DAY. MY ENGLISH GOLD
had been good for something at last, and I fancied myself
content. Céline and I had been together more than a year
when one summer evening I discovered that all my silver and
gold was not enough to keep her from wandering into
another man's bed."

BETRAYAL

A Paris Cafe—June 1806

A friend and I had just finished luncheon, but he had other business that day and was unable to stay. I ordered a *pousse-café* then watched the bustle go by for another hour or two. But boredom soon overtook me so I went on my way.

I wandered about Paris visiting a few night spots Céline and I had frequented. By day there was little activity, but after dark they would light up into exciting and boisterous places of pleasure.

As my imagination flamed with thoughts of *mon amoureux sauvage*, I burned to spend the night with her in my arms, for it had been many days since I had been to the apartment. Before long I was at her front door, knocking impatiently. When no one answered, I used my key and let myself in.

Perhaps she was napping, I mused, silently closing the front door. She often did so before a performance. Tiptoeing to the bedroom, I entered without a sound.

What a spectacular mess greeted me! The pillows, blankets and quilt were heaped in a pile on the bed. A dozen of her dresses lay scattered and draped everywhere, on the floor, the chairs, a dressing table. I smirked, grateful it had been her possessions and not me which suffered the wrath of some explosion of temper.

I was relieved to be spared another argument, yet at the same time irritated she was not here. I paced the sitting room, my annoyance growing by the minute. Where had she gone? She was due at the opera house in less than three hours. She was never late for curtain rise. Bathed in her scent of musk and amber, my desire only flamed hotter. The apartment was littered with fresh flower arrangements sent by admirers unknown. They filled the rooms with such a cloying sweetness that the air nearly choked me, so I escaped to the balcony.

It was a warm June evening but a breeze stirred and I breathed in drafts of fresh, summer air. Dropping into a chair, I propped my boots on the railing then lit a cigar. Soon, the fragrant tobacco scent calmed me. The street below was quiet enough, but soon would be crowded with fashionable carriages rolling toward the opera house. When Céline stopped here before going to the theatre, I would inform her that food and wine would be awaiting us after her performance. For tonight, I meant to have her all to myself.

I blew a circle of smoke into the air and watched it waft away into the summer night, thinking about the day we first explored these rooms together. She simply adored the place. Within her circle of influence, this address had become legendary for its boisterous, extravagant parties. Of course, I footed the bill for them all, but in those days I saw myself only through the eyes of every man who was jealous of her affection for me. In the beginning, I attended every one of those soireés, but latterly, had stopped coming. The routine had grown tiresome. The crowds which flocked to her beck and call were always the same empty-headed creatures who constituted her acquaintance.

Yes! A damning indictment upon me as well. But for some time, I had been thinking about leaving Paris and I wanted Céline to come with me. When first we met, she seemed excited by the idea of being my travel companion, of visiting other cities and taking in their musical theatre, perhaps even participating in it. But only in her narrow world here in Paris could she be the center of attention in a place where her devotees could nightly assemble to pay their homage.

Nevertheless, I was determined to convince her that a change of scenery would do us good. I was even prepared to bring the baby, the *filette* she had presented me with six months before. No doubt Céline would use her as an excuse not to go, but I was more than willing to bring her along. I would even hire a nursemaid to look after the child, so Céline could have no excuse.

At last, the sound of a carriage rolling to a stop on the cobblestoned street below caught my attention. With a thrill of expectation, I leapt up from my chair, snuffed the cigar then looked over the railing, prepared to greet her as she exited the equipage. Through the soft glow of gaslight, I saw her demurely step out of the vehicle.

"Mon ange," I whispered.

I was about to call down again, louder this time, but who was that? Someone else was getting out of the *voiture.*

When a hatted head appeared, then a booted, spurred heel rested upon the coach step, a green fist of jealousy clutched my heart. After everything I had given her, she would dare betray me with another man?

Her companion leaned out of the vehicle, pausing to glance in either direction before stepping down into the street. When he descended, she stood on tiptoe and put her arms around his neck. He kissed her eyes, her throat, her mouth. She laughed as he nuzzled her neck. I could easily hear their conversation in the yet uncrowded street.

"*Mon cher*," she laughed. "You have no patience!"

"You expect me to have patience, when your smile, your scent, your body, they beckon me?"

They soon disappeared under the arched *porche cochère* of the hotel. At any moment they would enter the apartment. Trembling with fury, I decided to ambush them. Leaving a narrow slit in the curtains to observe them, I left the balcony doors ajar to overhear the lovers' whispered conversation.

A chambermaid preceded them into the room. She lit a fire, then a lamp, which she left on a table. The couple soon tumbled in after, laughing and chattering. I clenched the door handles until my knuckles turned white as I fought the urge to burst into the room.

Peering between the curtains, I could see her companion clearly.

And I recognized him. A soldier, an officer, he was the Viscount Guy D'Arblay, a brutal, drunken youth whom I had occasionally met in society. He possessed a violent temper and a reputation with the ladies. His romantic escapades had given him ample opportunity to display his prowess on the dueling field, which was legendary.

Seeing him there, the anger drained out of me at once, and I let go of the door. Good God, what a simpleton I had been! The veil was ripped away and I could see it now. The missed rendezvous, the feigned headaches, the spur-of-the-moment visits from friends.

Céline had *never* cared for me. She only ever wanted my money and the fine things it could buy for her. What a damned idiot I had been! Would I never learn? Smoothing my hair, I took a deep breath. My indignation became a steely resolve to rectify that mistake.

The lovers' urgent whispers again drew my attention.

D'Arblay unbelted his sword, then fumbled at his uniform buttons. Céline helped him hurry off his coat, then lent against him as his arms came around her. He whispered in her ear and groped and clutched while she writhed with pleasure.

"First, a drink, *ma petite,*" he said breathlessly, tickling her chin.

He released her, then went to the wine rack and selected a bottle. As he reached for the corkscrew, he saw my card, which I had left on the table before going out to the balcony.

"Ah, it would seem your pig of an Englishman called while we were out."

"That barbarian?" She laughed, as he uncorked the bottle and poured two glasses. "The Devil take him, for all I care."

He handed her a glass. They each took a swallow, then paused, staring longingly at one another. Silently, he took her glass then set both on a side table. D'Arblay pulled Céline into his arms, kissing her face, her neck. She tugged his shirt from his pants while he began unlacing her gown.

At that moment, I stepped through the balcony doors.

D'Arblay's hands dropped at once, and he jumped back from Céline as if he'd been bitten.

"You will explain yourself at once, monsieur! What is the meaning of this intrusion? Why are you lurking about like a spy?"

"Since I pay for the privilege I will lurk wherever I wish," I replied. "But that woman," I pointed at Céline, "belongs to me."

She lunged at me. I caught both wrists then encircled her small frame with one arm, pinning her tightly against me.

"Be still, my dear," I admonished as she tried to squirm out of my grasp. I held my finger on her lips. "I promise to release you if you behave yourself. Will you?"

She squeezed her eyes shut in frustration and tried to

push herself out of my arms, but when she realized it was no use, she went still, then nodded. True to my word, I let her go. She ran to D'Arblay's side and clutched his arm protectively.

"Look around you," I glared at the Viscount. "Everything in this apartment is provided at my expense. The coach which brought you here and even the very English horses pulling it were bought with *my* gold, monsieur. Accordingly, you will forestall your feeble protests, for I very much doubt without such trappings, you would be here at all. You are as vain as she."

"Zis is too much—" he began to protest.

"Oh, I have not finished, not in the least." I was actually enjoying myself. "Céline, *ma chère*, you will kindly remove all your jewelry. Since you have chosen to abuse my generosity, I will have them returned at once. You may take a few of your dresses, shoes and wraps, but I'll thank you to leave the expensive Russian furs which I brought back from St. Petersburg. They will fetch a handsome price at market and I think they are best got rid of rather than you should keep them."

"Oh, *mon Dieu!* Edward, how can you…this is outrageous!"

"Not at all, my dear," I chuckled. "Not at all."

She was in complete shock. My appearance had been wholly unexpected, and my actions now were just as surprising. Céline believed herself secure in my affections and supposed I was so bewitched by her beauty that she could do whatever she pleased. But being so rudely dismissed by me? Never!

"Plead not to God, madam. It is I who now relieve you of the obvious nuisance of my attentions, as well as the burden of all these fine things. But never fear. I shall give you a small purse for immediate exigencies, and three days to pack what I leave you. If after that time I return to find you here still, I shall summon the police and have you arrested for trespassing. Once I inform the proprietor of your imminent departure, he will want to lease the apartment again as soon as possible. Your lingering presence will impede his ability to do that. And I'm sure he'll have no scruple about using whatever means are at his disposal to be rid of you."

She stamped her tiny foot in frustration, cursing me resoundly in the most elegant sounding French. Before she could raise another protest, I turned to the young viscount.

"And now, D'Arblay. Shall you compel me to go through the little ritual, or may I simply invite you to the Bois de Bologne tomorrow, if you have the courage to face me there."

"If I have the courage, monsieur?" He spluttered with the arrogance of a man overconfident in his abilities. "Perhaps you are unaware, but I have never been bested on the field. It may be wise for you to reconsider your challenge."

"I will be there at sunrise," I replied coldly. "And now, kindly leave us. I have more business with Mademoiselle."

D'Arblay hastily tucked in his shirt, pulled on his coat, then quickly belted on his sword. Snatching up his hat and cloak from the crimson velvet armchair where he'd dropped them, he looked at Céline, imploring her to do something. But she just stood there, unable to move or speak. I thoroughly enjoyed watching them twist helplessly in their embarrassment.

The Viscount buttoned his uniform jacket. Pulling it taut he eyed me haughtily, desperate to maintain some sort of dignity. "You are no gentleman, Rochester. If you are fool enough to appear at the Park in the morning, it will be my pleasure to end your miserable existence with whatever weapons you choose."

I merely smiled. He retreated to the door, snapped his heels, then was gone.

Céline, who now was weeping dramatically, sat on the

sofa, her face buried in her small hands. I applauded in admiration.

"Another grand performance, my dear. But your tears will not move me." I took a handkerchief from my pocket and dropped it onto her lap. "Dry your eyes."

She dabbed her cheeks. "*Mon Dieu*, how can you be so cru-el, to put me out into the cold?"

"It is June, my dear, not in the least cold. Besides, of all your many acquaintances, is there not one who will take you in for a night or two? Or will this sudden loss of your possessions and accommodations diminish your worth in their eyes?"

Céline stood up, and still dabbing her eyes and cheeks, went to the side table where I had laid my card. She took up a small toy laying there—a baby's rattle. Whirling about, she pointed it at me. "And *la fillette*, your daughter?" she cried. "You cannot abandon her!"

I laughed. "*My* daughter? You think I still believe Adele is mine? I have been a fool, but I've known for months she is not my child."

Céline gasped. "How could you possibly know?"

"Most offspring at six months bear at least some resemblance to its parents. I see a strong aspect of you, her mother. But there is not even a shadow of myself. Was our bed ever exclusive to us, my dear? Or has D'Arblay been there all along? Tell me the truth, this once. The Viscount is her father, is he not?"

She was silent.

I watched and waited as she wrestled with her frustrations. Her lip quivered as she struggled against the desire to confess and throw herself on my mercy, or continue her mutiny. In the end, however, her pride and vanity would not permit it.

She lifted her chin. "I will never tell you his name. Never!"

I shook my head. From my pocketbook I withdrew several hundred francs. "Here is the money I promised, and something extra for the child's sake. Remember. You have three days to get out. And take care to observe the conditions I have laid out. A scene with the police will only be an embarrassment."

As she cursed me again, I departed.

DUEL

AFTER LEAVING CÉLINE'S APARTMENT, I WALKED TO ANOTHER quarter of the city and called upon my old friend, Philippe L'Argent.

"Rochester, to what do I owe this pleasure? I have not seen you for many weeks. Have you been traveling?"

"No, Philippe, but I have been thinking about leaving Paris. And after tonight, I am fully decided to go." I related in few words what happened. He was not pleased I had challenged the Viscount.

"It is foolish, Rochester. He is quite the proficient. As far as I am aware, he has never been bested."

"I don't care, old friend. I cannot overlook his insult. He must pay for his arrogance."

"The dueling field is no place for your anger."

"I assure you that by tomorrow, I will be calm and unmovable. But I am resolved in this. It would honor me greatly if you would consent to be my second."

He bowed. "I am humbled by your trust. But you are certain? I cannot dissuade you from this course?"

I shook my head. "I will provide more details in the

morning, at the Park. But for now, there are things I must do, arrangements I must make before my rendezvous with the Viscount."

"Very well, *mon ami.*" He embraced me affectionately. "I will be there at sunrise."

After we said goodbye, I wandered around the city for an hour or two before returning to my flat. As I sat at my desk writing out my will and final instructions for my solicitor, I was surprisingly indifferent about the prospect of my own death. Why should I not be, when there was no one in the world who would mourn my passing.

The next morning I arrived at six o'clock, coming into the Park from the *Porte de Boulogne* entrance. We rode along the lane for about two hundred yards, then halted at the first crossing. Some distance down the path I could see the ruins of the *Château de Madrid.*

The sunrise glow behind the trees which formed the eastern boundary of the Park greeted me as I stepped down from the coach. A soft dew still clung to the grass. With a surprisingly lighthearted pace, I walked to the other end of the clearing where L'Argent awaited me.

"Philippe." He greeted me with his customary kiss on either cheek. "Thank you—I am grateful you have come."

"Rochester." He frowned at me. "You are determined to go through with this? D'Arblay is an opprobrious cur of course —but let me again remind you of his reputation."

"I am aware of his reputation."

"Then I pray you know what you are doing."

"He is a hot-headed youth who cannot control his temper. It will prove his undoing in the end."

"He has killed at least two men that I have heard, and seriously wounded several others. Those odds do not look good from my point of view."

"Ah, but his prowess is the saber, not the pistol."

"All I know is he has never lost a contest. But," he sighed, "as long as you understand the risk, I am willing to second you."

I nodded, and clasped his hand warmly. "Thank you. Here is the key to my apartment. There you will find the few important papers in my possession. I have prepared a letter to Stewart, my agent in England. Should I not survive this morning's encounter, you will kindly forward them all to him, and he will settle my affairs."

"You are very cavalier about all this, Rochester."

"Not at all. I am merely being practical. Besides, I have no intention of dying today."

"D'Arblay's proficiency is quite beyond dispute."

"I daresay he has never faced the cold-hearted resolve of a man who cared not whether he lived or died."

L'Argent sighed again, then pointed to the box under my arm. "You have brought the weapons?"

I handed him an ornately carved little beechwood trunk which held a pair of dueling pistols. "I think you will find them more than adequate to our purpose."

He took the box and held it while I withdrew a small brass key from my pocket. I turned it in the lock, then lifted the lid to reveal the weapons laying in the velvet cushion. They looked just as they looked that night so many years ago, when I contemplated putting a bullet in my brain with one of them.

"I cleaned them last night. You will find the balls and powder as well the other necessities in the small drawer at the front of the box."

Caressing the ivory carved handle, he asked, "How did you come by these, Rochester? They are quite beautiful."

I laughed softly. "They were a gift given to me long ago."

"Ah, you will excuse me, but it appears they are other than English origin?"

"It is Spanish craftsmanship."

"Ah, yes, I see. The flamboyant carvings on the grip." Lovingly, he ran his hand over the ivory, his fingertips touching the lines and swirls of the intricately carved patterns. "Quite beautiful, indeed."

L'Argent shut the box and withdrew to await D'Arblay's man, who along with himself, would load the pistols as we watched. As the challenged party, it was the Viscount's prerogative to choose the instruments of duel. Though he was skilled with the blade, I had so infuriated him with my challenge, D'Arblay had—whether he intended to or not—deferred to me by remarking I might meet him with 'whichever weapons you choose.'

Presently, another carriage drew up and three men stepped out. One was my foe, another most assuredly his second. Who the third man was, I could not say.

D'Arblay strutted across the field like a peacock, his uniform cloak flowing behind him. He appeared resplendent in his military dress, cutting rather a suave figure as he approached. Compared with my thick, blacksmith-like stature, the contrast was marked. I smiled however, knowing his long frame would provide me with an ample target.

"Rochester." He snapped his heels and honored me with a curt bow. "You at least have the courage to meet me this morning. That is more than I can say about many men who have dared to challenge me."

I gave a curt nod. "Don't flatter yourself. You are here at my invitation. Besides, I fully intend to kill you."

"Ha, ha, ha. That is quite ze boast, monsieur, for one who has never appeared on the field before."

"And just what do you know of my history on the field?"

Finger by finger, he tugged off his white, uniform gloves. "Let us just say I make it my business to be informed of the disagreements which are settled here in the Park." Casually, he handed the gloves over to his second. "Your name, as I recall, has never been mentioned."

"Paris is not the only city where such confrontations occur," I replied coldly. "The Bois de Boulogne is but one arena among many."

"Well...that is...quite true," he answered a little too casually. The possibility he could be facing an experienced rival gave him pause.

"Gentlemen," L'Argent began. "As challenger, Monsieur Rochester has chosen this field in the Bois de Boulogne. The Viscount Monsieur D'Arblay has agreed to participate with whatsoever weapon his opponent would choose. I now show you his choice."

Philippe held the carved box with the dueling pistols and opened it beneath the eyes of D'Arblay and his second, a Monsieur Ormon. The latter was struck by their workmanship.

"These are quite beautiful, Monsieur Rochester. I have never seen their like before. Are they of Italian design?"

"Spanish," I replied. "From the New World."

"Ah." Taking up one of the pistols, he turned it this way and that, then held it out, sighting down the barrel. He hefted it once or twice between his hands. Holding it again in his right, he cocked the hammer with his thumb, then pulled the trigger.

"It is a well-balanced weapon. I choose this one for Monsieur D'Arblay."

L'Argent bowed, then took up the remaining pistol. D'Arblay and I removed our cloaks and jackets as our seconds loaded the weapons then gave them to us.

"You will stand back-to-back then walk ten paces to the points as marked by the foils, each of which has a red bandana tied to its grip," commanded L'Argent. "When you reach that point, turn and face your opponent." He showed us a small square of cloth. "Fix your eyes upon this white kerchief. When I drop it, you may fire."

L'Argent fell silent. I pulled the hammer to cock my pistol. I heard the snick of D'Arblay's weapon as he did the same. We looked at each other.

"I hope, Rochester, you have prepared yourself?"

I bowed, but said nothing.

I believe it would give me great pleasure to kill you. Yet the satisfaction would be fleeting, as once you are dead, you will be unable to know the humiliation of losing. Besides, as I had watched him swagger across the field this morning, I remembered my conjecture from last night, the strong possibility he was Adele's father.

We stood at the marked center, and walked out to the points, ten paces. When I turned, D'Arblay was facing me. He looked eager and determined. I stood like a statue, my weapon at shoulder height. I stared at him. He tried to look defiant, but I could tell he was nervous.

"*Messieurs!*" cried L'Argent. "*Regardez moi!*"

Céline would never confirm my insinuation about D'Arblay, but what of it? Would I be the man to deprive Adele of a parent, no matter how unworthy of that calling he might be? As much as he had offended me, it was not my prerogative to execute him for it.

L'Argent lifted the handkerchief aloft. "Raise and aim your weapons!" he shouted.

I obeyed, as did my opponent. I sighted him at the end of the barrel, and looked him square in the eye, along the sight of his own weapon. In the instant before L'Argent let go of the kerchief, it fluttered in the breeze. In the next heartbeat, he dropped it. I fired a split second before D'Arblay, who recoiled with pain as his gun discharged. His shot went wide, and I saw him drop the pistol and clutch his left arm. He fell to his knees and moaned in pain.

Ormon and the other man standing by rushed to D'Arblay's aid. A dark, red stain spread rapidly over his shirt sleeve. The third man proved to be a surgeon, for he produced a small bag, and from it took a length of cloth, as well as a bottle of liquid. D'Arblay snatched the bottle, pulled out the cork with his teeth, took a long drink, then poured some on his wound.

The viscount was on his knees, hunched over and rocking back and forth in pain. How strange! As I watched him, I thought I would be filled with a kind of gloating, a deep satisfaction at thus wounding him. But I felt nothing. They say revenge is sweet, but at the moment, I found it a rather tasteless dish.

The surgeon bound up D'Arblay's wound then helped him to his feet. L'Argent retrieved the weapon from Ormon then walked back up the field.

"Thank you, Philippe, for attending me this morning. Your presence gave me much confidence."

"It is the least I could do for a friend, Rochester. One whom I do not see enough."

He now opened the box. "Your pistol?"

"Certainly." I took the gun and looked at it. Briefly I recalled again the time I held it to my own temple and nearly pulled the trigger. I laid it back in the box and shut the lid. L'Argent pulled my flat key from his pocket, laid it on top of the box then held it forth.

I took the key than pushed the box towards him. "Keep them."

"Rochester, you are not serious?"

"I am. You have been a good friend to me, Philippe. These pistols were given to me long ago by my brother. But he is dead, and I foresee no further use for them." I tugged the key chain out of my pocket then draped it across the lid of the box. "For services rendered to me faithfully and well, I should like you to have them. I trust they will never again be used for such a purpose. Perhaps they are something you would remember me by."

"*Mon ami*, I thank you from the bottom of my heart. But what do you mean, 'remember you?' Are you leaving Paris?"

"Within the week, and I shall be gone for some time."

"May I ask where you are going?"

I shook my head. "At this moment, I cannot tell you. It is more than a year since I have been back to Thornfield. I should attend to the responsibilities I have latterly neglected. You understand how it is when one has been away for so long."

"Of course, of course."

"So, take the pistols, Philippe. Do with them what you will."

He bowed. "*Merci.*"

I put on my coat and cloak. "And now—I must go."

We shook hands. Again, he kissed me on both cheeks. "May God go with you on your travels."

"*Au revoir, mon ami.*"

With the beechwood box tucked under his arm, he departed.

We had been out perhaps an hour. The sun was just cresting the skyline of Paris, and the apartments and trees and buildings were hallowed in brightness. The park would be full of visitors in another hour or two: lovers leisurely strolling the paths with no particular destination, or artists come to capture a pleasant landscape. The birds now were noisy, and the hush which greeted me this morning was no more.

I walked away from the field and did not look back.

DOOMED TO BLINDNESS

"So, Carter—where was I to go now? Though I had no desire to remain in Paris, I must stay long enough to make good on my threat to Céline. I spent the rest of that morning revisiting many of places she and I had been in what I could pretend to believe were happier times. I wondered if ever I should find contentment. It seemed that whatever I set my hand to, it ended poorly. Perhaps my father was right after all. I was doomed to failure."

Near noon we stopped at a small coaching inn to have lunch while Jack changed the horses.

"I roamed far and wide around the city that day. While at a favorite café, I realized how late it had gotten, and so returned to my flat to begin preparations for departure. The morning post had been delivered, and among the few letters was one addressed to me in the hand of an old friend, informing me of his recent engagement and forthcoming marriage to a Miss Emily Alworth of Scarborough."

"I was simply bursting with the news!" he replied. "I had no idea if you were in Paris, but I must make the effort to tell you nonetheless. Like Noah's dove, I sent forth that letter and hoped that somehow it would find you."

"Your happiness shone through every word." I sighed. "How I envied you, James. If envy is a sin, then I committed it with great vigor. But tell me again how you had come to meet your Emily." I took a bite of the meal which had just been set before us. "It was quite the whirlwind courtship, as I recall."

"It was indeed," he chuckled. "She had come into town to aid her brother's family during his wife's lying in. It was their second child, and so there must be someone to attend the first. She remained some weeks after the baby was born, and one evening was escorted by her brother to a country dance in Millcote, where we met. Before returning to Scarborough, she had consented to become my wife."

"Whirlwind is an apt description," I laughed. "You are a lucky man."

"How well I know it. But our wedding wasn't until October. You left Paris in June. Where did you go? What occupied you during those months before you returned to England?"

Just then, a stable boy ran in to inform us our coach was ready to get underway. We gobbled down the remainder of our lunch then hurried outside. I climbed into the vehicle and settled in. Pilot laid his great head across my lap. Idly, I scratched his ears. The journey had been tedious and I was glad for my friend's company. The endless miles and bumpy road made me long for a good night's rest in a decent bed. Strange it was to be looking forward to returning to Thornfield, if even only for a few days. But I knew once I was there, it would not be long before every feeling rebelled and I must depart yet again.

As our coach pulled away from the inn, I continued my tale.

"Within days of evicting Céline, I found my way to

Florence. I had visited there once or twice before settling in
Paris. It was a charming city. I discovered its theatre and
musical society were much to my liking. In one of the
groups, I was introduced to Giacinta. She was, by the by,
singularly beautiful, though certainly, it could not have been
any physical perfections of mine which attracted her notice."

I continued. "At a party or some such affair, I happened to
recount my recent, unhappy history in Paris, that I had lately
quit that city, having just banished an unfaithful lover whose
paramour I shot in a duel. I thought she would be repulsed
by such violence, but she was enamored by it. She wanted to
know every detail. That very evening she offered herself as
Céline's replacement!"

Carter shook his head. "Truly, Edward? I must be the
most naive man in the world."

"Humiliation leaves one singularly vulnerable, James. I
should have refused her at once. But at that moment, I was
beyond all self-respect. Falling into the arms of another *belle
amour* was a way of escape. To crawl in a hole and lick my
wounds. When she agreed to come back to Paris with me, I
was elated. Giacinta was a lover of the visual arts, painting,
sculpting and the like. Being from Florence, she fancied
herself familiar with all things avant-garde. She dabbled as a
painter, but soon discovered those who supported the arts
held the true power. They were highly sought after and flattered by every artist who needed their money."

"And had she the purse to carry this off?" he asked.

"Of course not," I laughed. "She had found me. So once
again, I took the foolish step of securing a woman's affection
with money. I funded a little gallery where she could woo the
bohemian community with whom she fraternized."

"At first," I continued, "it was amusing to watch them all
fawning over each other's work, lavishing praise and adulation where none was deserved. I soon became bored with it

all and spent less time with her and her friends, though now and then in the evening, I still found my way to her flat, which I paid for, of course. Sometimes, when she was particularly excited about a new prospect, she would meet me for breakfast at a favorite café to regale me with stories of disappointed young men whose artistic talents didn't quite measure up."

Carter looked askance.

"Yes. She took many lovers among those young men. If they pleased her, she would include them in her gallery."

"Edward, really—"

I held up a hand. "I know, I know. But I ended my association with her before I returned to England. When I discovered how she manipulated these young artists, it made me angry, somehow. I knew her deceitful character, but these young men blinded by passion for their art, gave in to her demands in exchange for her patronage. Giacinta needed me to keep her little enterprise afloat but when I threatened its survival, the depth of her true character was revealed."

"What happened?" asked Carter.

"It was the fall of that year. I remember because the leaves of the trees along the streets of the city were turning to gold. I met her one morning and told her I was planning a trip to England for your wedding...and that I was going alone."

PARIS—*SEPTEMBER, 1806*

I hurried into the café on the Montmartre where Giacinta and I on occasion met for a breakfast. She was well-known among its regular crowd, her little gallery having become a modest success. Her Florentine roots, her boisterous temper and unconventional taste had won a loyal following among them, though certainly their work would never be displayed at the *Salon de Paris*. Not that they aspired to such a goal, for she termed such art as *ottuso*, and *passato di moda*, and declared she would never promote such work on her own premises.

She sat at our usual table, perusing a few drawings given to her by a hopeful, young *artista*.

"Ah, another starry-eyed dreamer, *mia cara*?" I asked, pulling out a chair to sit down.

"*Certamenta*," she laughed, holding up one of the drawings.

It was an uninspiring likeness of one the many bridges across the Seine.

"He is like every other painter who comes to Paris. Look at these…it is all he sees. He strolls along the river, falls in love with a bridge, then paints it, many times over from every possible aspect. I will put him on the wall for a day or two, but nothing more."

"It gives you pleasure, I see, to wield such power over these young men."

"*Buon Dio*, my love, it is not that. I must be the *guardiano*, a gatekeeper for vision and originality. It is my duty to make sure the patrons who come to my gallery see only the best the city has to offer."

"If you must," I sighed, pressing her small hand to my lips. Idly, I stroked the back of her fingers. "I am glad you have your gallery to keep you amused. I will soon be returning to England for awhile."

"*Inghilterra*?" she asked, her voice rising with curiosity. Suddenly, she snatched her hand away. "*Mio amore*, for how long? Am I not to go with you?"

"I will be away for a month, perhaps two. But you couldn't possibly abandon your community for that long. They so depend upon you. Besides, it will be a dreary affair where you are concerned. My good friend is engaged to be married, and I must be at his wedding. I cannot imagine you would enjoy something so *tradizionale?*"

"*Matrimonio?*" she echoed. "So conventional. Ah, but to travel, and across the Channel? *Eduardo,* I have never been to England. Oh, I should love to go! I must make plans to staff the gallery, and will I have time for the small exhibition next month? *O mio,* there is much to do—"

"Giacinta, listen to me." I interrupted. "I shall be going alone."

"*Solo?*" Her voice rose. "But of course I must come with you. Are we not lovers? Do not lovers share everything?"

"Perhaps they do, *mia cara*. But our bed is not something I chose to share, though you have done so, very freely, it would seem. And don't try to deny it. I am aware of them all, the *scultori e pittori* you have bedded. Was it for sport? Did you believe in any of them, in their art? Or was it to spite me?" She started to protest, but leaning across the table, I touched a finger to her lips. "Oh, it is not that I mind them. Well, not very much, because I know you. I've known you all along, you see. You are not very loyal, therefore I feel no compunction to invite you."

Her mouth opened in shock. "But...but I must come with you! How would it look, you leaving me behind? Everyone knows we are lovers."

"Yes, but I am only one among many. I do understand it may perhaps look bad for you, to be forsaken by the rich and foolish Englishman who has single-handedly kept your wretched little gallery afloat. No doubt when the money runs out, they will abandon you without a second thought."

Suddenly, she slapped me across the face, then jumped up from her chair, upsetting the cups and spilling the coffee all over my lap and the drawings on the table.

"You...you are a *suino,* a beast! I demand to go with you. It is my right! I have paid dearly for it, with my body, with my honor!"

"Honor, my dear? I don't think you understand the meaning of that word. Besides, I have no intention of taking you among respectable people. Am I to introduce you as my mistress? Carter would forgive me, but I would never do that to his young bride who, I am sure, is everything you are not. No, I am resolved. I will go alone."

I stood to leave. While watching her face darken with displeasure, I tugged out my wallet, withdrew a wad of francs then tossed them on to the table. They landed in a puddle of coffee. "There is your final payment. It is time you find another fool to prop up your little enterprise."

"*Eduardo!* Don't leave me, *per favore!* I love you!"

She moaned, she begged me not to desert her. It was cruel. How could I do such a thing? I was nearly out the door when one dish, then another and another crashed to floor behind me as she screamed, "You are a beast! *Ti maledico!*"

I actually felt glad to be relieved of her society, and all the pretensions that accompanied it. I had not the heart to report the gossip behind her back, gossip I had overheard at a party, when I was informed by a very drunk young sculptor what many of them really thought of her. They despised her garish tastes, and her foreign ways, but being more interested in renown than integrity, they sold themselves for fame.

Much as I had done, I thought. Sold myself. For love, that is. No, it was never really love. Not from Giacinta, not from Céline. Idolatry, perhaps? Yes, of gold. Of my money. And of all the pleasures it could buy them. But at the end of the day, I was still the same, lonely man.

A few nights later, on the eve of my departure to England, I returned to that café to bid adieu to a few friends. Philippe L'Argent and I were having a quiet supper when she appeared out of nowhere and confronted me at my table."

"Eduardo!"

My former lover stood over us. Wrapped in a shawl, her long, black hair disheveled and dark circles of sleeplessness under her eyes, she swayed on her feet, obviously very drunk.

"Giacinta. How nice to see you. You look well—"

"Do not lie to me, you swine! I am miserable."

Calmly, I lit a cigar. "And why is that?"

"*Perché?* You mean to desert me for another, I know it."

"Desert you?" I laughed. "I think you have it backwards. You drove me away. Where are all your lovers now, your artistes and bohemian friends? How is the gallery?"

This was a low blow, but I could not help myself.

"It is no more!" She wailed. "Everyone has left me. I am destitute. I have no money, you miser! *Tu sei il diavolo! Vai all'inferno!*"

I sighed. "I am sorry, but I did warn you." I blew out a cloud of smoke, then tapped off the ash. "And now, if you would kindly go away, my friend and I would like to finish our dinner in peace."

"But *Eduardo!*" She clutched at my arm. "You love me! You must take me with you! What shall I do if you leave me? *Ti amo...ti amo...ti amo.*"

She stood there, mumbling and weeping so I feared she would fall onto the table. Philippe leapt up from his chair to assist.

Giancinta swayed violently. I reached to support her when suddenly from beneath the shawl she whipped out a pistolet.

Philippe gasped, backing away from the table.

She waved the weapon around her head, then cried, "If I cannot go with you, you shall not go!"

Gripping the gun with both hands, she wildly aimed then pulled the trigger.

A CHRISTMAS GALA

PRESENT DAY

"Good God!" exclaimed Carter.

"You say rightly," I agreed. "I was very lucky. She was too drunk to hold the gun steady, so her shot went awry. Philippe and the other patrons were just as fortunate. They restrained her to prevent further brutality. That is when we found the hidden dagger. That no one was was injured, or worse…"

"Providential," replied Carter, his eyes wide in wonderment. He exhaled a breath of relief. "Most auspicious, indeed."

"Yes, I see that you marvel at my continued stupidity," I answered with a wry smile. "Well, rather than take up with yet another ungrateful woman, for once I chose the wise course of action and returned straightaway to England for your wedding. I would not for the world have missed it, James. You were not the same man I had known three years before. Whatever wanderlust made you yearn for a naval career was gone. Your spirit was settled and content. I remember wondering if ever there might be such happiness for me."

"I was delighted you came, Edward. But when Emily and I returned from our honeymoon, you were still in Millcote. And to my further astonishment, you revived your mother's tradition by hosting the Christmas Ball."

"I suppose it was rather an impulsive thing to do. But really, James, you ought to give credit where it is due. It was all Lady Ingram's idea."

Carter frowned. "The Baroness Ingram? Whatever did she have to do with it?"

"You had no idea?"

"Of course not. You never said anything about it."

"Probably because I was so furious with her. I happened to discover her intentions the day I returned to Millcote for your wedding."

"And where was I?"

"Off to Scarborough to fetch your lovely bride."

He smiled. "Of course. With all the last-minute preparations, I didn't have much time to give you a proper welcome."

"No need for apologies. Emily deserved your every attention."

"Aye, she did." He sighed. "But what is all this about Lady Ingram?"

After I arrived in Millcote, I saw Obadiah Turner. He told me you asked him to meet my coach."

"Yes, I did. I had made arrangements for Emily's family to lodge at the Rochester Arms, where he was proprietor. When I asked him to do me that favor, he obliged without hesitation."

"Did you know he once worked for my father?"

"I did not." replied Carter. "As ever, you are full of surprises."

I smiled. "Well, Turner had his own surprise for me that day."

Millcote - October, 1806

"Mr. Rochester, sir!"

A stout, middle aged man hailed me from the doorway of the George Inn. I had just stepped down from the coach which only moments before had arrived in Millcote.

As he hurried out into the street, I recognized him. "Obadiah Turner. How are you?"

"Very well, Mr. Edward," he replied, shaking my hand. "Thank you. You're in town for Mr. Carter's wedding, then?"

"I am." In a solemn voice, I added, "You are one of the few people who knows what he did for Rowland and my father all those years ago. I owe him for that."

Turner removed his hat. "Mr. Carter was so very faithful in 'is care of Mr. Rowland and old Mr. Rochester. He is a good soul."

"Indeed he is. It pleases me to be celebrating a happy occasion for a change."

"Miss Emily will be a fair bride, sir."

"Not a doubt of it. The good doctor's letters to me are filled with her praises. I am anxious to meet her." I looked up and down the street. "And just where is he? He was supposed to meet my coach today."

"That's one reason I've come to town, sir. To inform you Mr. Carter will not be back from Scarborough until tomorrow. Last-minute arrangements and all."

"To be expected, I suppose. And what is the other reason you are here?"

"Makin' a supply run for the Rochester Arms, sir."

"The Rochester Arms?"

"Aye, the property you left me after your father passed. The old Queen Bess Inn?"

"Of course, of course," I nodded. "I was not aware of its new name."

Turner shrugged. "Well, sir. I wanted that to be a surprise, as it were. I'm afraid I didn't even tell Mr. Stewart my intentions."

"Quite all right. It's probably just as well he didn't know." I chuckled. "Likely he would have made too much of a fuss."

"After all you did for me, sir, I felt it was only right."

Turner had been my father's butler. I was but a boy when he came to Thornfield Hall all those years ago from *The Queen Elizabeth Inn* when the proprietor's health forced the closure of that establishment. When Henry died three years ago, Turner was left without resource. But a wild notion had struck me, and Turner and I had a very productive conversation before I made my way to the Continent.

"TURNER, now that my affairs are in order, I have decided to go to Paris. I am sorry, but there is no longer need for a butler at Thornfield Hall."

"Ah'm quite aware of that, sir. I do 'ave a bit of savings laid by."

"You have been very faithful in your service to my family. Wouldn't you agree all those years deserve something other than a sacking?"

He looked embarrassed. "Well, it ain't exactly that, Mr. Edward. I shall get on."

"What would you say to returning to your old line of work?"

"Sir?"

"You once were employed at the Queen Elizabeth Inn, were you not?"

"Aye." He hesitated. "I don't want to seem ungrateful, sir, but I was just a nip of a lad back then. I did the fetchin' and towin' for everybody."

"I understand. But suppose you were the owner?"

"The owner, sir?" He rubbed his chin. "But there ain't another such place within ten miles of The George Inn in Millcote."

"The Queen Elizabeth Inn is a mere two miles from Thornfield Hall, across the back fields."

"The Old Queen Bess, sir? That it 'tis. But the place 'as been closed for years. It's very rundown. It would take a deal of money and work to make her fit to receive guests again."

"And I believe you are just the man for the job. What do you say?"

He rubbed his chin thoughtfully. "I s'pose I could make a go of it, sir, but my pitiful little savings would never do."

"Don't worry about that. If you are willing to take on the challenge, I shall instruct my solicitor, Mr. Stewart, to provide whatever funds you require." I smiled. "Within reason, of course."

"Why, Mr. Edward!" He grabbed my hand and shook it, then looked even more embarrassed. "Forgive me, sir, but I don't know what to say." He swallowed hard, then looked away. "I shall always be in your debt."

"Do me proud, Turner. The Queen Bess is on Rochester land, after all."

"You can count on me, sir. I'll make it the prettiest little coaching inn in these parts."

"It's took me a good two years to brush her up to be fit to receive guests again," he said with pride. "But that old inn has given me a new purpose, thanks to you, sir. T'was out of gratitude I chose the name."

"Quite magnanimous of you, but hardly necessary."

"Perhaps not. But folks ain't half aware of your generous nature, sir."

"I'll wager they hardly think of me at all, since I've spent very little time here these past three years."

"They can think what they will, sir. I don't pay them no mind."

"So? You've been open for business about a year and a half, then?"

"Aye, sir. Things 'ave been slow and I've still a deal of work to do, but when the old road is reopened and coaches are goin' back and forth again, I won't 'ave a day's rest."

"Better to busy than idle, eh?

"Very true, Mr. Edward. Very true, indeed."

I tipped my hat. "Well, I must be off. Good day to you, Turner."

"Mr. Edward?" He seemed hesitant to leave.

"Is there something else?"

He toyed with his hat. "Aye, sir, there is. If I may be so bold, tis something you ought to be aware of. And I mean no offense by it, 'a course."

"None taken. What is it?"

Turner looked around, then up and down the street, as if to be sure no one was overhearing our conversation. Again, he dropped his voice low and asked, "Will you be long in residence at Thornfield, sir? I mean, 'ave you plans to remain awhile after the wedding?"

"I shall be here a fortnight, perhaps three weeks. Why do you ask?"

"Well, sir," continued Turner. "You know it was Miss Blanche Ingram's 18th birthday this past April?"

"I expect her come out ball was a splendidly garish affair."

He shook his head "That's just it, sir. There ain't been a ball as yet. What's more," he continued with astonishment, "Her ladyship said she intends to 'old the party this Christmas."

"The Baroness Ingram?"

"Aye, sir."

"Not until Christmas, you say?" My eyebrow arched.

"Miss Blanche now refuses to speak to her mother, I suppose?"

"It's not like that at all, sir!" Again, he stole furtive glances all around. "She ain't made any fuss a t'all. Ah've seen them in town once or twice, and they look as thick as thieves."

"Really? We are talking about the same young lady who gets whatever she wants?"

He nodded.

"Seems very out of character."

He looked up at me, pleased at this shared confidence. A sly smile crooked the corner of his mouth. "Far be it from me to disagree with you on that score, sir."

"You mean to tell me that a pompous, vain woman who never misses the opportunity for display is deliberately waiting until Christmas to put her daughter on the marriage market?"

"You're not gonna like it, sir."

"Why not?"

"Your sainted mother was much loved, God rest her soul. Her annual Christmas Ball was the talk o' the town."

I nodded. "And?"

Turner looked over his shoulder and shrugged. "Tis only a rumor," he muttered. "But I've 'eard folks say her Ladyship has always been jealous of that regard, that she's scheming to 'ave the ball at Christmas on purpose-like, so folks would think of her instead of Mrs. Rochester."

"Don't be ridiculous, Turner," I laughed. "My mother has been dead for many years. Any regard she once had I'm sure is long forgotten."

He shook his head. "Beggin' yer pardon, Mr. Edward, but it's true. When it was known you'd be attendin' the doctor's wedding, more than one soul made it known to me they'd prefer a party at Thornfield Hall to Ingram Park any day."

I tapped my chin in thought. "You're quite serious?"

He bowed awkwardly. "I am, indeed, sir."

Impulsively, I shook his hand again. "I am much obliged for your candor. But you must realize it's simply out of the question. I will be returning to Europe in less than a month."

Turner nodded. "Quite reasonable, sir."

I eyed him again. "People genuinely inquired about this?"

"That they did, sir. But as you 'aven't spent much time at the old Hall since your father passed, I knew it wasn't likely to 'appen."

"Too many bad memories, I'm afraid."

He nodded. "I perfectly understand, sir."

I touched my hat. "Good day to you, Turner."

He grinned. "Goodbye. And thank you, indeed, Mr. Edward. I am much obliged to you."

PRESENT DAY

By now we had arrived at the *White Hart Inn,* our last night's stop before Millcote. We decided to have a late meal and tea before retiring.

"Obviously," said Carter, after we were seated in the small dining parlor, "you did change your mind. But what ever possessed you to talk Lady Ingram out of her plans? Good God, Edward!" His voice rose suddenly. "You risked *everything* for the sake of your ego?"

I winced. "Perhaps it was selfish of me, but Turner's news created such strange feelings in me, such outrage, I can hardly describe them. You know why I went to Jamaica, and how angry I was with my father. In my heart, I wanted to believe my mother knew nothing about the scheme. Yet how could she not have known? They shared everything. But to believe that felt like I had betrayed her. When Turner revealed Lady Ingram's intentions, I could not abide the thought of that woman's name being mentioned in the same breath with Aurelia Fairfax Rochester." I sighed. "James, you know my temper."

"Yes," he agreed. "And it never fails to get you into trouble."

I shrugged. "But where's the use of scolding me now? When the idea of the party came to me, I simply acted."

"Edward," said Carter, his tone calm once again. "Did it never occur to you how the commotion from such an event might affect Grace's patient?"

"I confess, it did not. At least, not at first. But once I had committed to the project, there was no going back. Besides, what harm could come from a few hours' entertainment? I would be in the house at all times. And I made it quite clear to Lady Ingram that any out-of-town guests would be most welcome to lodge at the George Inn or even the Rochester Arms."

"To Turner's surprise and delight, no doubt?"

"And to Lady Ingram's considerable annoyance." I grinned. "I was merely doing my part to support a fledging business endeavor."

Carter shook his head, then gave me a sly smile. "Somehow, you always manage, don't you?"

"I try."

"And by which of your charms did you persuade Lady Ingram to go along with your scheme?"

"Can there be any doubt? While you were away on your honeymoon, I called at Ingram Park. No one was more surprised to see me than the baroness."

LADY INGRAM

INGRAM PARK - NOVEMBER, 1806

It was an unusually mild day for November as I rode towards Ingram Park. My most vivid recollection of the place was the time I accompanied my father and brother on a shooting expedition. Henry had a standing invitation from the baron to come any time during the season. Lord Ingram always had a houseful of guests whenever he was in residence—anything to avoid having to spend time alone with his shrew of a wife.

I smiled, knowing full well how Lady Ingram would construe this visit. After her husband died, her only son Theodore inherited his father's title. Besides the fact the estate was entailed, the baron had gambled himself into considerable debt. Not much remained to provide dowries for his daughters, Blanche and Mary. It had always been Lady Ingram's mission to find wealthy matches for them both, but now she was positively obsessed with it.

Passing through the gates, I rode up the long drive to the house. The grounds appeared to be in decent condition, though by this time of year, most of the trees had lost their leaves and the grass had stopped growing. A splendid fountain at the center of the circle drive was dry save for the stagnant, green water puddled at the bottom. I dismounted at the front door.

A shabby-looking groom hustled up the drive to take my horse. I handed over Mesrour's reins and the lad walked him back to a paddock. Assuring myself all was in order, I rapped on the front door.

After several minutes, an elderly butler answered. "His lordship is not at home."

"Edward Rochester to call upon his lordship's mother, the dowager Lady Ingram." I handed him my card.

He glanced it over, then looked down his nose at me. In an ancient, patrician voice, he rasped, "Do you have an appointment, sir?"

"I do not," I replied. "But if you would kindly announce me, I am sure her Ladyship will see me."

He eyed me with suspicion, but grudgingly accepted my hat and cloak then stepped aside. "Very well, sir. This way if you please."

I followed him down the long hall, noting the threadbare carpet. Halting at the end of the corridor, he laid my things on a side table. With a flourish, he pushed open the double doors into the drawing room and announced, "Mr. Edward Rochester to see her Ladyship, the Baroness Ingram."

I passed by him and went into the room. Seated on a new, red and gold brocaded sofa was the titled dame. Her youngest daughter Mary sat at her left. Blanche perched at a small table on the other side of the room. Several sheets of drawing paper lay scattered before her, though her pencil was idle. At my entrance, she glanced up and smiled with a conceited expression, as if she was somehow expecting my visit. For a moment I feared I was about to do something foolish.

I approached the baroness and stood before her. "Lady Ingram," I bowed. Accepting her outstretched hand, I said, "A pleasure to see you again."

"Mr. Rochester," she replied in her deep, imperious voice. Majestically rising from the sofa, she asked, "Did we have an appointment today?"

"No, madam. Forgive me for dropping in unexpectedly. Perhaps you are aware that I have been in town for Mr. Carter's late wedding to Miss Alworth?"

"I heard something to that effect," she replied.

Sensing some annoyance at the mention of Carter, I added, "But I did not have the pleasure of seeing you there. I am sure you received an invitation."

She peered at me through her lorgnette. "Certainly. I am sorry to say, we had a previous engagement and were unable to attend."

This was a lie, of course. She simply thought herself above attending the wedding of a country doctor, though Sir Basil Fairfax had been there. He would have been my dead brother's father-in-law had not his daughter Catherine died in the carriage accident several years ago.

Blanche rose from her work and approached.

"So splendid to see you, Mr. Rochester." She extended her hand, which I brushed with a kiss. "You know, we would have called at Thornfield after your poor father died, but you were gone from England before we had the opportunity."

"A pity. Perhaps you were not aware I remained in town half a year to sort things out with the lawyers before I departed for Paris."

"Were you?" A faint sheen of crimson dusted her cheek. "Well, I am sure your brother's death a year earlier complicated things no end. Such a shocking event." She held her throat. "Thrown from his horse, and not found for several days, why—"

"I am aware of the details, Miss Ingram," I interrupted. Not wishing to sound too harsh, I added, "But I have not come to discuss my deceased family. I heard a rumor in town and decided to verify in person whether or not it was true."

"And what rumor is that?"

I looked at her mother. "Is it true, madam, that you postponed the come-out ball for Miss Ingram until December?"

She stood very straight, and glancing at her eldest daughter, replied, "Yes I did. April is such a dreary time of year, don't you agree? So much rain. Of course, December can be frightfully cold, but most people are disposed to travel for the holidays. Why not give them somewhere important to go?"

"Yes, why not?" A large chair stood near one end of the sofa. I indicated it. "May I sit?"

"Please do."

I remained standing until Lady Ingram sat down again. Blanche took a seat beside her. Flanked by her daughters, the baroness waited expectantly.

Mary, busy with her needlepoint, giggled. I marked the differences between her and Blanche, the latter having dark hair and olive skin, while her fair-haired sister was very pale, and resembled her late father in countenance and temper. But Miss Ingram was like her mother in every respect. I must tread carefully if I was to pull this off.

As I sat down, Lady Ingram rang a bell. The elderly butler soon returned. "Featherby," she commanded. "Bring tea."

He bowed. "Right away, madam."

"Lady Ingram," I began after Featherby had departed. "There is something of great importance I should like to discuss with you."

"And what could that be?" The baroness again scrutinized me through her glasses.

Given the lady's temperament, I knew it was unwise to

beat about the bush. "Madam," I began. "Since you delayed Miss Ingram's come-out ball until Christmas, may I also presume you did not go to London for the season?"

"Certainly not," she replied haughtily. "My darling was not yet 18. Nor could I abide being in town for merely half the season. After consulting a few intimate acquaintance, I determined a Christmas ball to be just the thing to launch my eldest into proper society. I believe it will lend a certain *je ne sais quoi* to Blanche's debut in London next spring."

I smiled. Of course she had not ventured to London. The expense would have been dreadful and strained her already minimal resources to their utmost.

A maid appeared with the tea service. At Lady Ingram's direction, she served a cup to everyone then departed.

"Well, Mr. Rochester," said the baroness, pausing before sipping her tea. "To what do we owe the pleasure of your visit?"

"Yes, Mr. Rochester," interrupted Blanche. "You have rarely been in England these last three years, and yet you take the trouble to make this most particular visit. We are all impatience to know why."

The Dowager patted her daughter's arm. "How perceptive you are, my best. So, Mr. Rochester. Of what possible interest could Blanche's come-out ball be to you?"

"Oh, it very much interests me, as I should like to put a humble proposal before you."

Her eyes widened at the word *proposal*. She and Blanche exchanged glances.

"As Miss Ingram kindly pointed out, my brother's untimely death followed by my father's barely a year later cast a shadow over the Rochester name. In the last three years, a pall of gloom has descended upon Thornfield Hall. I am determined upon a course of action that will sweep it away."

Mary dropped her needlepoint into her lap. All three of them sat up quite straight.

Lady Ingram, almost holding her breath, asked, "And what sort of proposal do you have in mind that would accomplish that?"

I smiled. At that moment I was sure they were imagining Blanche Ingram as a fresh young bride, all in white, her incandescence illuminating every corner of such a gloomy place as they no doubt believed Thornfield to be. Likely they expected me to drop to one knee right here.

I sipped my tea, relishing their anticipation. "As you have said, madam. A Christmas ball would lend a certain fairy tale-like quality to an otherwise common affair."

"Precisely.

"It would be talked about for years to come, and no doubt your daughter would be the most sought after debutante in London next spring."

Lady Ingram visibly puffed up.

"Furthermore, if the venue emanates mystery, perhaps even a bit of peril when juxtaposed to that festive season of the year, your guests won't be able to contain their curiosity and will talk of nothing else until the day of the ball."

"Why, Mr. Rochester," interrupted Blanche. "I believe you mean to offer Thornfield Hall as the venue. Am I right?"

"You are as perceptive as ever, Miss Ingram."

"Thornfield Hall?" exclaimed the dowager. "But I couldn't possibly— "

"Madam," I interrupted. "For all the reasons I've stated, I believe Thornfield would be the perfect place for Miss Ingram's ball. And of course, I would never make such a proposal unless I was prepared to go all in."

"All in?" she repeated.

"All in," I confirmed. "In *every* way."

"It's such a delicious idea!" exclaimed Blanche, tossing her ringlets. "So completely unexpected. Besides Mama, if Thornfield Hall needs a bit of brightness, who better to be that beacon than Baroness Ingram of Ingram Park?"

Her mother smiled. "My dearest Blanche, how you flatter me. But of course, this is to be your gala, not mine."

"Oh, Mama, do let Mr. Rochester do it," blurted Mary. "Then you won't have to spend a farthing."

"Hush!" exclaimed the baroness.

"Madam, I am prepared to spend whatever is necessary to make this a most memorable occasion, and you shall not persuade me otherwise."

Miss Ingram glanced at me archly. "Mr. Rochester is such gentleman, Mama, therefore you must allow him his pride. I think his proposal a charming and splendid idea."

Lady Ingram deliberated. She had as much pride as her daughter, but in the end I knew her financial condition would overrule her heart. If someone else offered to foot the bill, why not let them?

She rose from the sofa. I did likewise. She extended her hand. I took it and brushed it with my lips. "Well, madam?"

Blanche and Mary clung to her like little schoolgirls. She stood rigidly, that autocratic eye glaring at me. With the merest hint of a smile, she sighed, then beamed in triumph at her eldest.

"My dearest Blanche. You know I can never refuse you anything. Thornfield Hall it shall be."

AN UNPLEASANT REUNION

PRESENT DAY

"Just as I suspected. And your story confirms it," said Carter.

"What is that?"

"I always knew Lady Ingram considered me beneath her, even though my father was a gentleman. I suppose it's typical for someone of her class, and I wouldn't have thought twice about it, except for Emily's feelings. I didn't want to send an invitation because I knew Lady Ingram would never respond, let alone attend. Emily thought it in bad taste to exclude her from the guest list, however. And of course she was right."

"Did your wife feel deprived by the grande dame's absence?"

"On the contrary," smiled Carter. "She was relieved. We peasants must adhere to proper social convention, but the Quality can step on whomever they please."

"All too true," I agreed. "I was surprised to see Sir Basil there."

"Yes, Catherine's father," added Carter. "The poor man. So

grateful I had been with her, that she did not die alone. His grief pushed him beyond the pretensions of rank. Emily actually felt sorry for the old man."

"No father should outlive his offspring," I said. "To lose a child in that horrible way? I can't imagine his suffering."

"It's a terrible thing," Carter replied, shading his eyes. "Even though I never had the chance to know my son, not a day goes by I don't think about everything that could have been, but never will be."

I was silent. I had no right to speak about such things.

"And you, Edward? Do you never think about the little girl now living at Thornfield Hall? Isn't it about time you told me why you brought her there?"

"Indeed, but it's late." I pulled out my pocket watch." Past midnight. "I have saved the best for last. Tomorrow you shall hear the final chapter, how little Adele came to be at Thornfield Hall."

He yawned. "I look forward to it."

After breakfast the next morning, we climbed into the coach for the final leg of the journey to Millcote. A brisk wind blew across the yard.

I yelled up at Jack. "How long until we arrive in town?"

"If the weather 'olds, sir, by the afternoon, I should say."

"Then let us away!" I replied.

Carter held his arms tight across his body, trying to get some warmth. I rubbed Pilot's head, and he plopped on the floor at my feet.

"So, Edward," said Carter, removing a glove to blow warmth into his hand. "I am all curiosity by now, as you must know."

"Your patience is exemplary, James. Do you recall asking me why a man would care for another's child?"

"Of course."

"I wanted to tell you everything about my past and how I

ended up in Europe because it all has a part in the decision I made about Adele. Though she is not my daughter, I feel responsible for her somehow."

"And why do you suppose that is?"

"When I broke it off with Céline, Adele was but six months old."

"I remember."

"It was more than three years later before I saw them again. After the Christmas ball, I returned to my wandering ways but visited more exotic and dangerous places of the world like the Peloponnese and Mesopotamia. I actually resided in Constantinople for some time, and became rather fond of Turkish coffee. But inevitably, I must return to Paris. It was a breezy September day when Philippe L'Argent walked into the café where I was having lunch.

Paris - September, 1809

"Ah, Rochester!" exclaimed a familiar voice. "How good to see you again."

"My old friend." We embraced. L'Argent kissed me on both cheeks. "How is it you always seem to know where I am?"

He chuckled. "I hear things. What have you been doing since escaping death at the hands of *cette femme folle*, Giacinta?"

"I went to England as I had planned. But instead of leaving after a week or so, I stayed there until Christmas."

"But you did not come back to Paris. I have not seen you in…" He tapped his chin then his eyes widened in astonishment. "It has been at least three years. Where have you been all this time?"

I smiled. "I have just returned from exploring the ancient sites and cities of Greece and Asia Minor."

"So now, *mon ami*—you are an adventurer as well as a treasure hunter, eh?"

"Not quite. But my ultimate quest remains the same."

"Ah, *l'amour de ta vie?* Rochester, do you really believe in such things?"

"I must. Life would not be worth living otherwise."

"You have been wandering the world ever since I have known you, but still you have not found it."

"Not yet, old friend." I smiled. "Not yet."

He shook his head. "I wish you *bon chance* in your search. Tell me. Are you planning to stay in Paris for awhile?"

"I have taken a flat in my old neighborhood."

"Ah, *trés bien!* I am invited to a special celebration tonight. Come with me, *mon ami.* I have friends you should meet."

L'Argent called for me about 8 o'clock that evening. He directed his carriage along a route that followed the Seine. As we weaved in and about the neighborhoods along the way, I was reminded of my first days in Paris, traveling everywhere with Philippe. I marveled at the beauty of the city and how well it suited me. There was always something to distract me in Paris, it seemed, something to make me forget for awhile the emptiness of my existence.

When we arrived at our destination, I heard the revelers above. A voice from a third floor balcony crowded with party goers, some of whom were already drunk, cheerily called down to the new arrivals.

"*Allo, mes amis!*" someone shouted. "*Viens prendre un verre de vin!*"

As we approached the stairs to the building's entryway, Philippe laughed. "Lucas has invited everyone, it seems."

We went in then pushed our way upstairs. Just inside the apartment's front door, someone shoved a glass of wine into my hand. The laughing young man who'd given me the goblet suddenly went quiet as he stared at me.

"*Reynard? Reynard?*" He put his hand on my shoulder. "*C'est vraiment toi?*"

I looked at him and shook my head. "My name is Edward."

"*Tu ne te souviens pas? Regarde moi. Je suis Pierre! Pierre Meyeux.*"

"Edward," said Philippe, ignoring Pierre's open-mouthed stare, pushing me toward the kitchen. "Come meet my friends."

I glanced back over my shoulder. Pierre had vanished into the crowd. As I was buffeted toward the group gathered in the kitchen, someone bumped my arm and I nearly spilled my wine on a tall man and the striking, dark-haired woman next to him. He laughed as she nuzzled his chin.

"Lucas!" shouted Philippe. "*Mon cher ami!*"

"Ah, Philippe," he replied. "*Bienvenu!*"

The two embraced, then L'Argent introduced me. "Lucas Frederick, may I present my old friend from England, Edward Rochester."

Lucas embraced me and kissed both cheeks. "Ah, any friend of Philippe is my friend also. Permit me to introduce my new wife, Madame Jacqueline DuMarché Frederick."

"Madame," I bowed. "Congratulations."

"*Merci.*" She took my hand. Her piercing, gray eyes seemed to know me. "Ah, Monsieur Rochester. Please, you must call me Jacqueline." Her gaze narrowed as she regarded me again. "We have met once before. Do you not remember?"

I looked again, then shook my head. "I am sorry, but you will have to enlighten me."

"It has been several years," she said. "Do you recall the party where first you met Mademoiselle Varens?"

"How could I forget?"

"I was also there that night, monsieur. Céline and I were in the opera company together, for awhile at least."

"You must forgive me. I am afraid I was rather smitten with Mlle Varens in those days."

She smiled knowingly. "I was but a chorus line girl, and never enjoyed such adulation as was heaped upon Céline. I did not stay long with the company."

"Well, if beauty were the only requirement—"

"Oh, monsieur, please," she laughed. "We both know how special was "The Varens." I am not so vain as to think I could ever be her equal. So you see, when Lucas and I fell in love and he vowed to spirit me away to the country, how could I resist?"

I bowed. "You are very wise."

"Monsieur Edward—may I call you Edward? You know, Céline came crying to me when you so cruelly cut her off."

"That I what?" Her bluntness shocked me, but then she touched my arm in a gesture of empathy.

"Oh, I do not blame you one bit, Edward," she added. "Céline is quite beautiful. Men are enraptured and it blinds them to her faults, which of course is what she counts on. But after awhile, they discover to their regret, she is loyal only to her possessions."

"On that point, Jacqueline, I cannot disagree with you."

At that moment, a petite, sing-song voice I would recognize anywhere called for the crowd's attention.

"*Venez tout le monde! Écoute ma fille! Elle va chanter pour vous.*"

"Ah, *la petite chanteuse*, Edward," whispered Mme Frederick. "As usual," she sighed, "Céline must be the center of attention in one way or another." She smiled, then tilted her head in the direction of the drawing room. "Of course you are curious. Go. But you may perhaps be shocked by what you see. If ever you are in Burgundy, you must come visit us."

I hoisted my glass. "I wish you both every happiness."

Making my way into the spacious drawing room where a crowd of guests had gathered, on a low table in the middle of the room stood a little girl. Dark-haired and petite, she looked a miniature of her mother. Surely it was Adele, who was now about four years old.

Céline whispered in the child's ear. She responded by pirouetting around the table, then stopped. Holding both hands together under her chin, in her small, high voice, Adele began to sing. The gathered crowd laughed and joked as I discerned the words of a bawdy love poem. Entirely inappropriate for such an innocent. As the drunken crowd responded with cheers and shouts for more, I turned away in disgust.

It was time to go. Thinking Philippe was still with the Fredericks, I moved in that direction, when my arm was grabbed from behind. It was Céline, with Adele in tow.

"Edward Rochester," she smirked, looking me up and down with contempt. "I knew it was you."

"Mama," whispered Adele, tugging on Céline's hand.

Crouching low, Céline replied, "Shh, *ma petite*." She reached out to smooth her daughter's curls. "*Je dois parler à ton père*."

I grabbed Céline's arm and yanked her to her feet. Pulling her close, I whispered, "Have you been telling that lie to the child all these years?"

She pushed me away, then glared. "Why have you come here?"

"Philippe invited me to meet Lucas and his new wife."

"Jacqueline is my best friend. Philippe knew I would be here."

"You will not attribute malice to our mutual friend. I have never met Lucas. Nor did I remember Mlle DuMarché until she reminded me of the party where you and I first met all those years ago."

"*Quel malheur!*" cried Céline. "I wish I had never met you that night. When I think of all I endured only to have you forsake me. It was cruel!"

"As I recall, it was you, *ma chère*, who invited another man into our bed. By the bye, I have not seen D'Arblay tonight. Where is he?"

She shook her curls. "Bah! *Ça n'a plus d'importance.*" Her dark eyes flashed. Biting off some murderous retort, she presented her daughter.

"Adele, *voici M. Rochester. Il te connaissait comme un bébé.*"

The child curtsied and replied, "*Bonjour, Monsieur.*"

I bowed, took her little hand and kissed it.

She giggled. "*Êtes vous mon père?*"

I shook my head. "*No, ma petite. Je ne suis pas.*"

"*Oh, c'est dommage. Maman a dit que tu es riche.*"

I bit my tongue. Céline merely smirked. "She will be an exceptional talent, don't you think?"

"She will become a flirt and coquette like you. Why do you put her on display like that? She is just a child who has no idea what the words of her pretty little song mean."

Céline laughed. "Which is what makes it so delicious, *n'est ce pas?*"

"You are not fit to be a mother."

Céline bristled, then thrust Adele's hand at me. "Then take her away with you right now. *Je vous défie!*"

"Your insincerity knows no bounds."

"*My* insincerity? I loved you!"

"Certainly my money. But me? Never."

"Mama?" Adele tugged on her mother's hand again. "*Puis-je danser pour vos amis maintenant?*"

Céline glared at me, then smiling down on Adele, touched her cheek. "*Un moment, ma petite.*" She turned and thrust her chin at me. Leaning close, Céline whispered, "It's true. *Je ne t'ai jamais aimé*. I hope I never see you again. *Bon débarras!*"

Something in me suddenly grew cold and angry. It all rushed upon me with wretched clarity, how I discovered her treachery, how she and D'Arblay heaped their scornful laughter upon me, and the agony of her betrayal. I thought I had purged her from my heart, but the anguish and feelings of resentment were yet there.

With a vengeful sort of glee I murmured, "Why don't you tell the child about her real father? The coward who deserted his daughter because he could not, or would not support a deceitful, selfish woman and her gaudy, pretentious *mode de vie*."

Céline's lip quivered and her ebony eyes watered. She glared hatred and I thought she would speak. But before I could react, she snatched my glass of wine then dashed it in my face.

Without another word, she grabbed Adele's hand and fled the apartment.

FINDING ADELE

PRESENT DAY

"Not very gentlemanly of you, Edward, to say such things."

"Even though they were true?" He started to protest. "I know, I know. I suppose you are right. But seeing her again after all those years and hearing her lies? Everything I said about D'Arblay was the truth and she knew it. It made her angry, at him and me. She wanted to wound me, just as she'd been wounded by him."

"And Adele?"

"Céline still refused to admit to my face that D'Arblay was the child's father. After witnessing that little demonstration, I knew what Adele was destined to become. But Céline so hated me, she would never allow me a place in her daughter's life."

"And what kind of place would that have been? What good did you think you could accomplish, if indeed, that was your intention?"

"Of course it was. I could see the future laid out for Adele, a pretty little girl warbling vulgar lyrics in cheap theaters and

243

French brothels. Céline would have no scruple against using her in any way to earn money. I thought I might help with Adele's support, at least in some small way, by sending her useful gifts."

"How could you know those gifts would benefit the child?"

"I made sure to know about the parties where Céline would be present, and even went to several at her own small apartment, while she could still afford it. I would bring Philippe with me so she couldn't refuse me admittance."

"Adele was always there?"

"Oh, yes. And quite happy to see me because I would bring something special just for her. It irritated Céline, but in light of her dwindling resources, she would have been a fool to refuse."

"Was Céline not grateful, at least for the child's sake?"

"If she was, she never said so. Still, I often left Paris for weeks at a time."

"Weeks at a time?" repeated Carter, shaking his head. "How can you pop in and out of a little girl's life like that and expect her to trust you? How do you explain to a child you must leave her to satisfy some primal urge to wander?"

"I'll admit, I could not deal with my conflicted feelings. I spent the next few years wandering about Europe, but always came back to Paris. Every time I returned, it took me longer and longer to track them down until one day, I could not find them. Céline had just disappeared."

"And no one knew where they were? Not even her friend, Mme Frederick?"

"No. And frankly, it had become a nuisance, having to search them out every time. Besides, if Céline wanted me to know where she was, she would have made sure of telling Philippe. So I gave up went back to Vienna. Some months before, I had met a young woman there, Clara. We ended up living together for awhile after I got back. But like every-thing else I touched, it was not long before the relationship soured. Clara, unlike all the others, at least was honest and never lied to me. Her company had become tedious because all she could talk about was fashion. But she had a real talent for it, so I set her up in a small milliner's shop. We parted on friendly terms."

He shook his head. "Well, I am glad there is one woman at least who can still stand the sight of you. This is progress."

I laughed. "Perhaps. But after all those years of roaming about, I was exhausted and went back to Paris simply to rest. To think. To decide what I ought to do."

"After all that happened there? The failed relationships, the heartache, a lost little girl who needed a father?"

"Even so. It was the closest place I had to a home. But not long after I returned, I received a letter from Madame Fred-erick with disturbing news."

Paris - July, 1811

Mon cher Monsieur Edward—

It is only after much deliberation I have decided to write to you.

Lucas and I lived and worked on his small farm for these many years. We were very happy and content until his sudden illness required we sell the land and return to Paris.

A few months ago, Céline contacted me. I had not heard from her in almost a year. She asked me to look after Adele while she settled some urgent business. I told her my present circumstances made that impossible. But she cried so and begged me. She gave me 15 francs and promised to send more in a week. So, we agreed. My husband's niece, Sophie, came to live with us to be Adele's nurse.

A month passed and still, I had no word from Céline. Nor had she sent the money she promised. After several more weeks, I received a letter from Philippe. It seems that Céline left France and went to Italy with a man, some musician or singer. I realized in that moment she had no intention of returning for her daughter.

Edward, I can no longer support the child. My niece will be leaving soon since we are unable to pay her. Lucas is very ill and I must devote my attentions to him.

Perhaps long ago, you loved Céline—she once intimated you are the child's father, but I see no such resemblance. I would be grateful for anything you might do for us.

Mme Jacqueline DuMarché Frederick.

"CÉLINE SIMPLY ABANDONED HER DAUGHTER?" ASKED CARTER. "How could she do such a thing?"

"Are you truly surprised, after all I've told you about her? I was angry at this news, yet I can hardly tell you why."

"Just admit it, Edward. You do care about that little girl. Why else bring her to England? Even if it was a foolish thing to do."

I shrugged. "Nevertheless, I decided to pay Mme Frederick a visit."

"Impetuous as always," agreed Carter.

"By the following month, I found myself in a coach drawing up to the small brownstone in a very poor section of the city. I am sure the woman never expected I would appear on her doorstep, but Adele's reaction took me quite by surprise."

PARIS—AUGUST, 1811

I knocked on the door. After some minutes, a young French woman answered. This must be Sophie.

"Monsieur," she curtsied.

"*Je suis Edward Rochester. J'ai besoin de parler avec Madame Frederick.*"

"Oh! *Bien sûr. Entrez vous, s'il vous plaît.*"

I took off my hat and came inside. There was a small sitting room and kitchen, and probably two small bedrooms down the narrow hallway. Jacqueline Frederick soon appeared.

"Edward!" She embraced me and kissed me on the cheek. "I am so surprised to see you."

I pulled out my pocketbook. "I received your letter."

She smiled as I handed her a wad of francs. "Oh, *merci. Je suis très reconnaissant,* but it was not necessary to come in person."

"Perhaps. Tell me, Jacqueline. If you are unable to keep the child, what will happen to her?"

She shook her head. "Edward, you cannot be so naive as that."

"I suppose not. What does she know about her mother's disappearance?"

"I told her that her mother has gone the way of the saints. It seemed kinder to me that the child should believe her mother is dead than that she ran off with some worthless lover."

"Perhaps you are wise. No doubt it would devastate Adele to know her mother abandoned her."

"My thoughts, also. Please, Edward. Wait a moment while I fetch the child. She will be upset if she does not see you before you go."

In a few minutes, Adele came skipping out of a back bedroom. She squealed with delight when she recognized me.

"*Monsieur de Rochester!*" she cried, leaping into my arms.

"Hello, Adele." I kissed her little cheek, then set her on the floor in front of me.

She craned her neck, trying to peer around me. "*Avez vous un cadeau pour moi?*"

I touched her chin. "Not today, I'm afraid."

"Where have you been, monsieur?" she asked in rather a solemn tone. "I have missed you."

"You remember me, then?"

"Oh, *mais oui*! You always brought me pretty presents when you came to visit mama's house, or the other parties where the gentlemen and ladies came to hear me sing." She sniffled, and stared down at her shoes. "But mama is not here anymore. She is gone to the Holy Virgin, and I will never see her again."

"I am very sorry, child."

I thought about all the times she sang at the parties. I thought of the laughter of the crowds, the lewdness of their remarks, how the innocent prattling of a child could fuel their basest appetites. Seeing her little, vulnerable self there, the solution suddenly came to me.

"Adele?" Again I crouched to her level, and gently lifted her chin to look up at me. "Would you like to come to England and live with me there?"

"Ah, Monsieur!" she clapped. "*D'Angleterre?*"

"Yes. I will take you to the coast where we will board a steamer ship to cross the Channel. Do you know what that is? It is a cold, narrow passageway of wild water that will transport you into a whole, new world."

She clapped her hands and twirled about. "Oh, *mon ami*, Monsieur de Rochester! I would like that very much. I have never seen England, or been anywhere but Paris!"

"We will go to my house in the country," I continued. "It is a very big house, with a beautiful garden to play in. What do you think of that?"

She promptly threw her arms around my neck and kissed my cheek over and over again. "Oh, *monsieur, merci,*

merci mille fois! When shall we go? May Sophie come with us?"

PRESENT DAY

"Mme Frederick had not exaggerated the wretchedness of her circumstances, James. The money I gave her would help them for a time, and certainly would last longer with two fewer mouths to feed. So, we packed up Adele and Sophie, and I brought them to England."

Carter shook his head. "Adele still does not know about her mother?"

"No. And Céline will never come looking for her. It's better the child doesn't know. To learn she was rejected by the mother she adored? Well, I hope you can understand."

"I suppose I do. It was very generous of you, though still, I don't believe it was wise to bring her to Thornfield."

"Only time will tell about that. Sophie and Adele had become fond of each other, and I thought it best to keep them together. In less than a month, we steamed across the channel to England, then on to Thornfield Hall. Mrs. Fairfax was quite surprised when I arrived with two strangers in tow.

> "Sir? Do I properly understand you? Miss Sophie and the child are to live here. Permanently?"
>
> "Indeed they are, Mrs. Fairfax. Miss Varens is now my ward, and I intend she should grow up here in the wholesomeness of the English countryside. I have brought Sophie to be the child's nurse. As they are quite attached to one another, it would have been cruel to separate them. And one more charge I give you, madam. You must hire a governess for Adele directly."
>
> "Certainly, sir," replied Mrs. Fairfax. "Do you have any partic-

ular qualities in mind? Perhaps a woman of a certain age or experience?"

"No, madam. Such details I shall trust to your discretion. You may advertise the salary will be £30 per annum. Apart from that stipulation, hire whomever you deem to be the most suitable person for the position. I shall leave it in your very capable hands."

"And Mrs. Fairfax never asked you about the child's father or mother?" inquired Carter.

"Of course not," I smiled. "She is not the curious sort of person. One reason she makes me an excellent housekeeper."

I pulled out my pocket watch. It was after one o'clock. Just then, the coach began clanking and creaking as we rumbled over the planks of the bridge into Millcote.

"Nearly home," said Carter, peering out the window.

The coach clattered across the river, and we soon pulled into the coaching yard of the George Inn, the establishment to which I had directed the delivery of my trunk. Jack jumped off his perch and opened the door."

"Gentlemen, we've arrived in Millcote."

JOURNEY'S END

I leapt out of the coach after Pilot, then Carter followed. How good it felt to be walking again! After hours of sitting I was cramped and stiff.

"Well," I patted the dog's head. "You may use your own four feet from now on, and I'm sure you'll be glad of it."

"Jack," I beckoned our intrepid driver. "Give me a moment, will you?"

"A' course, sir. I got no where to go just now. Take yer time."

I went into the George Inn and spoke to a rather timid looking young man standing behind the front desk.

"I am Edward Rochester of Thornfield Hall. My trunk was directed here from Dover. Have it brought outside and loaded onto my private coach."

His eyes widened and he gulped. "Dover, you say, sir? I should hope I would remember the delivery of a trunk that came all the way from there. But we've received no luggage or any such goods from Dover for weeks, I can tell you. None at all."

"That's the damnedest thing. I thought surely it would arrive ahead of me."

"No, sir. There has been no delivery. But I'll send word at once when it arrives."

"Yes, do that."

After making a few other arrangements, I left the inn, rather annoyed with this development, when I heard someone call my name.

"Mr. Rochester, sir!"

A plump man of late middle years conversing with Carter on the other side of the street waved to me.

"What a surprise, sir!" he exclaimed as I approached. "Tis good to see you again."

I shook hands with an enthusiastic Obadiah Turner. "The good doctor and I are just arrived from Dover."

Carter smiled. "Mr. Turner has been catching me up on all that has happened since I left Hay."

"Aye, sir," replied Turner. With solemnity, he added, "We all heard about your grief, Mr. Carter, yours and the missus. You both have my sympathies, sir."

"Thank you, Turner. I shall convey your condolences to my wife."

Turner tipped his hat. "Well, business won't wait, gentlemen. Good day to you. And goodbye, Mr. Edward. P'raps I'll see you again soon!"

"He still calls you that?" asked Carter.

"I suppose he has the same trouble with me as do I with Lord Ingram—can't imagine me as anything else but a mischievous lad."

He laughed. "No doubt. Well, I must be getting home. Your horse?"

"Mesrour is at the stabler's in town. But there is a little problem: my bloody trunk hasn't arrived yet."

"Well, well," smiled Carter. "Come home with me. Have

supper with us. From what I see, you have no excuse to decline."

He was positively grinning at me.

"You are enjoying this little difficulty of mine entirely too much, James. But I accept. Fetch Jack and tell him he must add another three miles to his tally."

We walked to the stabler's and collected my horse. And so, with a fine Arabian stallion trotting behind our dusty coach, we left Millcote for Marleton.

BY THE TIME WE ARRIVED AT CARTER'S COUNTRY FARMHOUSE, it was dusk. Jack turned up the drive and approached the house, warmly illuminated by candlelight. As the last rays of daylight lingered, its steeply pitched roof glistened with frost.

A dark-haired woman of perhaps seven or eight-and-twenty, wrapped in a woolen shawl, stepped out the door as we came around the half circle to a stop. Carter leapt from the coach the moment it halted and rushed into his wife's open arms. They clung to each other, then he took off his hat and kissed her tenderly. A wave of envy engulfed me as I observed them together.

She smiled as they spoke and held his face in her hands, but I was too distant to hear their conversation.

Pilot ran off to search for rabbits in the sparse, low shrubberies along the front of the house. Carter and Emily approached.

"Look who it is, my dear," said he, his arm tightly around her. "Owing to a fortuitous oversight of the shipping company, Edward's trunk has not arrived in Millcote. He has consented to have supper and spend the evening with us."

I removed my hat and bowed. "I hope I am not intruding."

Emily embraced me affectionately. "Don't be absurd, Edward. I am very glad to see you."

"Gerry, where are you lad?" Carter called out to the boy who did chores around the property.

A gangly youth loped out from the barn, wiping his hands with a tattered cloth. "Dr. Carter. A pleasure to see you again, sir."

"Thank you, Gerry. My friend has come to spend the evening with us. There's a good lad—put his horse into the stall next to Millie, will you?"

I handed over Mesrour's reins and we all watched as Gerry led my horse to the barn.

"Now, Edward," said Carter. "Emily and I will await you at table." And they walked into the house, arm in arm.

I turned to our driver and handed over several bills. "Here is the fare and rental cost for the rig and horses these last few days. An excellent coachman you are, Jack."

He tipped his hat as he accepted payment. "I thank you, sir, very much."

Taking another note from my pocketbook, I stuffed it into his coat. "This is just for you. If you return to the *George Inn*, you will find a hearty supper and a warm bed in which to spend the night."

Jack gripped my hand and shook it vigorously. "Why, thank you kindly sir, that's most generous 'o you. I shall enjoy it very much, sir."

"If you will just see to our meager luggage, I release you from your service."

"Right away, sir."

As Jack emptied the boot of our few bags, I went into the house to the dining room where Carter and his wife awaited me. I took her hand and kissed it.

"If you can accept such shamefully overdue condolences,

Mrs. Carter, you have my utmost sympathy for your recent loss."

"I can, and do," she smiled. "Thank you, Edward."

Marveling at Emily Carter's graciousness, I sat down with them to the simple meal before us. After the fare of last few days, it tasted excellent and more than satisfied my appetite. When coffee was brought, Mrs. Carter took up the topic no doubt on everyone's lips.

"I understand there are new residents at Thornfield Hall?"

"Quite true, I'm afraid. A little girl and her nurse, and a governess whom Mrs. Fairfax has lately hired. I knew the child's mother many years ago in Paris. But she deserted Adele to run off with her lover."

Emily sighed. "Oh, the poor, little dear."

I understood her gentle inference. "My sins have been many, Mrs. Carter, but Adele is not one of them."

"I am a doctor's wife," she replied softly. "Such things do happen. They always have, and I suppose always will. It is in the rebellious nature of our race, I think. It's just that…well, I do not doubt the wisdom of Providence, but occasionally I do wonder at the ways He works in this world."

Carter looked at his wife tenderly, then covered her hand with his.

"While I do not understand how any mother could abandon her own daughter," she continued, "why have you brought the child to England? Would she not be better off with her own relations in France?"

"She had no other family that I could discover," I replied. "I fear the child's future would have been unpleasant had she remained there."

Emily smiled and touched my hand. "Then you did right, I am sure. Thornfield was your own home for many years, was it not?"

"It was."

She rose from the table. "Shall I see you in the morning, Edward, before you are off on your business?"

"Of course. No one is expecting me save my solicitor. One or two old matters which require my hand."

"Well, it is good to see you. Sleep well." She smiled then left the room.

Carter and I retired to his study where he poured out two glasses of brandy. We drank and smoked in silence for a time, when abruptly I asked, "Do you remember the letter I wrote to you after Rowland's death?"

"Of course. I still have it if you would care to see it."

"Do you really?" I inquired, rather surprised.

"Yes, it's locked in my desk."

"Why on earth would you keep it? Full of horror and vengeance from beginning to end." I glanced at him over the rim of my tumbler. "I suppose it's a wedge, a reminder of your power over me, eh?"

Carter paused mid-sip, glared at me, then set his glass on the end table. Striding to the small roll-top desk, he dug into his pocket, yanked out a ring of keys then furiously sorted through them. After finding the one he wanted, he slipped it into the desk lock and savagely twisted it. Sliding open the roll-top, he snatched a folded paper from one of the lowest pigeon-holes.

"If you could truly believe such a thing, Rochester, then take it."

He held the folded letter in front of me. Now yellowed with age, the sight of it thrust me back in memory to the circumstances under which I had written it. I shook my head then pushed it away.

"Damn it, Carter. Sometimes I speak before thinking."

"How well I know that," he replied.

"Forgive me. Of course I know you would never…but

why have you kept it? Have you chanced ever to read it a second time?"

"Yes, actually, I have," he said, his anger all but dissipated. "I think to remind me of your circumstances then, as well as now. And to remind me why I agreed to help you all those years ago. I am sorry," he sighed. "After our travels, I do understand you much better. I have sympathy for what you have suffered, but for God's sake, a man can have only so much patience with his friends— especially those with too damned much pride and pigheadedness for their own bloody good!"

"Ah, James," I smiled, hoisting my glass. "Here's to you. I am fortunate that you have been, and remain, my truest friend."

He lifted his glass.

I told him I would meet with Stewart this week, and probably be busy with business for a few days. "No doubt, once word has spread that I am again in residence at Thornfield Hall, the parade of visitors will begin."

We laughed together, and not long afterwards, retired to bed.

But I could not sleep. I lay in the dark, listening to a low wind moan and whistle through the window casement. My head was full of thoughts of the last few days and the things I had shared with Carter. Though it had done me much good, still, it was my burden to bear, and the nearer to Thornfield I came, the heavier it grew. By tomorrow, the light-heartedness I felt in this house would be gone. The hopes he and his wife yet cherished in spite of their recent tragedy, their unaccountable optimism for God's provision—I would feel it no more once I walked out the door.

No doubt my stay would be shorter than ever, I supposed, as at last, I drifted off into a dreamless slumber.

The End

For a preview of Edward's continuing story, check out Chapter 1 of "FINDING JANE EYRE," which picks up the tale the very next afternoon.

PREVIEW: "FINDING JANE EYRE"

By three o'clock the next afternoon, I could avoid it no longer: I must go back. I must return to Thornfield Hall.

Carter and I walked down to the barn where I saddled my horse.

"James, I was glad of your company up from Dover." I lifted Mesrour's saddle from the wall hook then threw it over his blanketed back. "It made a tedious journey bearable."

"I was glad to do it, Edward. Besides, after discovering that a little girl had been living at Thornfield Hall since last August, I had to hear the explanation from your own lips. While I appreciate your confidence, can you assure me the child is in no danger?"

"What more must I say to convince you?" I shook my head. "You have been privy to my most intimate secret for years. And now that you know the whole of my wretched history, you should understand why I brought Adele to Thornfield. Besides, did you not tell me that Mrs. Fairfax hired a strict and proper governess to look after her?"

"I did. But you shall not escape the question so easily, for you know very well, it is not the child who worries me," replied Carter thoughtfully. "But we shall see. May I call upon you before you are off to the Continent again?"

We shook hands. "It would please me no end, but be quick about it, James. You know I never stay more than a few days." I mounted my horse. "Goodbye."

As I headed down the drive, I called out, "Pilot!"

The huge black and white Newfoundland dog bounded out of the nearby field. I urged my horse after him, and we sped along the road home. Home, to the oldest, most respected estate in the neighborhood, Thornfield Hall. It was a place I once loved with all my heart, but for these ten, long years, I have shunned it like a great plague-house.

The January afternoon was getting colder, and while the sky was yet clear, the crisp, chill air portended snow, likely by tonight. Strange. No matter how long I stayed away, I could never forget. How many years had gone by since last I endured a north-of-England snowy day? Or listened to the moaning wind on a bleak winter evening?

As the sun sank lower in the west, I turned onto Hay Lane, a shortcut road home. The narrow, cobbled path ran uphill from Thornfield all the way to Hay Common then sloped downhill into the great town, Millcote. At the top of the rise, I would be able to spy the house and grounds. Pilot, sensing that home was near, suddenly raced ahead of me. Mesrour picked up the dog's excitement and broke out of his trot into a gallop. I too, would be glad of a seat by the hearth, so I let my horse have his head.

It was late along this lonely way as we pounded up the lane, then over the crest of the hill down along the causeway. *Tramp, tramp, tramp*, the sound of his hooves shattered the deep and cold silence of the winter afternoon. The trees rushed by on the other side of the road where darkness lay, stretched out in a black blanket.

What was that? Was there someone sitting on that stile?
Suddenly, the horse skidded across the path.

"What the deuce?"

I found myself tumbling over the steed's neck. I grasped
his mane to keep my saddle, but pitched forward as he struggled to maintain his balance. My left boot, still in the stirrup,
slid to the ankle as Mesrour tumbled over. It wrenched sideways in an explosion of pain as I hit the ground. Pilot barked
furiously then ran back up the path from whence we had
come as I labored to free myself.

"Damnation!" I tried to ignore the throbbing fire in my
ankle as I struggled to free my leg pinned beneath my fallen
steed.

The horse appeared unhurt, but he could not right
himself with my foot snared in the stirrup. As I tugged and
twisted to free it, a voice asked,

"Are you injured, sir?"

"Bloody Hell, horse!" I exclaimed, still exasperated by my
predicament, unheedful of the young woman's inquiry (for a
young woman it was). Pulling myself close to Mesrour's
head, I muttered through gritted teeth, "What the deuce was
that?" His ears lay flat, and his nostrils flared as I whispered
to him. "Since when does a little ice cause you to lose your
footing?"

When finally I twisted my foot free, it came—a flood of
throbbing pain, pounding in my boot from toe to knee.

"Might I help you, sir?" the young woman asked again.

"Just stand over there," I muttered. The little figure,
cloaked in dark wool, obeyed my command without
hesitation.

From my knees, I whispered to the horse, "Up, get up."
There followed a tumult of snorting and stamping as he
heaved himself to his feet. The frenzied dog barked and

barked while Mesrour, annoyed with all the commotion, trotted away to a distance.

"That's enough, Pilot," I growled.

Taking another deep breath, I stood up on the uninjured leg, then bent over and squeezed my boot. The bones felt intact. I had not broken the ankle after all, only sprained it. That was a relief. With excruciating effort, I limped to the stile where the small stranger had been sitting. She approached me again.

"You are hurt, sir. May I not fetch someone to help you?"

"Thank you, young lady, but that won't be necessary. It's only a sprain."

I stood up to walk.

"Ugh." A sharp, stabbing pain forced me to sit down again.

I heard her quick intake of breath; she took a step towards me, then as abruptly, halted.

I looked up at the young woman again. The moon waxed bright, but something of daylight still lingered. Bolder than brass, she stood waiting upon me, quite at her ease with a perfect stranger. Her serenity was a contrast to my exasperation, but I was in no mood for conversation so waved her away.

"I cannot abandon you now, sir." She sounded almost annoyed. Glancing up the lane towards Hay, she chided, "Certainly not. It is late, and you have only me to assist you."

Cheeky little thing.

"Stubbornness does not become a young lady," I said. "Besides, it grows late. You ought to be at home instead of traipsing about the countryside like some gipsy. What can you be about?"

"I am going to Hay, to post a letter."

"Are you indeed?" Again I was impressed by her ease and confidence. "And why have you ventured forth at such an hour? Night is upon us, and there will be a storm soon. If you have no care, you will be caught out in the weather."

"I am not far from home, sir. It is there, just below. Besides, I rather enjoy an evening walk when there is a full moon to light my way. As for the weather..." She peered at the darkening clouds on the horizon. "It is but two miles to Hay, a brisk walk. I have no intention to linger, unless you wish me to find someone there to assist you."

My curiosity now wrought to a pitch, I could not help but scrutinize her after such a speech. She was not tall but very slender. She carried herself well, quite erect, but without arrogance or guile. The eye was clear, the chin firm and resolute. Her face, however, was a riddle unto itself, for though it was unlined and youthful, the eyes were deep and possessed wisdom. Not precisely handsome, but it was an uncanny face. There was strength and resolve, an air of assurance that quite struck me. Yet it was difficult to say how old she was. Probably no more than two or three and twenty.

"You come from 'just below,' do you? Do I take you to mean that house down there with the battlements?"

I pointed to the old Hall, which looked rather like something out of novel, sitting square under the full moon, whose pale beams cast a ghostly light over its outline. I could see the hoary old thorn trees, like gaunt skeletons with bony arms upraised in fright.

"Yes, sir. It is called Thornfield Hall."

We stood for several moments gazing upon the manor. Seized by a strange impulse, I suddenly asked: "Well, whose house is it, then? Yours?"

"Oh, no sir," she laughed. "It belongs to Mr. Rochester."

"Mr. Rochester? Who is he?"

"He is the owner."

"Do you know this Mr. Rochester?"

"No sir, I have never seen him."

Nor I you, young lady. I should never forget such a face as that. My garrulous old housekeeper, it seems, has enlightened you about the absent owner of Thornfield Hall. Ah, Mrs. Fairfax—how much have you revealed about me?

"Can you tell me where he is?"

"I cannot."

I stopped to examine her garments: a plain cloak and black beaver bonnet—not half fine enough for a ladies' maid. A deuced puzzle to be sure.

"You are not a servant at the Hall, of course," I began. "Then you must be—"

I could not quite make up my mind. She helped me.

"I am the governess."

"Of course, the governess. How could I forget?"

On our journey up from Dover, Carter told me when he had been to Thornfield last fall, Mrs. Fairfax confessed to having some difficulty in finding a governess for Adele, but at last had found a willing applicant through an advertisement in the newspaper.

As the young woman stood waiting upon me to make a decision, it struck me that our situation was rather humorous. Well, well, perhaps I ought to introduce myself.

But after a moment's consideration, I thought the better of this idea. It may unnerve her to face her employer so unexpectedly. Besides, I was not in a very advantageous position at the moment. Better to wait for a warm hearth and a clearer view. Again, I stood and tried to walk.

"Ugh." The ankle throbbed anew with pain sharper than ever.

And again, she moved towards me as if to help. "Truly, sir, you cannot walk on your injured ankle. And in good conscience, I cannot depart until I see you are fit to mount your horse."

"There's no need to fetch help if you can assist me yourself."

"Of course, yes, sir."

"Perhaps you have an umbrella I might use as a walking stick?"

"Regretfully, no."

"Then take hold of my horse's bridle and lead him to me." She hesitated.

"You are not afraid, are you?"

Was that irritation in her glance? She set her muff on the stile, then approached the tall steed where he stood munching the grass. With effort upon effort she attempted to snatch his bridle, but Mesrour was a spirited beast. He shook his head, rattling the reins and bit, dangling them completely out of reach. I smiled at her heroic attempts to ensnare him, but it was hopeless. He jumped and stamped and snorted his displeasure.

"This will never do." I laughed. "Come here."

She ceased her efforts and approached me.

"Do excuse me, but I must beg of you to help me walk to my horse."

In the next moment, I laid my hand on her shoulder. A strange shock of sensation suddenly pulsed through me. Like a blow to my gut, it knocked the breath out of me and I stumbled, just catching Mesrour's bridle. For an instant, I leaned against his flank, senseless. Then she stepped away, unaware of the effect which had stunned me to the core.

"Steady now." I breathed fast and spoke low in his ear. Still reeling from the tremor of her touch, I eased my injured foot into the stirrup, then pulled myself up. Springing into the saddle, I wrenched the sprain once more.

"Be so good as to fetch my whip." I bit my lip, trying to ignore the fresh wave of pain. "It lies over there, under the hedge."

She looked around a moment, found it, then brought it to me.

I snatched it away. "And now! Make haste with your letter to Hay, and return as fast as you can."

I spurred my horse forward, and away we bounded down Hay Lane towards Thornfield Hall.

ACKNOWLEDGMENTS

Thanks to FBG for their unwavering support.

Thanks to my husband for putting up with my idiosyncrasies.

Thanks to my narrator, Dallin Bradford, for bringing Edward and the rest of my characters to life!

ABOUT THE AUTHOR

R.Q. Bell can't seem to stick to one genre, and is an author of historical romances, middle grade science fiction, high fantasy and cozy mysteries.

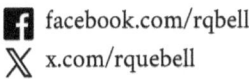

facebook.com/rqbell
x.com/rquebell

www.ingramcontent.com/pod-product-compliance
Lightning Source LLC
Chambersburg PA
CBHW031123210626
46816CB00016B/1958